A PUZZLE FOR FOOLS

Patrick Quentin is the pen-name of Hugh Callingham Wheeler, who was born in Hampstead in 1912. He was educated at Clayesmore School and at the Universities of London and Berlin. In 1934 he went to the United States, where he has lived ever since; he is an American citizen. Apart from a period in the U.S. Army Medical Corps his work has been writing. He spends six months of the year in his eighteenth-century farmhouse in New England and his New York apartment, the other six in his house on the island of St Kitts in the Caribbean. His interests apart from writing include music, modern painting and gardening.

Until 1952 'Patrick Quentin' was a collaboration involving Richard Wilson Webb. Wheeler and Webb also wrote under the pseudonyms 'Q. Patrick' and 'Jonathan Stagge'.

Several of Patrick Quentin's books have been published in Penguin, including *The Wife of Ronald Sheldon* and *The Follower*. His final mystery story was *Family Skeletons*, published in 1963. After this he totally changed his career and began to write plays under his own name. His Broadway plays include *Big Fish, Little Fish* and *Look We've Come Through*, as well as several musicals, including *A Little Night Music* and *Sweeney Todd* in collaboration with Stephen Sondheim, and *Candide* in collaboration with Leonard Bernstein. He has also written the opera *Silverlake* with Kurt Weill, and *Impresario*, using the music of Mozart. He has won many awards for his plays, including three Tony Awards, four Drama Critics' Circle Awards and several *Evening Standard* awards.

A Puzzle for Fools
PATRICK QUENTIN

PENGUIN BOOKS

PENGUIN BOOKS
Viking Penguin Inc., 40 West 23rd Street,
New York, New York 10010, U.S.A.
Penguin Books Ltd, Harmondsworth,
Middlesex, England
Penguin Books Australia Ltd, Ringwood,
Victoria, Australia
Penguin Books Canada Limited, 2801 John Street,
Markham, Ontario, Canada L3R 1B4
Penguin Books (N.Z.) Ltd, 182–190 Wairau Road,
Auckland 10, New Zealand

First published in the United States of America by Simon & Schuster 1936
First published in Great Britain by Victor Gollancz 1936
Published in Penguin Books 1986

Copyright Simon & Schuster, Inc., 1936
Copyright renewed Hugh C. Wheeler, 1964
All rights reserved

CIP data available
ISBN 0 14 00.8081 3

Printed in the United States of America by
R. R. Donnelley & Sons Company, Harrisonburg, Virginia
Set in Monophoto Plantin

Except in the United States of America,
this book is sold subject to the condition
that it shall not, by way of trade or otherwise,
be lent, re-sold, hired out, or otherwise circulated
without the publisher's prior consent in any form of
binding or cover other than that in which it is
published and without a similar condition
including this condition being imposed
on the subsequent purchaser

I

It always got worse at nights. And that particular night was the first time they had left me without any kind of dope to help me sleep.

Moreno, the psychiatrist in charge, had given me one of those dark, impatient looks of his and said: 'You've got to start standing on your own feet again, Mr Duluth. We've coddled you long enough.'

I told him he did not make sense; that surely I paid enough per week to cover the expense of a triple bromide. I pleaded; I argued; finally I got fighting mad and vented on him that remarkable vocabulary which is vouchsafed only to alcoholics who have been shut up for a couple of weeks without liquor. But Moreno just shrugged as much as to say:

'These drunks are more trouble than they're worth.'

I had started to swear again and then I thought: 'What's the use?' I could not tell him the real reason why I wanted dope. I was not going to admit that I was afraid, blindly, horribly afraid, like a kid that is going to be left alone in the dark.

On the outside I had been drinking to an eight-hour-a-day schedule for close on two years. That was how it got me after that fire in the theatre which had killed Magdalen. But a quart per day does not mix with a working man's life. In my few lucid moments I had begun to realize that my friends were getting tired of being sorry for me; that I was throwing down the hatch what reputation I had built up as New York's youngest theatrical producer, and that, if I went on, I should soon be ringing down the curtain on the tragi-farce of my own life.

I was not particularly reluctant to drink myself to death. In fact I was prepared to go merrily and deliberately to hell. But one of those things happened. On the day of its publication, thirteen friends presented me with thirteen copies of Bill Seabrook's *Asylum*. It was a gentle hint which even I could not overlook. I skimmed the book and discovered the comparative delights of a sanatorium cure. In a moment of impulsive determination I made the great gesture. I disembarrassed Broadway of a tiresome drunk and threw myself on the tender mercies of the well-known and discreetly titled Sanatorium of Doctor Lenz.

It wasn't a sanatorium really. It was just an expensive nuthouse for people like me who had lost control.

Doctor Lenz was a modern psychiatrist with a capital P S Y. After a brief period of tapering off, I had spent three liquorless weeks taking hell and giving it to the poor devils who looked after me. Hydrotherapy, physical jerks, sun-ray treatments had been sandwiched between unsuccessful attempts to sock male attendants on the jaw and occasional maudlin passes at pretty nurses. I had been one of the least attractive types of soaks, but I was making progress.

At least, that was what Miss Brush, the beautiful day nurse, had told me that afternoon. I guess that was why they had taken me off sleeping-powders.

All I needed now, she had said, was the will to pull through. Long after Doctor Moreno had gone, I lay in bed trembling and jittery – thinking it would be quite a while before I had any will at all.

I do not know whether all drunks get the same symptoms, but without stimulants or sedatives I just felt scared. And it wasn't a question of pink rats or purple elephants. It was just this frightful fear of being left alone in the dark; the violent need of someone to hold my hand and say: 'It's all right, Peter, I'm here. It's all right.'

I might have told myself that there was nothing tangible to be afraid of. I knew all the nuts around me. They were perfectly harmless, less dangerous perhaps than I was. My room or cell or whatever you call it, was comfortable, and the door was open. Mrs Fogarty, the night nurse, was in her little alcove at the end of the passage. All I had to do was to summon her through the house telephone at my bedside, and she would come rustling in like a horse-faced Florence Nightingale.

And somehow I could not pick up the receiver. I was ashamed to tell her that I was so scared of the vague shadow of the washbasin spigots on the white wall that I had to use every ounce of will power to keep my eyes from that side of the room. And I was not going to tell her that the corroding memory of Magdalen being burned to death almost before my eyes kept flashing blindingly through my mind – like the recurrent theme of a nightmare.

I shifted in the narrow, antiseptic bed, turning my face towards the comforting blackness of the inner wall. I would have given anything for a cigarette, but we were not allowed to smoke in bed, and they didn't trust us with matches anyway. It was very quiet. Some nights old Laribee, in the room next door, would mumble last year's stock prices in his sleep. But there was nothing like that now.

Quiet, lonely, not a sound . . .

I was lying there, straining my ears at the silence, when I heard the voice. It was faint, but very clear.

'*You've got to get away, Peter Duluth,*' it said. '*You've got to get away* NOW.'

I lay absolutely motionless, caught up in a stillness of panic far worse than mere physical fear. The voice seemed to have come from the window. But I could not think of things like that at the moment. All I knew – and it dawned on me with sickening clarity – was that the voice I had heard so distinctly was my own voice. I listened and it came again, *my own voice* whispering:

'*You've got to get away, Peter Duluth. You've got to get away* NOW.'

For a moment I knew that I really had gone mad. I was talking to myself and yet I could not feel my lips move. I had no sense of speaking. With a sudden, desperate motion, I lifted a quivering hand to my mouth and held it tightly across my lips. At least I could stop myself – stop that quiet, dreadful sound.

And then the voice – my voice – came again.

'*You've got to get away, Peter Duluth.*'

There was silence – an infinitesimal silence, before it added, softly, intimately:

'*There will be murder.*'

I hardly remember what happened next. But I have a vague recollection of jumping out of bed and rushing wildly down the long, lighted corridor. It was a marvel that I did not come across Mrs Fogarty, the night nurse. But I didn't.

At length I found the unbreakable glass door which led from the men's quarters into some of the outer quarters. I swung it open and, in pyjamas and bare feet, ran on with only one thought in my mind – to get away from my room, to shake the echo of that voice from my ears.

I was in some place I had never seen before when I heard footsteps behind me. I glanced over my shoulder and saw Warren, our night attendant, sprinting after me. The very sight of him seemed to clear my head, to give me a sort of desperate cunning. Before he could catch me, I turned and dashed up a flight of stairs.

I reached the top and, after an instant's hesitation, ran towards a door, opened it and slammed it behind me. I had no idea what room I was in, but I felt a crazy sense of triumph. Bending, I started to fumble for the key. I could lock the door, keep Warren out. No one would ever be able to take me back to my room.

But while my fingers were still moving futilely along the woodwork, the door was thrown open and I felt myself caught in a steel headlock. It was dark and I could not see Warren. But I fought, scratched, and yelled curses at him. I might as well have tried to argue with a steam shovel. Warren was thin and slight, but as tough as an electric cable. He merely held my head under one arm and warded off my erratic blows with the other.

We were still in this loving clinch when the room was suddenly flooded with light, and I heard a cool female voice saying:

'It's all right, Warren. Don't be rough with him.'

'But he's gone haywire, Miss Brush.' Warren's arm had tightened around my neck, hurting my ears.

'He'll be all right. Let me deal with him.'

Slowly I felt myself released. I blinked and gazed across the room. It was a bedroom. A shaded light burned by the bedside, and Isabel Brush, our day nurse, was walking calmly towards me in white silk pyjamas.

Most of my fears drained away when I saw her. They always did. In those pyjamas, with her blonde hair loose around her face, she looked like an extremely healthy angel – a sort of celestial hockey captain.

'So you came to visit me, Mr Duluth,' she was saying with a bright smile. 'You shouldn't, you know. It's against regulations.'

I knew she was humouring me because I was a nut, but I didn't care. I wanted to be humoured. I wanted to be mothered.

I hung my head and said: 'I had to get away, Miss Brush. I couldn't stay in that room – not with my own voice talking about murder.'

Miss Brush's deep-blue eyes looked at me steadily. 'Why not tell me what happened?'

Warren was standing by the door, still suspicious. But Miss Brush gave him a reassuring nod and sat down at her dressing-table. Before I knew what I was doing, I had slipped to the floor at her side and was laying my head in her lap like a five-year-old instead of a grown man past thirty. I babbled everything out to her, and she made soothing, matter-of-fact comments, stroking my hair with fingers which could probably have ju-jutsued me into helplessness if I had started to act up.

Gradually I felt myself giving way to a delightful sense of warmth and comfort. I was not aware of Doctor Moreno's presence in the room until his voice rang out curtly:

'Well, Miss Brush!'

The fingers paused on my hair. I looked up to see Moreno in pyjamas and dressing-gown. He had been on the stage for a while, and he always looked like a handsome young stage doctor – the type who gives the heroine a third-act turn-down in the interests of Humanity. But at that moment he seemed more like a stage villain. His black, Spanish eyes flared with some emotion which in my confused state of mind I could not interpret.

'Really, Miss Brush, this is quite unnecessary – and very poor psychiatry.'

Miss Brush smiled serenely. 'Mr Duluth has been frightened.'

'Frightened!' Moreno crossed the room and pulled me to my feet. 'Mr Duluth ought to have more sense. There's nothing wrong with him. Heaven knows, we have enough trouble looking after the really sick patients without these theatrical scenes.'

I could tell what was going on in his mind. He thought I was just acting up in the hopes of being given something to help me sleep. He did not approve of Doctor Lenz taking alcoholics, I knew. He thought we were a waste of good psychiatry and a damn' nuisance. I felt suddenly ashamed of myself. Most likely I had wakened him up from a much-needed sleep.

'Come on, Mr Duluth,' he was saying sharply. 'Warren will take you back to your room. I can't imagine how you got out.'

When he mentioned going back, all my panic returned. I started to struggle and was summarily handed over to Warren. As the attendant's lean fingers clamped on to my wrists, Miss Brush drew Moreno aside and said something which I could not hear. Immediately the expression in his eyes changed. He crossed to me and said quietly:

'I shall have to take you to Doctor Lenz at once, Mr Duluth.'

I looked at Miss Brush doubtfully, but she said with bright persuasiveness:

'Of course you'd like to see Doctor Lenz, wouldn't you?'

She took a blanket from the bed and wrapped it around my shoulders. Then she found woolly bedroom slippers which somehow were large enough.

Before I had time to register an opinion, I was bundled unceremoniously out into the passage.

2

I saw by the large clock on the mantel that it was one-thirty when Moreno and Warren brought me to the director's study.

In his own sanitorium, Doctor Lenz was like God. You saw him very rarely and then only in a cloud of pomp and circumstance. This was my first informal visit, but I was still impressed. There was something indestructibly divine about that large man with his arrogant beard and calm grey eyes.

As a quasi-celebrated producer, I had met most of the contemporary personalities. Doctor Lenz was one of the few who bore up under close inspection. He was aloof but vital. He had enough electricity in him to run the New York subway.

He listened gravely while Moreno outlined my recent misdemeanours, and then dismissed him with a slight inclination of the head. When we were alone together, he watched me closely for a moment.

'Well, Mr Duluth,' he said with his almost imperceptible foreign accent, 'do you feel you are making progress with us?'

He treated me like a human being, and I began to feel fairly normal again. I told him that my spells of depression were not so frequent and that, physically at least, I was improving.

'But I still get scared in the dark. Tonight, for example, I acted like Little Lord Fauntleroy. And I can't do anything about it.'

'You have had a difficult time, Mr Duluth. But there is no real cause for worry.'

'But I swear I heard my own voice – heard it plainly as I hear you. That's pretty screwy, isn't it?'

'If you thought you heard something,' said Doctor Lenz with a sudden change of tone, 'there was probably something to hear. You must take my word for it that you would not imagine things of that sort.'

Instantly I was on my guard. I felt he was trying to humour me, just like the rest of them. And yet I was not sure.

'You mean there might have been something?' I asked doubtfully.

'Yes.'

'But I tell you I was alone. And it was my voice – my own voice.'

Doctor Lenz did not speak for a moment. A faint smile lurked in his beard as the large fingers tapped reflectively on the desk. 'I am not concerned about your case, Mr Duluth. Chronic alcoholics are like poets. They are born and not made. And usually they are psychopaths. You are definitely not a psychopath. You started drinking merely because the whole focal point of your life was suddenly taken from you. Your wife and your theatrical career were bound up together in your mind. With the tragic death of Mrs Duluth, your interest in the theatre died, too. But it will come back. It is merely a question of time – possibly even of days.'

I did not see what he was driving at, but suddenly he added:

'In the seriousness of your own problem, you have forgotten that other people have problems, too. You have lost contact with life.' He paused. 'At the moment I myself happen to have a problem, and I would like you to help me. Perhaps in helping me you will also be able to help yourself.'

It was strangely comforting not to be treated like a case history in a book on morbid psychology. I pulled Miss Brush's blanket more closely around me and nodded him to continue.

'You tell me you heard your own voice this evening,' he said quietly. 'It is possible that your condition was responsible for your believing that voice to be your own. But I do not doubt that there was something definite and actual behind your experience. You see, this is not the first disturbing thing which has been reported to me recently.'

'You mean –?'

Doctor Lenz's grey eyes were grave. 'As you know, Mr Duluth, this sanatorium is not run for the incurably insane. Everyone who comes here has been suffering from some nervous condition. Many of them are just on the fringe – in real danger of losing their reason permanently. But I do not accept the responsibility of hopelessly demented patients. If such a case develops here, we advise the relatives to have them committed to a State institution. From several unexplainable little incidents, I feel that there may be at this moment someone in the sanatorium who ought not to be here.'

He pushed a cigarette box toward me and I took one eagerly.

'You would be surprised how difficult it is to put a finger upon the cause of unrest, Mr Duluth. We cannot really tell from charts, from physical examinations, or even from the closest supervision, just how mentally sick a person is.'

'And yet you think one of the patients is deliberately causing this trouble for some crazy reason of his own?'

'It is possible, yes. And the damage which such a person could do is incalculable. With the type of patients we have here, even a slight shock might be sufficient to retard their progress for months, might possibly prevent their ever getting well. As a theatrical producer you must have been thrown in contact with highly strung, temperamental people, and you know how little things can upset them.'

He had stirred my interest all right. Forgetting that I was a semi-mental case wrapped up in a blanket, I asked questions curiously. Doctor Lenz was surprisingly lacking in reticence. He told me frankly that he had no means of localizing the disturbance to any particular place or person. All he could say was that there was a subversive influence, and that he was worried about his institution.

'My responsibilities are great,' he remarked with a slight smile. 'Naturally, it means everything to me as an individual and a psychiatrist that my patients should make good progress. But there are other complications, too. Take the case of Herr Stroubel, for example. He is certainly one of the greatest conductors of our age. His return to health is eagerly awaited by the musical world. The board of directors of the Eastern Symphony Orchestra have even offered to donate ten thousand dollars to the institution on the day he leaves us, a well man. He had been showing splendid progress; but recently there has been a distinct set-back.'

Doctor Lenz told me no details, but I guessed that the famous conductor must have been frightened – just as I had been frightened earlier that night.

'There is another case,' continued Lenz slowly, 'which is even more delicate. Mr Laribee, as you know, is an immensely wealthy man. He has made and lost several huge fortunes on the stock market.' He passed a hand across his beard. 'Mr Laribee has appointed his daughter and myself as trustees of his estate. By the present arrangement a great deal of money will come to the institution at his death, or at any time when he should have to be certified permanently insane.'

'And you mean he's being upset, too?'

'No. Not yet.' The grey eyes stared at me fixedly. 'But you can imagine

12

how worried I am lest this – er – influence should affect him. He is doing well at present. But if he should suffer from any shock while under my care, you can guess what people would think – the scandal.'

He broke off and for a moment neither of us spoke. Until then I had been too intrigued to wonder why Doctor Lenz should have confided so casually in a half-cured drunk. Now the thought came into my mind and I asked him point-blank.

'I have told you this, Mr Duluth,' he said solemnly, 'because I want you to help me. Of course, I have absolute confidence in my staff, but in this particular case they can be of no great assistance. People who are mentally sick are often reserved. They do not like to tell their medical attendants about the things which upset them – especially when they fancy that those things are part of their own sickness. Patients who would not talk to their physicians might talk to you as a fellow inmate.'

It was a long time since anyone had put me in a position of trust. I told him so and he smiled slowly.

'I have deliberately asked your help,' he said, 'because you are one of the few patients here whose mind is basically healthy. As I have said, I feel that you need nothing more than an interest in life. I thought this might help to give you that interest.'

I did not speak for a moment. Then I asked: 'But that voice said there would be murder. Aren't you going to take that seriously?'

'You seem to have misunderstood me, Mr Duluth.' Lenz's voice chilled slightly. 'I take everything very seriously indeed. But this is a mental hospital. In an institution of this type, one does not take everything which is heard – or seen – literally.'

I did not grasp his point, but he left me no time for questions. He spent the next few minutes making me feel good, as only expensive psychiatrists can. Then he rang the bell for Warren to take me back to my room.

As I waited for the night attendant, I happened to glance down at the bedroom slippers which Miss Brush had provided for me. There was nothing particularly unusual about them except that they were large and obviously male.

Miss Brush, I knew, was the most efficient of young women. But it showed almost excessive efficiency to keep slippers in her bedroom against the chance visit of a neurotic male patient in bare feet.

I might have tried to puzzle it out. But Doctor Lenz was speaking again.

'Do not worry, Mr Duluth. And remember that, if you see or hear anything out of the ordinary, that thing is real and has its basis in fact. Do not let anyone or anything persuade you that you are suffering under a delusion. Good night.'

3

I had no objections now to going back with Warren. Of course, if I had been a little more – or a little less – crazy, I might have thought that Lenz had been putting up an elaborate song and dance to get me interested in something besides myself. But I didn't. Although I had been unable exactly to grasp his attitude toward it, I felt that he did actually believe strange things were going on in the place. Well, it was exciting, something to break the clinical monotony.

Back in Wing Two, as the men's quarters were officially titled, Warren handed me over to the dour care of the night nurse, Mrs Fogarty, who happened also to be his sister.

Apart from the celestial Miss Brush, the staff on Wing Two was a family party and, according to rumour, not a particularly happy one. We patients spent hours of prurient speculation upon their complicated relationships, which were worthy of Dostoievsky or Julian Green.

The angular Mrs Fogarty was the wife of Jo Fogarty, our day attendant, and, either by choice or by accident, their work shifts gave them practically no time together by day or night. The union, if it was one at all, was obviously of the spirit. And Mrs Fogarty, as though suffering from a sort of spinsterial hang-over, spent most of her time and her grim affection upon her brother.

Incidentally, she was as plain as Miss Brush was pretty, presumably on the theory that we mental patients needed stimulation by day and sedation by night.

Mrs Fogarty greeted me with an antiseptically anxious smile and a rustle of starched cuffs. Owing to a slight hardness of hearing, she had cultivated the habit of never speaking herself when a facial expression or a gesture was sufficient to convey her meaning. A nod of the head indicated that I was to go back to my room, and together we started down the corridor.

We had just reached my door when there was a scuffling sound in Laribee's room, next to mine. As we paused, old Laribee ran out into the corridor, his grey woollen pyjamas flapping in unbuttoned abandon. His florid face was creased with fear. His eyes had that blank, hopeless look which a few weeks in the sanatorium had made me know only too well. Dazedly he came up to us, clutching shakily for Mrs Fogarty's large-boned hand.

'Tell them to stop,' he moaned. 'I've tried not to give way. I tried to keep quiet. But they've got to stop.'

Mrs Fogarty's equine face registered professional consolation, and then, as though sensing that the situation demanded words, she added mechanically: 'It's all right, Mr Laribee. No one's hurting you.'

'But they've got to stop.' He was a tall, heavy man, and it was somehow shocking to see the tears rolling down his cheeks like a baby's. 'Tell them to stop the ticker. It's way behind the market. Stocks must be crashing. Don't you see? I'm ruined. Everything's going. The ticker – make the ticker stop.'

The night nurse's fingers gripped his firmly and she drew him back into his room. Through the wall I could hear him, quite hysterical now.

'Put in a stop loss order on my Consolidated Trust – crashing – crashing.'

Mrs Fogarty's answering voice was placid and reassuring. 'Nonsense, Mr Laribee. Stocks are all going up. Now you go to sleep and read about them in the paper tomorrow.'

At last she calmed him down. I heard her creak past my door.

What a job, I thought, spending the night looking after nuts like us.

After her footsteps had faded and the room was quiet again, I found myself thinking about old Laribee. I did not have much sympathy with him, or with any other of the Wall Street wizards who in 1929 had wizarded away their own money and, incidentally, quite a bit of mine, too. But it was pathetic to think of a man who still had a couple of million going crazy because he thought he was broke.

And yet I remembered how Doctor Lenz had said that he was making progress. A few stray words which I had absently overheard that morning between Miss Brush and Moreno passed through my mind. They had been talking about Laribee, about his improvement. 'It's been weeks now since he's heard that ticker,' Miss Brush had said. 'Looks as though he's picking up.'

It had been weeks since he had heard that ticker! Why had he had this relapse – I wondered. Was it perhaps due to what Lenz had called the subversive influence?

Mrs Fogarty must have given him something to make him sleep, because he was not whimpering any more. There was silence again – that deep, institutional silence which had scared me earlier in the evening, but which somehow had no fears for me now. I listened to the stillness, not expecting to hear anything. Then for the second time that night I had a shock. But this time it was a shock that intrigued me, not one that set me off blubbering like a frightened kid.

I sat up in bed. Yes, there was no doubt about it. Too soft and muffled for Mrs Fogarty's ears to have caught, but quite distinct, I could make out a quick, rhythmic ticking, quicker than a clock.

Tick, tack – tick, tack!

It came through the wall from somewhere in Laribee's room.

Tick, tack – tick, tack!

There were only two ways for me to think. Either I was catching old Laribee's bug, or else there was something in that room ticking, something quite separate from the sinister sounds in Laribee's broken brain.

Tick, tack – tick, tack!

4

Next morning I felt pretty fair considering my hectic night. Jo Fogarty, one-time champion wrestler and now the night nurse's problematic husband, woke me at the usual, ungodly hour of seven-thirty.

As I stumbled out of bed into my slippers, I noticed that the ones lent me by Miss Brush had vanished. The day nurse, too, it seemed, was an early riser.

We all had our daily treatments, and mine consisted largely of a thorough pepping up. Doctor Stevens, whose job it was to look after the patients' physical as opposed to their mental frailties, had prescribed an extensive course of physio-therapy and massage. He was a pleasant fellow and I did not hold it against him, but I always felt injured at being dragged to the slaughter before breakfast. That morning I sulked as Fogarty took me down to the physio-therapy room and made me atone once again for my years of soaking, with the pin shower, the electric camel and various other outlandish exercises.

Fogarty was one of those half-ugly brutes just past their prime with a sense of humour and a Tarzan attractiveness for the women who like that sort of thing. And quite a lot of them did, judging from the tales he told me. I could not help wondering sometimes whether he was equally frank with his grim-faced wife.

For some reason he was crazy to get into the show business – stunts and strong-man acts, or something of the sort. I think that was why he liked me, or played up to me, at least. Anyhow, we had grown quite friendly and he told me sanatorium gossip out of school.

While I lay naked on the slab, waving my legs, he started to kid me about the night before.

'Gettin' into Miss Brush's bedroom!' he said. 'You'll have old man Laribee after you if you don't watch out.'

'Laribee?'

'Sure, he's nuts about her, asks her to marry him twenty times a day. I figured everyone knew that.'

I thought he was being funny, but he convinced me that he was serious. And after all, there was nothing particularly fantastic about it. Usually Laribee was perfectly normal. Last night was the only time I had seen him acting up. He was a widower with a couple of million and a good chance of getting well again. And even if he was hovering around the crazy sixties, he was still young and sane enough to know an attractive girl when he saw one. I was interested to hear Miss Brush's reactions to these proposals, but Fogarty had gone off at another tangent.

'So my sissy brother-in-law threw a headlock on you,' he was saying as he kneaded my muscles. 'He reckons he got the leverage even if he don't have the weight. Had the nerve to challenge me for a tumble the other night – me an ex-champ! But I say, what's the use of chewing up a little guy like that anyway?'

I had a look at his muscles and felt he could chew up anyone – even the steel-cabled Warren. I knew that no love was lost between the two of them, and I imagined that, if it came to blows, he could beat up his brother-in-law with one hand tied behind his back. I told him so and he seemed pleased.

'It's kind of nice to have a drunk to look after once in a while – someone who isn't out-and-out cuckoo,' he said. 'They're more human, if you see what I mean.' He gave me a final slap and asked, 'How's 'at?'

I said it was fine, and that for the first time since I had been in the place I felt like eating something for breakfast.

And I did. Despite a slight return of jitteriness, I managed to get some cereal down without kidding myself the milk was rye. Miss Brush, who presided in the dining-room as a kind of hygienic hostess, noticed immediately and showed her approval.

'Night life seems to agree with your appetite, Mr Duluth.'

'Yeah,' I said. 'And I never thanked you for the blanket and the bedroom slippers.'

She smiled disarmingly and moved away.

Since my talk with Lenz, I found myself feeling an almost convalescent interest in the people around me. Before, patients and staff alike had just been sombre caricatures on a monotone backcloth. I had been too wrapped up in myself to pay any attention to them. But now I began to figure out the relationships between them and do a bit of wondering. After all, from my own experience I knew that Lenz's 'subversive influence' lurked somewhere in the building. Maybe it was tangible.

Maybe it was right here in the room. Drunk, sober or convalescent, the detective instinct is as fundamental as birth or sex.

We had small individual tables in the dining-room, just two or four at a table to kid us we were on a boat or something and not in the hatch. I ate alone with Martin Geddes, a nice, quiet Englishman who superficially had nothing worse wrong with him than a tendency to talk too much about the Empire, and India, where he had been born.

He was in for a disease which seemed like sleeping sickness, but which his chart called narcolepsy, complicated with cataplexy. He was liable to fall off into a rigid, profound sleep at any moment.

That morning he did not appear for breakfast, and, consequently, I had more time and opportunity to observe the others.

From a casual glance it would have been difficult to tell that there was anything wrong with any of us. Laribee was over the way from me. Apart from a slight twitch around his heavy mouth, he might have been any successful Wall Street financier taking breakfast anywhere. But I noticed he was up to his old tricks of pushing away the food and whispering:

'It's no use. I can't afford it. With Steel down below 30, I've got to economize – economize.'

Miss Brush was watching him with an angelic brightness which almost hid the worried cloud in her deep blue eyes. I remembered what Fogarty had told me and wondered just how much of the day nurse's worry was professional.

Laribee sat at a table with a very beautiful, lustrous young man with perfect tailoring and the mouth of a saint. His name was David Fenwick, and, although usually he was no more peculiar than the average young aesthete, he occasionally heard spirit voices. You could see him suddenly break off in the middle of a sentence to listen to phantom messages which were to him far more important than the conversation of his fellow inmates. Spiritualism had got him as successfully as spirits had got me.

There were about six others, but I only knew a couple of them. Franz Stroubel sat by himself, a fragile, paper-thin little man with a shock of white hair and the eyes of a fawn. He had been in Doctor Lenz's sanatorium ever since that night six months before when, instead of conducting the Eastern Symphony Orchestra, he had begun to conduct the audience, and later had stood bare-headed in Times Square trying to conduct the traffic. The rhythm of life had become confused in his mind.

As I watched him at the breakfast table, his beautiful hands never stopped moving. There was no other means of telling that he had suffered a set-back.

The most popular inmate was Billy Trent, a swell kid who had been hit on the head playing football. It was only a superficial brain lesion. He thought he was serving in a drug store, and he would come up all smiles and eagerness to ask your order. You couldn't resist him. You had to take a chocolate milk shake and a liverwurst on rye. Miss Brush had told me the lesion would heal soon and he would be well again. It made me glad.

After breakfast I began to wonder about the non-appearance of Geddes. I knew that he, like myself, had a bad time at nights. I could not help thinking that perhaps something had happened to him, too.

I asked Miss Brush about it when she conducted us to the smoking-room, where we were supposed to digest our breakfast over the highbrow magazines. So she did not reply. She never did when you asked her anything about the other patients. She just struck a match for my cigarette and told me there was a good article on theatrical producing in *Harper's*. To please her, I picked up the magazine and started to read.

Geddes looked pretty shaken when he appeared. He strolled over to me and sat down on the couch. He was one of those thirtyish men who look like Ronald Colman: handsome, groomed, and with a moustache which you feel must be a whole-time job. He had been in America several years but, like Rupert Brooke's grave, he was for ever England – or, rather, Anglo-India.

I noticed that his hand trembled as he lifted his cigarette for Miss Brush to light. I asked him quite bluntly if he had had a good night. He seemed surprised that I had started the amenities, because I was usually pretty glum.

'A good night?' he echoed in that type of English voice which in the Lonsdale era used to set Broadway by the ears. 'As a matter of fact, I had a rotten night.'

'I had a pretty bad time, too,' I said encouragingly. 'Maybe I disturbed you.'

'There was a bit of a row, but I didn't pay much attention.' I felt that he was edging around to say something.

'I guess it's fairly grim for you here,' I tried. 'After all, you're not a mental salad like the rest of us. Your trouble's more or less physical.'

'I suppose it is.' He spoke quietly but with a strange faltering in his voice. 'You're better off than I am, though. They'll cure you, but none of these doctors seems to know the first thing about narcolepsy. I've read a few medical books and I know as much as they do. They say you've got a screw loose in the central nervous system. They say something snaps and you go to sleep fifteen times a day and that if you've got cataplexy, too, you're liable to turn as rigid as a five-bar gate. But they can't do anything about making you well. I came here because I heard Stevens and Moreno were having a big success with a brand new drug, benzedrine sulphate. For a while I hoped – but it doesn't seem to do me any darn good.'

'It must be tough,' I murmured.

Geddes bit the lip under his moustache and said surprisingly: 'Moreno's one of those supercilious blighters. Jolly difficult to tell him anything, if you get me.'

I said I got him and showed what I hoped was the correct amount of impersonal interest.

'Listen, Duluth,' he said suddenly. 'Something happened last night, and I've got to tell someone about it, or I'll go off my bean. Of course, you'll say it was one of those damnable nightmares of mine. But it wasn't. I swear I was awake.'

I nodded.

'I got off to sleep quite early, and then I woke up. I don't know how late it was, but things were pretty quiet. I was in one of those half dozes when I heard it.'

'Heard what?' I asked quietly.

He passed a hand across his forehead with that curious English languidness which is cultivated to conceal any emotion.

'I think I may be going mad,' he said in a very slow and deliberate tone. 'You see, I heard my own voice speaking quite plainly.'

'Good God!' I broke in, suddenly alert.

'Yes, my own voice. And I was saying: "You've got to get out of here, Martin Geddes. You've got to get out now. There will be murder."'

He had clenched his fists in his lap and now he turned toward me with a look of sudden terror. His mouth was half open, as though he were about to say something more. But he did not speak. As I watched, I saw the muscles of his face freeze. The mouth locked half open. The eyes stared. There was a sort of wooden hardness about his cheeks. I had seen him fall asleep several times before, but I had never seen one of these cataplectic trances. It wasn't pretty.

I touched him and his arm was stiff and inhuman, like a sack of cement. I felt suddenly helpless. My fingers started to shake, and went on shaking. It made me realize what a wreck I still was.

Somehow, Miss Brush got on to the situation. She nodded to Fogarty, who was constantly on guard. The attendant hurried forward and picked Geddes up.

Not a muscle of the Englishman's body moved. It was amazing to see a man like that – still in a sitting position when he was being carried across the room. With his dark complexion and wide-open eyes he looked like a solemn Indian fakir giving a demonstration in levitation.

I had returned to the magazine to steady my nerves when the ethereal David Fenwick came up. I saw at once that he had that far-away, ghost look in his huge, deer-like eyes.

'Mr Duluth,' he said, almost in a whisper, 'I'm worried. The astral plane is not propitious.' He glanced over his shoulder as though eager to make certain there were no phantom eavesdroppers. 'The spirits were about last night. They almost got through to me – to warn me. I couldn't see them. But I could hear their voices faintly. Soon I shall be able to take their message.'

Before I had time to ask more, he had floated away, gazing in front of him with that dazed, other-worldly stare.

So Laribee, Geddes, and I were not the only ones who had been disturbed last night. In a sense, it was comforting to have this further proof that my imagination had not been playing tricks on me. But even so, I did not like it. Imaginary voices do not prophesy murder for nothing – not even in a mental hospital.

I picked up *Harper's* again, trying to revive the old theatrical enthusiasm, which used to effervesce in my blood, but which now had gone as flat as yesterday's champagne.

The article told me the stage was this and the stage was that. It even threw a bouquet at a play I had done a few years before. Well, what of it? It was a relief to see Billy Trent coming over to me, his young face smiling.

'Hello, Pete,' he said, standing in front of me as though there were a soda fountain between us. 'What's it to be today?'

I grinned at him. Crazy as he was at the moment, there was something intensely healthy about young Trent, with his clear blue eyes and athletic build. You knew it was all the fault of a crack-up on the football field, and you could take it in the spirit of good clean fun.

'What's it to be, Pete?'

23

'Oh, I don't know, Billy. Give me a couple of nut sundaes. And for the love of Mike, get yourself a hard-liquor licence. The stuff you serve is ruining my stomach.'

5

The usual routine of the day went on. Discipline at Doctor Lenz's sanatorium was strict but never obvious. However planned one's schedule might be, it was allowed to progress with a seeming spontaneity. It was faintly reminiscent of the organized fun to which cruise passengers are forced to submit on board ship.

Ten o'clock was the hour for my visit to the surgery where Doctor Stevens, pink and smiling like a substantial cherub, thumped and prodded me, looked at my tongue and eyes, while he kept up a running commentary on the weather, the decline of the American stage, or other non-controversial subjects. He told me that day that we were due for more snow and that there was no longer any albumen in my urine. He asked my opinion of Katherine Cornell and went on to more intimate and personal questions to which I was able to give a more satisfactory answer. Finally he said that if I was satisfying the psychiatrists as well as I was him, there should be nothing to prevent my leaving them and producing plays on Broadway again within a very few weeks.

After that, Moreno gave me my daily mental once-over. He had only been with Lenz a short time, having been imported with Stevens from the most up-to-date medical school in California. Miss Brush had assured me that he was a first-class psychiatrist, and I could believe her. Although I did not like the bright young doctor type, I rather admired the man. He had a hard matter-of-factness which does a lot to give jittery people confidence. But that particular morning he was different. I could not put my finger on what was wrong, but I felt he was on edge, jumpy.

When he was through with me, Miss Brush rounded us all up for our morning walk. It was a cold March and there was deep snow on the ground, so we were wrapped up with maternal care. I noticed that Miss Brush herself tied old Laribee's scarf and put on his rubbers. She gave him one of those quick, intimate smiles of hers, and I saw a jealous look come into young Bill Trent's eyes. He worshipped Miss Brush. But then we all did. I guess she was part of our cure.

At length we started out, ten or eleven grown men, walking two by two, in a rather uncertain imitation of schoolchildren. Miss Brush was ostensibly taking care of us, but my wrestler friend, Jo Fogarty, lounged along behind as though he just happened to be going in the same direction.

I was surprised and glad to see that Geddes was with us. He made no reference to his attack. I suppose he did not even know he'd had one. We strolled along together, getting quite 'pally'.

We all behaved pretty well until we had left the sanatorium behind and were walking across country over some of the hundred or so acres which belonged to the institution.

Old Laribee had been very quiet, striding along with a blue scarf fluffed around his puffy red face. Suddenly he stopped in the snow, and that look I had seen the night before came into his eyes.

The others stopped, too, gazing at him with idle curiosity. He had gripped Miss Brush's arms and was saying hoarsely:

'We've got to go back.'

We gathered around him, all except Billy Trent, who was throwing snowballs vigorously. Jo Fogarty had come up and was hovering at Miss Brush's elbow.

'We've got to go back, Miss Brush.' Laribee's lower lip was trembling distractedly. 'I've just had a warning. Steel's going to drop ten points today. If I don't get to a telephone and put in some selling orders, I shall be ruined – ruined.'

Miss Brush tried to calm him down, but it was no use. He was sure he had heard his broker, he said, heard his voice in his ear. He pleaded, argued with a kind of desperate doggedness, as though to assure himself rather than her of his sanity.

Miss Brush showed a certain amount of brisk sympathy, but she said she couldn't have the walk broken up, not even if the whole of Wall Street were collapsing. I thought she was being rather tough with him. But he seemed to like it. The strained, wild expression left his face, giving way to a sort of cunning hopefulness.

'Miss Brush – Isabel, you've got to understand.' His hand gripped her arm again. 'It's not only for me – it's for us. I want you to have everything money can buy; everything my daughter has had and more ...'

His voice rambled on, low and quick so that I was not able to hear. Billy Trent had stopped throwing snowballs and his eyes were smouldering. None of the others seemed particularly interested.

Miss Brush was smiling again – a smile which seemed a fraction too unprofessional.

'Of course it'll be all right, Dan. Hurry up and get well. We can take care of the stocks later on.'

Laribee was all excited. He even hummed a little tune as we resumed the walk. He seemed to have forgotten about the warning and his broker's voice in his ear.

But I hadn't.

Of course, I had no idea then of the fantastic and horrible things which were so soon to happen in Doctor Lenz's sanatorium. I had no means of telling just how significant these minor and seemingly pointless disturbances were. But I did have a distinct impression that something was vitally wrong. Even then I felt that behind all this madness there was method. But whose method it was, and just how sinister its motive, was at that time a problem far too intricate for my post-alcoholic brain.

I started to talk to Miss Brush to cheer myself up. That girl had a way with her. A few words and a couple of her famous smiles made me feel a helluva fellow. I strode along as though the whole sanatorium belonged to me, with its large acreage of parkland.

This accession of virility put me ahead of the others. I turned a corner around a small wood and almost collided with some of the female patients, who were also taking their daily exercise.

As a general rule, we saw nothing of the other sex except during the polite social hour after dinner, when the better behaved of us were allowed to mix in the central hall for bridge, conversation, and the formal Saturday dance. To date I had never been a good enough boy to rate an invitation, so this was the first time I had seen the women. I had to thank the snow which restricted us to the footpaths.

Most of them wore very smart clothes, but there was something a little wrong about the way they wore them. Their coats and hats had been put on carelessly, rakishly. They looked like fashionable patrons leaving a night-club in the early hours of the morning.

The other men had come up now, and Miss Brush prompted our chivalric instinct by stepping off the beaten track to let the ladies pass.

They filed by uneventfully enough until the last one of them suddenly stopped dead. She was young, dressed in an expensive fur coat, and with one of those little Russian fur caps on her black hair.

Maybe it was because I had been away from women for a long time, but I thought her the most beautiful girl I had ever seen. Her face was pale and exotic, like those amazing white flowers they rear in hot-houses. Her eyes were large and incredibly sad. I had never seen such tragic, hopeless sadness before.

Her gaze was fixed intently on one of the men in our group. No one moved. It was as if we were all caught up in the fascination which held her there, spellbound.

I was standing only a few inches from her. Slowly she put out a small gloved hand and touched my sleeve. She did not look at me. I do not think she was even aware of my existence. But she said in a low, toneless voice:

'You see that man there? He murdered my father.'

Instantly the women's equivalent of Miss Brush drew her away. There was a certain amount of confused chattering among the females and the males. But it did not amount to much.

I took one final glance at that girl with the exotic flower face and the tormentingly sad eyes. Then I turned to see who it was she had been looking at. I could tell at once. There was no possibility of doubt.

The man who had 'killed her father' was standing very close to Miss Brush. He was Daniel Laribee.

6

When we were back in Wing Two and Miss Brush had seen to it that our socks were changed, I took Geddes on for a game of billiards. We had just finished when Jo Fogarty came in to take me away for my pre-lunch work-out.

As we started operations in the physio-therapy room, he began to talk about Geddes and what a nice fellow he was. He said he liked the English, and that Geddes was a typical Englishman. He'd been in London in '29, when he beat up the British wrestling champ, and all the guys seemed to look like Geddes. He rambled on about the other male patients. For some reason of his own he didn't approve of them. Fenwick was limp and soft as a girl; Billy Trent was muscle-bound and hard to handle.

Muscles always brought him back to his favourite topic – himself. With excusable pride he started in about his own strength and how he was a better wrestler than any of the framed phonies who were now disgracing the mat. There was a lot more concerning his bouts with the London women, but I was not listening very hard. Usually I found him amusing, but just then I could not think of much else but the girl with the sad eyes and the Russian cap.

As soon as it was decently possible, I brought the conversation around to her. Fogarty's pleasant, bulldog face grinned knowingly.

'Yeah,' he said, 'she's a good looker all right.'

'But what's her name?'

'Pattison. Iris Pattison. One of those Park Avenue dames. Her father lost his dough and threw himself off his penthouse roof-garden. The girl saw him jump. That did something to her. And then when she found she didn't have more than a few grand to her name, and her boy friend had given her the air, she went cuckoo. They brought her here, and she's been here ever since.'

There was a pause while he pounded my back. Then I said: 'What's wrong with her?'

'I never get on to the fancy names they use. It's something like melancholy.'

'Melancholia?'

'Sure. She sits most of the time and don't do nothing. Mrs Dell over in the women's wing tells me it gives you the creeps. Sometimes that girl don't say a word for a week on end.'

Poor Iris. I felt frightfully sorry for her. And I realized with a sort of shock that it was the first time I had felt really sorry for anyone, but myself, since Magdalen died. Maybe I was picking up.

'But you heard her today, Fogarty,' I insisted. 'What did she mean about Laribee murdering her father?'

Fogarty had muffled me in a warm towel now and was rubbing me up and down vigorously.

'She may be nutty, but that makes sense all right,' he said. 'Laribee and her father were in a sort of stock pool together. Laribee got out while the getting was good and left the others holding the bag. It was on account of that old Pattison committed suicide.'

I was putting on my bathrobe when Fogarty said cheerfully:

'D'you know, Mr Duluth, you've got a pretty swell physique for a guy who's been soaking for years.'

I thanked him for the doubtful compliment and he went on:

'How about me teaching you a couple of wrassling holds? Maybe when you're out, you can do me a good turn, too, and get me in the show business. That's where I belong.'

It seemed a rather one-sided bargain, but I agreed, and then Fogarty began to initiate me into the mysteries of the full Nelson. He had twisted me up somehow with my hands behind my neck when there were footsteps in the passage outside.

The door was open and we were standing near it. I felt pretty foolish when Miss Brush appeared. It pricked my male vanity for her to see me helpless in the grip of a great baboon like Fogarty.

But she did not seem to feel that way. She paused and watched in interest. Then she smiled that bright, fixed smile of hers.

'So you're learning to wrestle, Mr Duluth. Next time you misbehave you'll be harder to deal with.'

I couldn't have felt less hard to deal with, but she added suddenly:

'How about teaching me that hold, Jo? My ju-jutsu's a bit rusty and

I want to meet Mr Duluth on common ground next time we – come to grips.'

Fogarty let go of me like a hot cake and smiled broadly. I suppose he liked the idea of fooling around with Miss Brush, just as any of us would.

Calmly she walked over to him and let herself be manhandled. She was an amazing person. She took it all perfectly casually, as though she were being taught to knit. I sometimes wondered whether she knew how we men reacted to her. If she didn't, she was dumber than I thought.

She and Fogarty were in a kind of crazy embrace when there was a violent commotion in the passage.

'Lay off that . . . !'

I glanced at the door just in time to see a male figure in a blue bathrobe hurtle across the threshold. He sprang on Fogarty and started to strike out with his fists. For a few seconds I could distinguish nothing in the confusion. Then gradually that human thunderbolt with the naked chest and legs and the flying blue bathrobe made itself clear to me as young Billy Trent.

The boy was in a white-hot fury and his strength seemed almost superhuman. As Miss Brush staggered sideways into safety, the writhing mass collapsed to the floor with Billy Trent on top. With his tousled blond hair, his naked torso and his blazing eyes he looked like a movie magnate's bowdlerized conception of a jungle man.

'You're going to leave her alone, see?' His voice came quick, jerky. 'You're not going to hurt Miss Brush – no one's going to hurt Miss Brush. You leave her alone or . . .'

Fogarty started to put up a weak professional defence against those flailing young arms and legs, but he had been taken off his guard and his much vaunted muscles seemed surprisingly ineffectual now that Billy Trent had got his fingers around his throat.

For the first time since I'd known her, Miss Brush had lost her magnificent composure. She was hovering distractedly, exclaiming:

'It's all right, Billy. He wasn't hurting me. I asked him to do it . . .'

I made a very indifferent referee. I supposed something was expected of me, but my old jitters had returned and I had started to shake.

I don't know what would have happened if Moreno had not come in at that moment. Although my back was turned to the door, I was conscious of him as soon as he crossed the threshold. There was something about him – a commanding force. He gripped Trent's shoulder and said very quietly:

'You'd better stop that, Billy.'

The boy glanced up into the doctor's dark eyes; his gaze seemed to be held there as though hypnotized. Slowly his fingers relaxed from Fogarty's throat.

'But he was hurting Miss Brush! He tried to hurt . . .'

'No he didn't. You made a mistake. It was nothing.'

Trent drew away from Fogarty and the attendant scrambled ashamedly to his feet. Bill had risen too. He tied the cord of his bathrobe with an embarrassed, almost timid, look at Miss Brush.

'I'm sorry,' he murmured. Then he showed his splendid teeth in a dazzling smile. 'I'm sorry. I guess I kind of lost my temper. Silly of me. Anyone would think I was a nut or something.'

He mumbled an awkward apology to Fogarty and then, blushing like a school kid, hurried out of the room.

'It wasn't anything,' began Fogarty lamely, as soon as the door closed. 'Miss Brush just wanted to be taught a couple of wrassling holds.'

'Don't bother to explain,' cut in Moreno coldly. 'You'd better go and change.' He glanced at me. 'You, too, Mr Duluth . . . it's almost lunchtime.'

Fogarty slouched off, muttering something about being hit below the belt. Moreno and I stood there while Miss Brush patted her blond hair into some semblance of tidiness. Then I hurried away.

I hurried too fast. I had reached my room before I realized that I had left my towel behind. I suppose there was no real need to retrieve it, but it seemed like a pretty good excuse and I was curious to see if there was to be any sequel.

The door of the physio-therapy room was shut when I got back. I was just going to open it when I heard Moreno's voice, high and angry.

'Oh, he's just like me, poor kid. He can't bear to have another man touch you.'

To my shame I did not move, but they had lowered their voices and I could only catch disconnected phrases. I did hear Moreno mention Laribee's name, however.

And then Miss Brush laughed derisively.

'I rather fancy myself as the she-wolf of Wall Street,' she said.

I pushed open the door. They were standing very close together; Moreno with his hands clenched at his sides, Miss Brush serene and angelic, but with a determined set to her jaw.

As soon as they saw me, they relaxed. Moreno's eyes narrowed. Miss Brush smiled the specially-reserved-for-patients smile.

'I'm sorry,' I muttered lamely. 'I'd forgotten my – er – bedroom slippers – er – I mean my towel.'

7

It was Saturday, and I knew there would be the weekly formal dance-cum-bridge party in the main hall that evening. After my little act of the night before, I had not expected them to let me go. I was surprised when Moreno said it would be all right – surprised and delighted. I might have another chance of seeing Iris Pattison.

Iris had done something to me. That afternoon I had forgotten to start agonizing around cocktail time, and in spite of my shaking fit in the physio-therapy room, I felt pretty good.

I was almost childishly excited when Fogarty brought me my dress clothes, which he had produced from some mysterious place. He had to help me with my tie, but otherwise I managed. A furtive glance in the mirror was fairly satisfactory. I looked almost human, with my artificial sun tan and eyes that were no longer either yellow or blood-shot.

After dinner Miss Brush appeared, radiant in a slinky white dress, with a red corsage which added an intriguingly diabolic touch to her angelic blondness. The staff always dressed for these Saturday nights. Everything was very correct and none of us was allowed to remember we were in the polite equivalent of a bug-house.

Apparently the good-behaviour laws had been modified, because all our crowd was dolled up for the dance – even Billy Trent. Miss Brush marshalled us with tranquil determination and conducted us to the main hall. I walked with Geddes and young Billy. The Englishman was bored and a bit depressed, but Billy seemed to have forgotten his Tarzan act and was boiling over with enthusiasm. He was going to dance with Miss Brush, he told me. That was his idea of heaven.

The women were already assembled when we reached the co-educational lounge. The middle of the floor had been cleared for dancing, and there were bridge tables and couches grouped around the sides. The radio was playing soft dance music. Immediately I looked for Iris Pattison. I could not see her anywhere.

But everyone else was there – nurses, doctors, attendants, patients. Doctor Stevens, cheerful and cherubic, was chatting uproariously with a beautiful, and presumably crazy, redhead. Moreno was being the distinguished psychiatrist with a group of the non-resident medical staff. A grey-haired duchess of a woman was bowing with great dignity to imaginary acquaintances. The place fairly bristled with white shirt-fronts and *décolleté* gowns. It was quite impossible to tell the staff from the inmates. The whole thing looked like a fashionable Broadway first night.

Miss Brush was shepherding us around, presenting us to the women like a Park Avenue hostess, when I actually saw Iris. She was sitting alone in a corner, wearing a long purple dress. Forgetting the formality of the occasion I clutched Miss Brush's arm and pleaded loudly to be introduced. She gave me one of those knowing smiles and took me over.

'Miss Pattison – Mr Duluth.'

The girl looked up indifferently. It was an amazing shade of purple she was wearing – soft, subtle, like an iris, like her name. Her eyes met mine and dropped away. I sat down hopefully.

As I did so, they started to dance. I noticed Billy Trent hurry up to Miss Brush with an eager smile. She smiled back, but, as he moved towards her, she turned and stepped on to the dance floor with old Laribee. I saw the crushed disappointment on the kid's face, and for an instant my opinion of Isabel Brush dropped off like Laribee's imaginary stock market.

I tried to talk to Iris. I tried everything I could think of, but it was no use. Sometimes she answered in that quiet, expressionless voice. But there was no spark. It was like talking to a dead woman. And yet she was so young. One felt she could be so vibrantly alive.

I asked her to dance and she said, 'Thank you very much,' like a little girl. She danced perfectly, but there was a strange aloofness in her movements, as though she were doing it in a trance.

'You're very kind to me,' she said once, very softly – humbly.

I couldn't answer. The words just wouldn't come.

Meanwhile the party glittered around us with unruffled respectability. The nearest approach to unconventionality came paradoxically from Moreno. He stood in a corner, talking with Fogarty and Geddes, but his gaze was fixed on Laribee and Miss Brush. Suddenly when Miss Brush's head was rather too near the millionaire's shoulder, he strode through the dancers and cut in. It was all done politely, but there was an unbridled gleam in his eyes.

The music stopped. As I took Iris back to the couch, Mrs Fogarty rustled towards us. The night nurse had made an heroic attempt at an evening dress, but it bulged in the wrong places, as though she still wore her uniform underneath. She brought with her a faint whiff of antiseptic and a grey-haired woman with one of those stream-lined, aristocratic faces that suggested old brownstone houses and Back Bay.

Mrs Fogarty arranged her expression to register the sentiment: 'I feel you two would have a lot in common,' and then reluctantly permitted herself to speak.

'Mr Duluth, this is Miss Powell. She has seen several of your plays in Boston and she wants to talk about them.'

I didn't. I only wanted to be alone with Iris. But Miss Powell sat down with determination on the extreme edge of the couch and started to talk condescendingly and volubly about culture and the stage. I took it for granted she was some visiting psychiatrist or philanthropist who knew how to humour us unfortunate inmates. I reacted accordingly, being bright and humoured; but my eyes were on Iris most of the time.

I was looking at her when old Laribee came up. I had my back to him and could not see who it was. But his presence was mirrored plainly on Iris's face. Her pale cheeks flushed with a sudden expression of distaste. She rose to her feet and, after an instant, moved hurriedly away.

I wanted to go after her, to tell her that I'd sock old Laribee on the jaw – that I'd do anything if it would make her feel better. But Miss Powell was too quick for me. Before I had time to move, she had laid a strong, rather masculine hand on my arm and was drawing me back into the endless stream of her discourse.

Laribee lingered at our side, and eventually I managed to shift her on to him. He knew and probably cared less about culture than I did, but that did not seem to matter to Miss Powell. All she needed was an audience.

I was about to slip furtively away from them, when I noticed something curious. Miss Powell's alert eyes never met the financier's. They remained fixed with strange intensity upon the platinum watch-chain which stretched across his broad vest.

'Small cultural groups, Mr Laribee –'

The deep voice flowed tirelessly on. Then with infinite stealth, her right hand began to move forward.

'As our dear Emerson might have said –'

I stared in utter astonishment. Her fingers were almost touching the chain now. And then, without the slightest diminution of dignity or the least break in her monologue, Miss Powell had flicked the watch out of his pocket and was slipping it with ladylike delicacy under one of the pillows of the couch.

Laribee had noticed nothing. It had all been done in one elegant split second – a superb demonstration in pickpocketing, worthy of the Artful Dodger himself. Miss Powell had soared in my estimation.

'It is a very worthwhile endeavour, Mr Laribee. I'm sure you would be interested.'

Obviously, Laribee was not interested in worthwhile endeavours. He seemed to want to follow Miss Brush on to the dance floor. And the only means of doing so was to ask Miss Powell to dance. She accepted with surprising alacrity, and they sailed away like any ordinary, unhappily married couple. But that predatory look was still in the Bostonian spinster's eye. I wondered whether she was planning to start work on his diamond shirt-studs.

After they had gone, I felt under the pillow. The watch was there. But it was not alone. It lay in a little nest of other treasures. I found a bandage, a pair of scissors, a half empty bottle of iodine and a clinical thermometer. Miss Powell, like a health-conscious squirrel, must have been storing up medical supplies for the winter.

I slipped the watch into my pocket, meaning to return it to old Laribee myself. But I had no idea what to do with the rest of things. I glanced helplessly around the room and Mrs Fogarty caught my eye.

'Take a look at this,' I said as she hurried over.

The night nurse pulled at the sleeves of her evening dress as though it were a uniform.

'Poor Miss Powell,' she clucked agitatedly. 'She was so much better and now she's started taking things again. Such a good mind as she has, too.'

'I don't know about the mind,' I said. 'But she's got million-dollar fingers. It's kleptomania, I suppose?'

Mrs Fogarty nodded absently but did not give me a verbal reply. This little incident seemed to worry her more than I would have expected. She gathered up the treasure-trove and carried it to Doctor Stevens who was standing near by. I heard her say:

'Here are some of the things that were missing from the surgery, doctor. There's nothing else except two bandages and the stop-watch.'

Stevens's cherubic face had gone grave. Muttering something about being a doctor and not a detective, he hurried out of the room.

A few minutes later Laribee came back from the dance floor alone. I congratulated him on disposing of Miss Powell, but he seemed jumpy, nervous. As he sat down at my side, I noticed that his face was unusually pale. Suddenly, as though with an effort, he said in a low, earnest voice:

'Mr Duluth, if I ask you a question, you won't think I'm mad, will you?'

By tacit consent we inmates made a point of accepting each other's sanity. I asked politely what he meant and, thinking he referred to his watch, was about to produce it when he added:

'Do you or do you not hear a low, fast ticking like a –?'

He broke off. I knew he meant a tape-ticker and that he could not bring himself to say the word. For a moment I imagined it was just one of his delusions. Then I realized that it was nothing of the sort. Distinctly I could hear a rapid ticking – far faster than a watch. It seemed to come from the neighbourhood of Laribee's left coat pocket.

'Yes, I can hear it,' I said, feeling almost as surprised as he looked. 'Try your left-hand pocket.'

Dazedly and with trembling fingers, old Laribee thrust his hand into his pocket. It came out clutching a round metal object, which I recognized immediately as one of those gadgets Stevens used in the surgery to take pulses, blood-pressure rates, and what-nots. It was obviously the clinical stopwatch which Mrs Fogarty had referred to as missing.

It was ticking very fast and somehow its sound took even me back to the panic days of 1929.

'A stopwatch,' Laribee was murmuring softly. 'It's only a stopwatch.' Then he turned to me and added sharply: 'But how on earth did it get there?'

'Perhaps some one traded it for this,' I said, handing him back his watch.

He stared in astonishment and then took it from me with a pitying smile. Obviously he felt that it was I rather than he who was on the shady side of the fringe. As he fingered the cold platinum of the watch, I noticed an almost beatific expression pass across his face.

'So you see,' he said to himself, 'they're trying to frighten me. That's all it is. I'm not mad, of course I'm not mad.' He nodded his head sagely. 'I've got to tell Miss Brush.'

He rose and lumbered away through the dancers.

After he had left me, I felt a strange sensation of threatening danger. I had thought that Miss Powell was merely comic relief. But now, even she seemed to have become tied up in the development of this strange drama which was acting itself out so deviously in Doctor Lenz's sanatorium.

The Boston spinster had stolen the stopwatch. I felt pretty sure of that. But had she just slipped it into Laribee's pocket when they were dancing together? Or was it responsible for the ticking I had heard in the financier's room the night before? And if it had been, how on earth could it have got into the men's wing? I knew enough about stopwatches to realize that they could not run for many hours continuously. Someone must have wound it up again. But who? Miss Powell? Someone else who, for some reason, wanted to frighten Laribee? Or could it be the millionaire himself, working out some crazy, intricate plan of his own?

And then another thought struck me – a thought slightly more sinister in its implications. Laribee's sanity – or rather his insanity – meant a great deal of money to the institution. Was it possible that . . . ?

I would have given anything for a quart of rye to help me figure it out. But as there was not a Chinaman's chance of that, I went in search of fresh air. That opulent lounge, with its expensive dresses, its expensive psychiatrists, its dancing puppets, was beginning to get me down.

I had hoped to find my friend Fogarty in the lobby, but only Warren was there. I asked him for a cigarette and we started to chat. Despite his efficient headlocks, our night attendant was a mournful, rather ineffectual man. He always had a grievance, and this time, as usual, it was his brother-in-law. With uncharacteristic frankness, he hinted at Fogarty's marital short-comings and bemoaned his sister's fate for having married a 'four-flusher' like that. In a remarkably short space of time, he managed to explain how even a kid like Billy Trent had shown Fogarty up as a bum wrestler; how his brother-in-law was not a champ in America, but only in England and anyone could beat an Englishman at wrestling, anyway.

'He's scared to take a tumble with me,' he said darkly. 'He knows darn well he'd get eaten up. One day it'll happen and you'll see.'

This opened up another set of lugubrious thoughts. In the past, it appeared, Warren had himself hoped to become a professional wrestler. He and his sister had had a bit of money, but they had both been lured into the stock market and had lost it all.

'Yeah,' he said with strange viciousness, 'If I had that cash, I might have been a champ by now. And here I am, having to look after a guy like Laribee, the kind of bird who lost my dough for me.'

I had often wondered vaguely what happened to would-be wrestlers like Warren, superannuated champions like Fogarty and superannuated speculators like Laribee. As I left the night attendant for the dubious delights of the lounge, I felt that I knew the answer. In some rôle or other, they must all inevitably end up in a place like Doctor Lenz's sanatorium.

When I re-entered the hall, the dancing had stopped and everyone was clustered around the far end of the room. At first I could not make out the centre of attraction. Then I saw it was Doctor Lenz himself.

With his beard gleaming black against his white shirt-front, he looked like God in his younger and more tolerant days. As I joined the group I could feel his personality just as though I had come into his magnetic field. He moved around, giving a moment's attention, an omniscient word, to everyone. He was an extraordinary man. I wondered whether he was conscious of those electrical discharges that emanated from him.

I had the vague intention of reporting the stopwatch incident to him, but I forgot it when I caught sight of Iris. She was sitting alone again in a corner. I hurried over to her eagerly and asked rather fatuously whether she had enjoyed the evening.

'Yes,' she said mechanically, as though I were a dull host, who had to be thanked, 'I've enjoyed myself very much.'

There seemed no point in carrying the conversation further. I just sat and looked at her – at the exotic, flower face and the shoulders thrusting like white petals from the sheath of her iris dress.

Suddenly I felt an overwhelming desire to see her walk across the stage. There was something in that girl – something you see only once in a lifetime. A subtle curve of the neck, an indefinable beauty of gesture – the thing that every theatrical man from Broadway to Baghdad is looking for. My old enthusiasm started to tingle in my veins. I had to get out of that place, to take this girl with me, to train her. With the proper build-up she could go anywhere – anywhere. Already my mind was five years ahead of itself. It was the healthiest feeling I'd had in years.

Ideas were still tumbling over each other in my brain as I glanced back at the others. They were all there, patients and staff, gathered around Doctor Lenz and the bridge tables.

As I watched, a man detached himself from the group. I did not pay much attention at first. Then I realized it was David Fenwick, our spiritualist. In the black and white of his evening clothes he looked even more ethereal than usual. And there was something purposeful about the way he was making for the centre of the empty dance floor.

No one else seemed to have noticed him, but my eyes were fixed on him as he turned suddenly and faced the others. He lifted a hand as though for silence, and even at that distance I could see the gleam in his large eyes. When he spoke, his voice was curiously penetrating.

'At last they have got through,' he announced in a toneless half chant. 'At last I have been able to take their message. It is a warning for us all, but it is directed particularly toward Daniel Laribee.'

Everyone spun around. They were staring at him in a sort of fascinated stillness. I was gazing at him, too, but out of the corner of my eye I caught a glimpse of Miss Brush moving hurriedly forward.

She was within a few feet of him when he spoke again. I suppose there must have been something about him that made her pause. For she stood there absolutely motionless as he said:

'This is the warning which the spirits sent me. Beware of Isabel Brush. Beware of Isabel Brush. She is a danger to us all, and especially to Daniel Laribee. She is a danger. There will be murder . . .'

The silence was tense. For a second, the two of them stood there like figures on a stage – Fenwick in a sort of trance, Miss Brush very pale and rigid.

Then a voice suddenly cried out:

'David . . . David!'

To my amazement it was Doctor Stevens who had spoken and who now sprang forward. His round face had lengthened to an anxious oval. He put his arm almost caressingly around Fenwick's shoulder and whispered something in his ear.

As he drew him away, the spell had broken and the room was in an uproar. Miss Brush disappeared somewhere in the milling, agitated crowd. Moreno, Lenz, Mrs Fogarty, Warren – I had fleeting glimpses of them all as they hurried about trying to restore the polite veneer which Fenwick's startling announcement had so completely shattered.

For the first time I realized how synthetic, how superficial was this built-up pretence of normal men and women brought together for an evening's social entertainment.

That scene of half-panicky confusion was horrible and infinitely sad. As a symbol of it, I remember Franz Stroubel, that small, distinguished man with the beautiful hands, standing in a corner, gazing serenely over the jostling crowds in front of him and moving his arms rhythmically – conducting with an unseen baton, weaving a pattern into the chaos.

People were streaming past me, but I did not see them as I turned toward Iris. She had not moved from my side, but her hands were covering her lovely face.

'Murder!' I heard her whisper. 'Murder. It's – it's terrible.'

At first, when I realized she was crying, I felt helpless and miserable. But suddenly, I was glad. She was frightened, worried, but, at least, she was showing some emotion.

I suppose my nerves must have been rather shaken up, too. Before I knew what I was doing, I had taken her hand and was whispering urgently:

'It's all right, Iris. Don't cry. Everything's going to be all right.'

8

But everything was not all right as far as those in charge of us were concerned. We men were taken back to Wing Two, and some of us were pretty jumpy. Fenwick was nowhere to be seen. Miss Brush made no appearance. Laribee, pale and distraught, was put to bed by Mrs Fogarty.

The rest of us were herded into the smoking-room. I spent the few minutes before bedtime with Billy Trent, who seemed to have forgotten the soda fountain in his anxiety over Miss Brush.

'It doesn't mean anything, does it, Pete? We don't really have to beware of Miss Brush.'

'No, Billy,' I said. 'It's just a lot of hooey.'

'And all that about murder?'

'Bunk.'

I seemed to be successful in reassuring the kid. But I myself was not so easily reassured. I set very little store by spiritualistic warnings, but it did seem more than a strange coincidence that, within twenty-four hours, three different persons should have heard that ominous prophecy, 'There will be murder.'

After I had gone to bed, those four words repeated themselves in my mind; first in my own voice, as I had heard them last night; then in Geddes's voice, just before his attack that morning. And finally I seemed to hear them again, intoned mechanically by the dazed Fenwick in the crowded lounge.

And if there were murder, I asked myself, who would be the victim? Each of the day's incidents, whether trivial, amusing or sinister, seemed to point to only one person, to the man lying in the room next to mine – to Daniel Laribee.

I wondered whether Lenz were still attributing all these curious incidents to a subversive influence. Or whether he, just as myself, were beginning to believe that it all went deeper, all had some basic, alarming significance. After all, Laribee seemed to have plenty of enemies, even here in the institution. If any sane person wanted to murder him, they could hardly choose a safer setting for the crime than a mental hospital.

My reflections were taking a distinctly morbid turn. I decided to go to sleep – and did.

Next morning I woke up with the sunlight, having no idea what the time was. We did not have clocks in the rooms.

I felt a bit hang-overish, but that was nothing new. For an unconscionable time I lay in bed, waiting for Fogarty to take me down to the physio-therapy room. He did not come. At last I gave way to impatience and, slipping on my bathrobe, strolled down the corridor to look for him.

The passage clock said twenty minutes to eight. Fogarty was ten minutes overdue. I expected to encounter his wife somewhere, but her little alcove was empty and she was not around the corridors. In fact, no one was in sight. The place had a strange, deserted atmosphere.

I knew the physio-therapy room was always locked and Fogarty had the key. There was no chance of getting in without him. But I kept on my way. The ex-champ might already be down there, I thought.

When I reached it the door was shut. I was about to take my mild irritation back to bed with me when I saw the key in the lock. It surprised me, for I was not used to inefficiency on the part of Doctor Lenz's staff. Feeling curious, I turned the handle and went in.

The physio-therapy room was a kind of miniature Turkish bath without the Turkish baths. There were all types of electrical gadgets along one wall; showers on another; and small alcoves on the third, where we took rubdowns and other uncomfortably beneficial treatments.

A casual glance showed that Fogarty was not with the electrical equipment. I called his name and strolled to the showers. He was not there. And then, outside one of the alcoves, I saw, lying on the floor, the suit which he had been wearing the night before. For a moment I thought Jo must have been out on a bender and was giving himself a rubdown to help sober up.

I was smiling when I pushed back the curtain. Then, suddenly, I realized what writers mean when they talk about a smile 'freezing' on your face. I had started some fool phrase, reproving Fogarty for his unpunctuality, but the words stuck in my throat.

Lying on the marble slab in that tiny room was a thing more ghastly than the furthest horrors of delirium tremens.

'There will be murder.' The phrase was familiar enough, but I had not expected anything quite like this.

I could hear a sound re-echoing against the hard stone floors and walls – a muffled, persistent, sound. It was my own teeth chattering as they had done those first days without alcohol, here in the sanatorium.

I couldn't think coherently for a moment, but, when reason returned, I knew this was no hallucination. It was still there – that thing on the marble slab, that thing which had been Jo Fogarty.

There was no blood, no mutilation. It was the *position* of the body that was so shocking. The man was lying on his chest in his trunks and socks. And the upper part of his body was bound in a strange garment, the significance of which I did not immediately recognize. Only gradually did it identify itself in my mind with pictures I had seen of strait-jackets.

The stout canvas was strapped tightly across his great naked torso, pinioning his arms to his sides. Around his neck had been tied an improvised rope, made from woven strips of towel. This rope was also attached to his ankles, drawing his head back and his legs forward so that he looked like a swallow diver, caught and trussed in mid-air. I noticed vaguely that his feet were secured by his own tie and belt; and his own handkerchief was bound around his mouth to hold in place a gag of torn towel.

The whole tableau was like some mad modern sculpture, symbolizing the apotheosis of agony. And it was the very strength of the man that made it so horrible; the strength of that powerful frame, those swelling muscles straining against the bonds, straining, it seemed, even in death.

For he was dead. Instinct would have told me that immediately, even if I had not seen the towel cord, tight round the bull neck, the unnatural set of the head, jerked backward by the weight of the sagging heels. I do not even want to think of the expression on that contorted face, the desperation in those dead eyes.

Suddenly the realization dawned on me that I was alone with death – alone in a small room of vault-like marble. I was seized by a violent claustrophobia – a fear that I should go mad if I stayed another minute in that cramped, low-ceilinged alcove.

I remembered the key in the lock outside. Swiftly I hurried out of the room and, with trembling fingers, locked the door. I slipped the key into my pocket, looked up and down the corridor, and then started forward.

My thought processes were hopelessly confused. But one phrase repeated itself time and time again in my mind.

'. . . Doctor Lenz – must go to Doctor Lenz . . .'

I did not hear Moreno as I turned a corner in the passage. He seemed suddenly to have appeared from nowhere, standing in my path and looking at me with that dark, smouldering stare of his.

'You're up early, Mr Duluth.'

Inside my bathrobe pocket my fingers gripped the key. 'I've got to see Doctor Lenz,' I said with sudden decisiveness.

'Doctor Lenz is not up yet.'

'But I've got to see him.'

Moreno's eyes seemed to penetrate mine, trying to read my thoughts. 'Will you go back to your room alone, Mr Duluth? Or do you want me to go with you?'

'I have no intention of going back to my room.' I stood there a moment, trying to get a grip on myself. Then I added: 'Something very serious has happened.'

'Has it?'

'Something that only Doctor Lenz must know about. Now will you let me go?'

'Listen, Mr Duluth –'

Moreno started to humour me in his quiet, relentless fashion. Suddenly there seemed no point in holding back what I knew. Moreno would hear about it soon enough, anyhow.

'Come with me,' I said grimly.

He followed to the physio-therapy room. I unlocked the door, but I could not go near the alcove. As he pulled the curtain back, I saw his jaw drop slightly. But his voice was brisk, dangerously calm, as he said:

'When did you find this?'

I told him.

Slowly, deliberately, he took out a handkerchief and passed it across his forehead.

'Now will you let me go to Doctor Lenz?' I asked.

'We will go together,' he said quietly.

9

I had a nasty attack of jitters after my interview with Doctor Lenz. They sent me to bed, and a pale and very solemn Miss Brush brought me some breakfast. After a cup of black coffee, I felt better and able to think more coherently.

But even so, nothing seemed to make sense. This horrible and utterly unexpected death only added to the confusion of those other strange incidents which the past twenty-four hours had been piling up. Last night I had known there was danger, but that danger had seemed to be connected with Daniel Laribee and Miss Brush. Fogarty had no place in that pattern. There seemed no conceivable reason why anyone should want to kill the attendant whose worst fault had been his boastfulness.

And it seemed incredible, too, that anyone had been able to murder him in that beastly way. It would have needed amazing strength – the strength of a madman, a homicidal maniac.

Maniac! I remembered the look on Lenz's face when he had said: 'I feel there is someone in this sanatorium who ought not to be here.' Lenz might think it the work of a madman. Yet my own instinct told me it was not. The whole thing was either too deliberately crazy – or too horribly sane.

It was a relief when Miss Brush came in and suggested that I should get up.

I strolled into the library, hoping to find Geddes for a soothing game of billiards. He was not there. The room was deserted except for Stroubel, who sat in a leather chair, staring in front of him with an ineffably sad expression on his sensitive face.

The famous conductor looked up when I entered, and smiled. I was surprised, for he had never paid any attention to me before. I moved to his side and he said quietly:

'This is a tragic world, Mr Duluth. We do not realize that others beside ourselves suffer.'

I was going to ask what he meant, when he lifted one of those beautifully moulded hands of his.

'Last night, lying there in the darkness, I was sad. I rang for Mrs Fogarty. When she came I saw that she had been crying. I had never thought of that. Never thought that a nurse could have sorrows like mine.'

Instantly I found myself interested. It was rather pathetic to think of the grim-faced Mrs Fogarty crying. Surprising, too.

Last night she could not have known what had happened to her husband. Had she, like the rest of us, heard that strange prophetic voice? I hoped Stroubel would tell me more, but at that moment Miss Brush came in and said I was wanted again in Doctor Lenz's office.

She took me there herself. As she walked briskly at my side, I glanced at her curiously. She still preserved her brightness, but I suspected her composure of being as artificial as the pinkness of her cheeks. I asked her if she had been bothered by Fenwick's little scene of the night before. Immediately her lips moved in that fixed smile of hers.

'We expect these things, Mr Duluth. For a while Doctor Lenz felt I should be transferred to the women's wing. But we decided it was best for me to stay.'

We made no reference to Fogarty.

She left me at the door of the director's office. Doctor Lenz himself was sitting behind the desk, his bearded face gloomy. Moreno was there, too; and Doctor Stevens. A couple of plain-clothes men lounged by the wall, and in the seat usually reserved for interviewed patients sat a solid individual whom Lenz introduced to me as Captain Green of the homicide bureau.

They seemed to take very little notice of me. Lenz explained briefly that I had discovered the body, and then continued with a discourse which my arrival had interrupted.

'As I was saying, captain, I must make one point clear before there is any investigation in the sanatorium itself. As a citizen, I have an obligation to the State, an obligation to see that justice is done. But as a psychiatrist I have an even greater obligation, and that is to my patients. Their mental health is in my hands. I am responsible for them and I must absolutely forbid any kind of police cross-examination.'

Green grunted.

'Any shock of that sort,' Lenz went on, 'could cause irreparable damage. Of course, Doctor Moreno and other members of the staff will do all they can in a tactful manner, but I cannot allow anything more direct than that.'

Green nodded rather curtly and threw a suspicious glance at me. I suppose he took me for one of the sensitive patients in question.

Lenz seemed to read his thoughts. He assured him with a slight smile that I was a little different from the other inmates and suggested that I might prove useful.

'You can be perfectly frank in front of Mr Duluth, captain.'

From the conversation which followed between the captain and Lenz, I gathered that Fogarty had been dead for three or four hours when I discovered him. He had last been seen when he left the social hall to go off duty. It appeared that both Mrs Fogarty and Warren had already been questioned. They had had nothing to report and were able to account for one another's movements during the night.

Throughout this exchange of question and answer Moreno had preserved a cold silence. At length he leaned forward in his chair and said rather acidly: 'Isn't it perfectly possible that the whole thing was an accident? After all, we have no reason to believe that anyone would have wanted to murder Fogarty. I don't see why some practical joke –'

'If it was a practical joke,' interrupted Green tartly, 'someone around here's got a pretty queer sense of humour. If it was an accident it was a pretty queer accident. And if it was deliberate murder, it's one of the cleverest jobs I ever came up against. Doctor Stevens here says it's impossible to tell when the man was put in that strait-jacket. It could have been done any time last night, and whoever did it could have established a hundred alibis.'

'It's not only clever,' broke in Doctor Stevens quietly. 'If it was a crime, it's just about as brutal a one as you could imagine.' His normally cherubic face was pale and contoured with lines. 'The medical examiner and I believe that Fogarty was probably conscious up to the end. He must have been dying there in slow agony, maybe for six or seven hours. The gag kept him from calling for help and every movement he made to free himself would only have increased the pressure around his throat. It was the tightening of the towel rope, caused by the gradual constriction of his leg muscles, that eventually strangled him.' He looked down at his hands. 'I can only hope with Doctor Moreno that the death turns out to be the result of some unfortunate accident. People have been known to tie themselves up.'

'Yeah?' broke in Green impatiently. 'And put a strait-jacket on themselves and then run a cord from their necks to their ankles? You'd have to be a super-Houdini to do that. No, sir. We're dealing with murder or else I'm about ready for a cure in this sanatorium.'

He turned sharply to me and asked me to run through the events of my discovery in the physio-therapy room. While I spoke, he stared at me suspiciously, as though he expected at any moment to see me gibbering like an ape or climbing up the curtains. When I had finished he said:

'What did the patients think of Fogarty? Did they like him?'

I told him that the ex-champion had been popular with us all; and that he was rumoured to be especially popular with the ladies. He pressed me for further details and I mentioned his desire to get into the show business, and also his pride in his physical strength.

'That's just the point,' said Green exasperatedly. 'With a man of his physique, it would have needed at least six or seven ordinary people to get him into that strait-jacket. And yet the medical examiner and Stevens here say there's no sign of violence. The blood's been tested in your own laboratories and there's no trace of anaesthetic. I don't see how it was done, unless –'

He broke off and gazed at Lenz. 'This whole business seems crazy to me,' he continued. 'Isn't it possible that you've got someone in this sanatorium who's more dangerous than you think – some out-and-out maniac? They're supposed to have incredible strength, and maybe they'd get a sort of sadistic pleasure out of seeing a man in pain.'

I watched Lenz with interest. This theory seemed to fit in so well with his remarks about a subversive influence. To my surprise, his eyes hardened. Sadism, he explained coldly, was a common manifestation in the most normal individuals. But motiveless murder would imply an advanced condition of dementia which was most unlikely to exist in his sanatorium. He was willing to have any State alienist examine the inmates, but he did not feel it necessary.

'Because,' he concluded coldly, 'no homicidal maniac could have committed so deliberate a crime. When a maniac kills, it is in a moment of acute emotional disturbance. He would never have the patience to put a man in a strait-jacket and truss him up so elaborately – not even if he had the strength and the opportunity.'

Green seemed unconvinced. 'Even so, could any of your patients have gone to the physio-therapy room during the night without being seen?'

'I suppose so.' Lenz moved a hand up and down his beard. 'I do not believe in too much restriction here. With the type of patient I treat, it is essential to create the atmosphere of normality. I try to make the sanatorium seem as much like a hotel or a club as possible. Unless they cause any disturbance, the patients are given considerable licence.'

'So they could have got hold of one of those strait-jackets,' said Green quickly.

'No.' It was Moreno who spoke. 'We have only two in the institution. Both Doctor Lenz and myself consider them old-fashioned and dangerous. We do not believe in forcible coercion. The strait-jackets we have are kept for extreme emergencies. They are locked in a closet in the physio-therapy room. Only Fogarty and Warren had keys. I doubt if anyone else in the institution knew of their existence.'

Suddenly there flashed into my mind the recollection of my talk the night before with the gloomy Warren.

'I suppose there's nothing to this,' I suggested. 'Fogarty and Warren were talking about taking a tumble with each other. Maybe they used the strait-jacket as a trial of strength and – as Doctor Moreno suggests – there was an accident.'

A quick glance passed between Lenz and Moreno.

'Yes,' said Stevens urgently, 'surely some explanation of that sort would be more satisfactory.'

Green grunted non-committally. He asked me a few more questions and then said:

'There's another possibility. Mr Duluth here mentioned that Fogarty was popular with the women. Apparently it was impossible for a man to have tied him up against his will, but a woman might have persuaded him to put the strait-jacket on himself. You say he was proud of his strength. It would be easy to get him to show off. And once he was in the jacket, even a woman could manage the rest.'

Immediately I thought of Fogarty's little act with Miss Brush the day before – the act which had ended so sensationally with the intrusion of young Billy Trent. I could tell that Moreno remembered it, too, for his dark cheeks flushed slightly. Before I could make up my mind whether or not to mention it, he said abruptly:

'Mr Duluth is still suffering from the shock of his discovery, and excitement is not good for him. Unless the captain wants to ask him any more questions, I feel he should be excused.'

Green shrugged and Doctor Lenz nodded agreement. As Moreno crossed to my side, I could not help wondering at his eagerness to get me out of the room. And that was not the only thing that puzzled me. Lenz knew as well as I that strange things had been going on in the sanatorium. He himself had first called my attention to them. And yet he seemed to have made no attempt to tell Green.

Moreno conducted me to the door and paused on the threshold.

'Of course,' he said curtly, 'you will tell none of the other patients about this, Mr Duluth. And you mustn't think too much about it yourself. You are not a normal man yet, you know.'

10

As I stepped out into the corridor, I heard Doctor Stevens's voice from the room behind me.

'If you gentlemen can do without me, I'll be getting back to the surgery. I'll be there if you need me.'

He hurried out of the room and joined me in the passage. As we walked away in silence, I had the distinct impression that he wanted to ask me something. He proved me right by exclaiming with rather forced heartiness:

'Well, Duluth, that's a bad way to begin the day, but the old schedule must go on. How about coming to the surgery with me? We can get your daily check-up done.'

I agreed and followed him to the surgery, one of those gleaming, hygienic places with white-painted closets and glass topped tables. There's something about a surgery that always intimidates me. The smell of antiseptic, the gleaming knives in the glass cabinets, the rolls of bandages, they remind one with unpleasant force of one's inevitable exit. I sat down in a hard, shiny chair and watched Stevens pace restlessly up and down, his hands clasped behind his back. With his plump pink cheeks and china blue eyes he looked like a large cherub giving an impudent imitation of an agitated doctor.

Erratically he ran through his regular questionnaire and made the correct hieroglyphics on my chart. Then, instead of dismissing me, he sat down and stared at me over the instruments and bandages.

'What do you think about all this?' he asked bluntly.

By now I had grown used to being treated like a prison trusty. Apparently there's no one who inspires more gratuitous confidences than an alcoholic in a mental home.

'I don't think anything in particular,' I replied wearily.

'But that Green fellow,' persisted the anxious cherub, 'he won't even consider the possibility of an accident. Do you think it's murder?'

'My stage training has taught me that people who are found trussed up in grotesque positions are always the victims of some dastardly crime,' I said, trying out of sheer self-preservation to take the whole business flippantly. 'There seems no motive, but then – you don't need motives in a place like this.'

'That's exactly the point.' Stevens rose to his feet, crossed aimlessly to a closet and sat down again. 'Listen, Duluth, I want to ask you something in confidence. I'm not a psychiatrist. I'm just a plain medical man whose business it is to keep tabs on your bowels and bellyaches. But I'm particularly interested in this beastly affair and I'd like to know whether you as an inmate have any suspicions. Of course, I've no right to ask, but even so . . .'

'I'm afraid I haven't a single idea,' I put in quickly. 'And I'd let you know if I did. From what I see of my fellow sufferers, they're a pretty harmless lot, and I for one wouldn't expect any of them to murder me.'

Stevens picked up his stethoscope and started to toy with it nervously. 'I'm glad to hear you say that, Duluth. And there's a special reason. You see, I have a relative who's a patient here in the sanatorium. He's my half-brother, in fact. He got into quite a nasty mess, and I persuaded him to come all the way from California because I thought so highly of Lenz. You can understand my problem. I wouldn't want him to stay if I felt there was any real danger. And yet I don't want to send him away unless it's absolutely necessary. They've been decent to me here, and as a resident member of the staff I have a – er – financial interest in the sanatorium. If my half-brother left, it would set a bad example, and in twenty-four hours all the others would have gone, too.'

'I see your point,' I murmured, still marvelling at my ability to collect confidences. 'But as a moral adviser I'm pretty much of a broken reed right now.'

'Of course, Duluth. Yes,' Stevens's pink face broke into a quick smile and then settled once more into solemnity. 'If Fogarty's death is connected with one of the patients,' he said slowly, 'I feel there's one perfectly simple way of clearing the matter up.'

'How do you mean?'

'By psycho-analysis. I suggested it, but Lenz and Moreno don't approve, and it'd be as good as my job's worth for me to butt in.'

He paused and glanced at me. For a moment I thought he was going to ask my assistance in some extra-official psychological experimentation. But he didn't. He shook his head and said briskly:

'It's a pity Lenz wouldn't try that.'

'But how would you work it?' I asked.

'By an elementary process of thought-association. I happen to be very interested in that despised field of psychology.' Stevens laid down the stethoscope with a faint clatter. 'All one would have to do is to mention some word associated with the crime and watch the reaction on the patient.'

'Such as Fogarty's name, for example?' I asked, feeling suddenly interested.

'In this case, no. It would be too dangerous. The patients will be wondering about Fogarty anyhow, and a lot of damage might be done. One has to be extremely careful.'

'How about "strait-jacket"?' I inquired.

'Emphatically, no.' A slight smile moved across Stevens's lips. 'In a sanatorium of this type, that word would receive a violent reaction from anyone. It would have to be some phrase which normally had no particular significance – something that struck you for example when you discovered the – er – body. But I'm just riding my hobby horse, Duluth.' He rose and looked a little embarrassed, as though he realized he had overstepped the bounds of discretion.

'I wish you'd forget all this,' he murmured. 'I guess I'm a little unstrung. But I'm worried, you know – my half-brother.'

As I left the surgery and started back to Wing Two, I found myself wondering about that half-brother. Which, I reflected, of my fellow patients had this unsuspected connection with the staff? Then I remembered Fenwick's little act in the central hall the night before. I remembered how Stevens had dashed forward, heard his voice crying:

'David . . . David. . . !'

The would-be psycho-analyst, I guessed, was the half-brother of the spiritualist.

I was so absorbed in my reflections that I did not at first notice the girl with a mop who was swabbing the floor in front of me. Or if I did, I dismissed her from my mind as one of those nondescript females who occasionally cleaned and polished about the building. I had stepped on to a damp, freshly mopped patch before I saw her properly. And then it didn't make sense.

It was Iris Pattison with a white apron and a cute white cap on her

55

dark hair. She was manipulating the mop with more than professional concentration.

'Don't walk on the clean part,' she said, and her expression, as she glanced up, was irritated rather than sad.

But I hardly heard what she said. I was busy watching her. Maybe she was only pushing a mop around, but there was something about her – something that got the theatre in me all excited. The movement of her hips, the fragile profile half turned away, the slight droop of her mouth – all perfect. Instinctively I was back at rehearsals again.

'Superb!' I exclaimed. 'Now turn and come this way. That's right . . . no, not so quickly . . . head more to the left so's it gets the footlights . . . that's better . . .'

She was staring at me now, half in alarm, half in disappointment, as though she had hoped that I wasn't as nutty as the rest of them and had found out her mistake. But I was too worked up to mind. I gripped her arm and said:

'Miss Pattison, have you ever been on the stage?'

'You'd – you'd better go away,' she said. 'You're not allowed here.'

'Not until you've told me whether you've been on the stage.'

'Why, no, never. And I know I couldn't act.'

'Nonsense. You don't have to be able to act. I can teach you that. You've got everything, see?' I waved my arm in an abandoned gesture. 'Listen, Miss Pattison, you're going to get out of here and I'm going to do something about you. Given patience and six months, I could get you anywhere. And . . .' I broke off. Even I could not fail to interpret the expression on her face now. 'And I'm not mad,' I added testily. 'I happen to be a Broadway theatrical producer. I'm in here because I was a soak, but I'm getting better now and what I say goes.'

Her mouth moved in a faint smile. 'What – what a relief,' she said. 'For a moment, I thought –'

'All theatrical producers are crazy,' I broke in. 'And what the hell are you doing with that mop, anyway?'

'Doctor Lenz told me to clean the corridor.' Iris turned and started in again vigorously, as though she were being paid piecework. 'He said I had never done anything useful in my life. But I rather like doing this.'

I thought a hundred a week rather a lot to pay for the privilege of mopping corridors. But Lenz seemed to know his psychiatry. Iris was obviously interested.

I told her what a good job she was doing, and she seemed childishly grateful. An instant of radiance lit up the white flower of her face.

'I've done all that other corridor, too,' she said proudly.

There were so few opportunities of seeing her alone that I couldn't bear to tear myself away. There were a thousand things I wanted to say, but I seemed suddenly to have become inarticulate. All I could do was to start talking lamely about the night before, saying how sorry I was that Fenwick's spiritualistic warning had upset her.

I realized at once that I had been stupid to remind her of it. She turned her head away and manoeuvred a corner with her mop. 'Oh, it wasn't that which upset me,' she said softly.

'It wasn't?'

'No.' Her voice was low. She moved so that she was facing me and I saw the fear in her eyes. 'It was something I heard.'

I felt a moment of alarm. Suddenly the recollection of Fogarty's death and all the other grotesque incidents of the past days came flooding back into my mind, making even this charming interlude seem sinister.

'It was a voice,' Iris was murmuring. 'I don't know where it came from, but I heard it when everyone was running past. It said very softly: "Daniel Laribee murdered your father. You must kill him." '

She looked up, staring at me with an expression half of pleading, half of defiance.

'I know it was partly Mr Laribee's fault that father died. I understand. I can remember everything plainly. But I don't have to murder him, do I?'

There was something terribly pathetic about it. I felt almost physically sick to think that now Iris was being drawn into this beastly affair. I knew she was really sane; some instinct surer than reason told me that this was just another facet of the malignant scheme which was working itself out in the sanatorium. She was imploring me to help and yet I was so hopelessly inadequate. I tried to tell her it was all a mistake; that even if she had heard a voice it was only someone trying to frighten her.

'Yes,' she said surprisingly, 'I expect it was. I don't believe in spirits or anything. I know I'm in a mental hospital, and I know I'm trying to get better. It's just that I want to be left alone. I wouldn't mind, if only I was sure I didn't have to do what they told me.'

I said a lot of foolish things that were meant to be reassuring, but probably my psychiatry was all wrong. She seemed caught up in some reflection of her own, and I felt that she hardly heard what I said. She had started to work on the floor again, deliberately, mechanically.

At last I tried to be flippant.

'When you're through with that corridor,' I suggested, 'you might get Lenz to put you on the windows in Wing Two. They don't need cleaning, but it would be nice to see you again.'

As I spoke, I heard footsteps coming down the corridor behind me. Iris glanced up, the mop motionless in her hand. Her eyes were staring fixedly with an expression of almost mesmerized intensity.

'You mustn't tell him,' she whispered breathlessly. 'You mustn't tell him about that voice. He'd keep me shut up in my room. He wouldn't let me work.'

I turned to follow the direction of her still hypnotized gaze. The approaching figure was bearded and godlike. It was Doctor Lenz.

I spent the rest of the morning by myself, trying to piece together all the crazy ramifications that had led up to Fogarty's death. I was so angry at the idea of Iris being dragged into the miserable business that I could not concentrate. Something told me I ought to report to Lenz what she had said. But she had asked me not to, and I did not want to let the poor kid down.

I suppose I was reprehensible. Maybe I could have prevented a lot of tragedy if I had gone to the authorities there and then. But after all, I was only a jittery ex-drunk trying to get on my feet again. And my ethical standards were still a bit twisted.

No one in Wing Two had been told about Fogarty's death. But, despite the discreetly normal behaviour of the staff, there was a certain restiveness. People on the border-line are particularly sensitive to atmosphere.

Billy Trent asked Miss Brush three times why Fogarty was not on duty. She gave non-committal replies. But I could see that he was not satisfied. In fact, he was unusually silent and did not jerk a single soda.

I had missed my morning work-out. But when we got back from the afternoon walk, Warren appeared, tired and rather irritable. He was running both shifts temporarily, he said. And heaven alone knew when he was going to get any sleep.

The physio-therapy room was closed, and, from the muffled sounds which I heard as we passed it, I guessed that some of Green's men were still in there. Warren took me to the little-used gymnasium. There was not much equipment down there, so he suggested wrestling as the most effective type of exercise.

We wrestled. At least, he did. I suppose it was good for me, but I did not think so at the time. Although he claimed to be tired, he put up a pretty good imitation of an animated steel vice.

We were alone there, quite some way from the main part of the wing. At one instant he twisted me into a particularly complicated hold which he described with grim inappropriateness as a very pretty cradle. As he rocked me to and forth, stretching my legs in a manner worthy of the Spanish Inquisition, I was suddenly assailed by a feeling of blind, almost overwhelming panic. I suppose it was stupid of me, but I could not stop myself thinking of the night before, of Fogarty and the strait-jacket.

This curative torture went on for a good ten minutes. Warren threw me about far more than was necessary. And when it was over, I saw the reason why. As I reproached him mildly for contorting me into a human *pretzel*, he replied sourly:

'Well, you got me into a pretty tough spot telling the cops what I said last night about me and Fogarty.'

I was surprised at his frankness, surprised, too, at the truculence of his attitude. After all, I was an expensive and fragile patient.

'I'm sorry,' I said. 'They asked me to give all the dope I had.'

'Yeah. They kept me answering questions for a couple of hours, tried to make out me and Fogarty had quarrelled. Lucky my sister could check up on me. Otherwise I might be in jail by now. Those dumb cops always want to arrest someone.'

'That's too bad,' I murmured. 'You shouldn't go around shooting your mouth off if you don't want people to repeat what you say.' We were moving to the door when I remembered something. 'By the way, why was Mrs Fogarty crying last night?'

He wheeled toward me, and there was a different expression on his cadaverous face.

'What are you driving at?' he said.

'I thought there might have been some domestic trouble,' I replied lightly.

We were standing very close. I was startled by the look in his eyes.

'And what's my sister's domestic trouble got to do with you?' he exclaimed.

'Nothing,' I said. 'Nothing at all. I was just asking.'

I might have given him a homily on service, courtesy and the tactful handling of his bread and butter, but I didn't. I merely hurried out of the gymnasium in a rather undignified manner.

While I put on my clothes, I found my thoughts returning automatically to the 'subversive influence' and its widespread effect upon the inmates of the sanatorium. Already it seemed to have caused everything from surliness in the staff to an epidemic of fear, aggravated neuroses and possibly even murder. And I myself was becoming monotonously involved in each new manifestation.

I was buttoning up my pants when I recollected my talk with Doctor Stevens, and in that instant my theatrical idea was born. Stevens had dilated upon the efficacy of psycho-analysis and had explained how he could not dabble in it himself. But I was under obligation to no one. Both Iris and myself had been haunted by that elusive voice; both of us were potentially menaced. I seemed more than justified in trying an experiment.

And the experiment, according to the cherubic Stevens, was an elementary one. I had to think up some significant phrase, repeat it to my fellow patients and watch their reactions. It seemed innocent enough. The problem was to find the phrase.

With an effort I forced my mind to run over those dreadful moments in the physio-therapy room. I saw once again that distorted dead thing on the grey marble slab. The phrase, of course! 'The thing on the slab ...' That could have no alarming significance to the uninitiated. But for a guilty person it should come as a distinct jolt.

I finished dressing and moved out into the corridor, feeling a little nervous at my projected rôle of amateur psycho-analyst.

The passage itself was deserted, and I found most of the others in the smoking-room under the bright control of Miss Brush. But the day nurse was not as bright as usual. She had lost a great deal of her customary candlepower. She moved about restlessly and could not keep the harassed look out of her eyes. She even forgot to smile when Billy Trent brought a cigarette for her to light. Things seemed to be getting on top of her.

I spotted Fenwick alone in a corner. It seemed rather mean to use Stevens's experiment upon his presumed half-brother, but I'd made up my mind and there were to be no exceptions. I sat down at the young spiritualist's side and said softly and guiltily:

'The thing on the slab.'

The effect was sensational if not informative. Fenwick turned slowly toward me, his huge eyes glowing with a light that never was on land or sea.

'The thing on the slab?' he repeated. 'You mean a manifestation. It is often like that at first – an indeterminate shape floating and something grey. So you saw that! They're in touch with you, too!'

For a moment I thought this might lead to something, but it didn't. He went on talking rapidly, excitedly, about ectoplasm and other abstrusely technical phenomena. His loquacity grew with his enthusiasm and he welcomed me as a brother, a convert. I could trace nothing more sinister behind his effusions than excitement at finding a kindred spiritualist. Feeling rather ashamed of myself, I rose and hurried away.

My next chance came when Billy Trent strolled out into the corridor. I followed and engaged him in conversation. Somehow I disliked the idea of applying my hocus-pocus to a kid like Bill. He was so young, guileless and charming. But finally I quashed my scruples and, in the middle of a sentence, lowered my eyes and mumbled the phrase:

'The thing on the slab.'

His reaction was instantaneous.

'Oh, that!' he exclaimed. His eyes looked down and I could tell at once that he was scrutinizing the imaginary marble slab of a soda fountain. 'You mean those coffee cakes? They're a new line. We're trying them out – two for eight cents.'

I gazed at his fresh, eager face and shrugged resignedly.

'What the hell!' I said. 'Give me a couple.'

After that I thought I'd let the psychology lie a while. I bummed a cigarette from Miss Brush and crossed to Geddes, who was lounging in a chair by one of the bridge tables. He had picked up a novel, but he put it down when he saw me.

'Where've you been all day?' he asked with a smile.

I felt a violent urge to talk the whole crazy matter over with him and get his sane British reaction, but I didn't feel courageous enough to break Moreno's specific injunctions.

'Oh, I was just sparring with Lenz,' I said vaguely. 'He gave me a thorough check-up and reports a remote chance of ultimate recovery.'

Geddes became Anglo-Indian for a while and talked about polo in Calcutta. I found it soothing, although I did not know the first thing about polo – or Calcutta, for that matter. While he talked, he idly fingered the novel which he was still holding in his hand.

'What you reading?' I asked in a pause.

'Oh, I'm not reading it. Just something I found on that table.'

Casually he flicked the book open and simultaneously we both gave a little grunt of surprise.

Slipped between the pages was a small scrap of paper. It was lying face upward, and printed there in large, shaky capitals, were the words:

BEWARE OF ISABEL BRUSH
THERE WILL BE MURDER

Neither of us spoke for a moment. There was something about that familiar phrase when written down – something even more sinister than the disembodied voice. My mind was crowded with unpleasant speculations.

'D'you suppose Fenwick's up to his tricks again?' asked the Englishman at length.

'Heaven and the astral plane alone know,' I replied grimly.

Geddes suggested showing it to Miss Brush, but I dissuaded him. I thought it would be wiser to keep her out of it. After all, if anyone was to know, it ought to be Lenz.

I put the piece of paper in my pocket and said I would look after it. Geddes seemed only too glad to have the problem taken off his shoulders.

I was extremely eager to know for whom the note was intended, but I did not have to wonder long. We were still talking about it when old Laribee came in. He looked around the room and then made straight for us. Grunting something about having forgotten his book he picked up the novel from the table.

Geddes and I glanced at each other. Then obeying a momentary inspiration, I remarked:

'The thing on the slab.'

Once again my audience's reaction was startling. Geddes stared at me as though he were unable to believe his ears; Laribee stood stockstill. For a moment his lower lip trembled and he looked like a little boy on the verge of tears. Then, with an effort, he controlled his features and made one of those imperious gestures which might once have set Wall Street trembling.

'There is to be nothing on the slab,' he said firmly. 'Nothing but my name and the date of my death. And the funeral, that must be very simple, too. I have to economize, economize . . .'

He shook his head sadly, as though wondering upon the transience of human existence, and wandered away. Once again I had drawn a blank – and a rather foolish blank at that.

As soon as we were alone again, Geddes turned to me, his eyes still wide with astonishment.

'What on earth did you say that for?' he asked.

I grinned. 'It's all right. I'm not cuckoo. Just a fool joke.'

'Oh.' His expression of concern turned to one of relief. 'For a moment I thought our solitary specimen of sanity had gone off the deep end.' He smiled diffidently. 'That would have been the last straw, Duluth. Having you around is about the only thing that keeps me going.'

'Two orphans in the storm,' I said. 'We'd better stick together.'

I was grateful to him for expecting something of me. But the fact that he was worried on my account somewhat heightened my sense of guilt. So far I had succeeded merely in bewildering or upsetting four of my fellow inmates. It was ironical to think that I was rapidly becoming a subversive influence myself.

For a while we sat together in silence. It was Geddes who finally expressed the thought uppermost in both our minds.

'So that note was meant for Laribee,' he murmured reflectively.

'Yes,' I said, 'it was meant for him all right. And I'd give quite a lot to know why.'

Geddes stroked his moustache and said quietly: 'I don't like it, Duluth. I've got a feeling that something pretty queer's going on.'

I shrugged.

'You're darn tootin',' I agreed wearily.

12

Sunday, like weekdays, became co-educational in the evening. Of the regular gaieties only dancing was omitted as a gesture to the Sabbath. After supper on that particular Sunday, a listless Miss Brush conducted us to the central lounge as though nothing had happened to affect the normal curriculum. I was rather surprised, but I suppose it was a sound idea. When people are on edge, it is better for them to be kept occupied. I was hoping to be kept occupied by Iris.

But I was disappointed. She was not there. I taxed Mrs Dell, the women's Miss Brush, with her absence and was told brightly that Miss Pattison felt a little tired. For a while I agonized about it, imagining countless different disasters. Then I remembered the mop and reflected that anyone had a right to feel tired after all that manual labour.

Sunday's mood seemed to have impregnated the patients that evening. Although most of the male and female inmates were present, the sexes did not mix much. We kept in little celibate groups despite sporadic attempts on the part of the staff to start sociabilities.

Geddes, Billy Trent and I played rummy for a while, but we gave it up when Geddes fell asleep. Miss Brush tried to inveigle me into a bridge game with three of the women, but I declined politely. I felt depressed and rather jittery.

The Bostonian Miss Powell was by herself in a corner near the grand piano, playing solitaire. I strolled across and sat down in a leather chair at her side. She greeted me with an impeccable courtesy but did not seem particularly talkative. The whole force of her 'good mind' was concentrated upon the game.

As I watched I began to wonder whether she stole cards from a concealed pack and finally decided that she must be doing something crooked. Her demon came out three times running.

Memories of the stopwatch incident rose in my mind and with

them the recollection of my psycho-analytical experiment, which had temporarily slipped from my thoughts. Somehow Miss Powell seemed involved in the intricate undercurrent of mystery and confusion. I decided to try my luck with her.

'There's something very Bostonian about a Sunday evening, don't you think, Miss Powell?' I began tentatively. 'It always reminds me of the thing on the slab.'

Miss Powell turned to me haughtily, the half shuffled cards suspended over the table. Her forehead rippled in a slight frown, then she said:

'If you refer to the fish-markets, Mr Duluth, I cannot agree with you. Besides, they are closed on Sundays and very properly, too.'

She averted her eyes as though suddenly she associated me with all the uncooked fish in Boston. Her face was puckered with distaste. There seemed nothing for it but to get up and go on my way – none the wiser.

My aimless wanderings led me finally to Herr Stroubel. The celebrated conductor stood by a table, idly turning the pages of some musical magazine. As I joined him, he bowed with Viennese courtesy and started talking about the stage.

I listened with interest to his startling but sound ideas on the theatre. Apart from the uncertain restlessness of his eyes he seemed perfectly normal. He asked whether I had done any operatic direction and suggested that he would like to work with me. As he expounded his theories on Wagnerian production his enthusiasm increased. He gesticulated and his words poured out mellifluously.

'It is rhythm that they all lack, Mr Duluth. Take *Tristan*, for example. All of them, they play it with reverence, treat it as though it were something dead – some museum piece which must be approached with infinite respect. But *Tristan* must live, if it is to be anything. It must have rhythm – rhythm in the playing, the singing, the acting, the direction. Rhythm . . . vitality . . . something arresting!'

'Like the thing on the slab,' I put in sheepishly.

'The thing on the slab!' His eyes shone with sudden excitement. 'That is a grotesque phrase, and an arresting one.' A quick smile lit up his face. 'I see rhythm in that, Mr Duluth; rhythm pulsing through the phrase.'

He hurried to the piano, opened up the keyboard and started to play. I resumed the leather chair which was equidistant from the piano and Miss Powell and sat there, listening.

It was remarkable. As though inspired by the macabre quality of my fool phrase, Stroubel was improvising the weirdest, most alarming piece of music I had ever heard. Chords crashed sombrely after one another, seemingly disconnected and yet somehow bound together with a subtle, disturbing rhythm.

Everyone in the room was staring at him now. I noticed Miss Brush's face set with sudden apprehension. I was beginning to get rather panicky myself, when he broke off abruptly and slipped into a peaceful Bach chorale. The cool, soothing notes gradually slackened the tension.

Although I had often heard him conduct, I had never before heard Stroubel play. There was something rather wonderful about it. He had superb technique and a lot more. Maybe it was his own sadness which lent the notes that strange, nostalgic melancholy. I forgot about Fogarty, about the complexities of the sanatorium, about my own self-inflicted problems. I listened.

The others listened, too. One by one they left what they had been doing and moved toward the piano, until Miss Powell and I were the only two who remained seated. I suppose that people who are a bit off the mental balance react more immediately to music. Billy Trent stood quite close to me, caught up in a kind of trance of attention. Fenwick was there, too, with a strange, almost opalescent gleam in his eyes. I could see all the others, Geddes, Laribee, Doctor Stevens, the women. Even Miss Brush and Moreno had come up. Their shoulders almost touched. They were very still and silent.

I watched Stroubel's hands. They were the focal point of the room. Power seemed to flow from them with the music. The uneasiness had left the atmosphere, had given way before his calm, hypnotic spell. I glanced at Miss Powell. She sat motionless, her eyes straight in front of her and the jack of diamonds clasped rigidly between her finger and thumb.

At last the music stopped. There was a long, vibrant silence. No one stirred. It was as if they were all consciously unwilling to break the tableau.

A slight sound made me turn back to Miss Powell. Her hand still hung in mid-air, gripping the jack of diamonds. But the expression of her face had changed. The thin aristocratic mouth was set. There was a bright, almost exalted look in her eyes. Slowly her head bent over the cards.

And then I heard her voice. It was soft but perfectly distinct.

'There are lovely shining knives in the surgery – lovely shining knives. They are so easy to get. And they gleam. They are bright. I can hide them in the musical place.'

I heard no more of this incredible monologue, for everyone had started to talk again. Stroubel had risen and was gazing serenely in our direction. I saw him, and then I glanced back at Miss Powell.

She had resumed her solitaire. The jack of diamonds descended upon the queen of clubs. But her hand was trembling. That strange, almost hypnotized expression was still in her eyes. Hypnotized! The word rose up in my mind and lingered there. I found myself thinking furiously.

Shortly after Stroubel had stopped playing, Miss Brush took us back to Wing Two. Usually she stayed around until we were all in bed, but that evening she disappeared immediately with hurried good nights. She seemed fagged out and nervous.

Warren supervised us while we took last cigarettes in the smoking-room. He had put in a couple of hours' sleep in the afternoon, he grumbled, but he was still as tired as a dog. A new attendant had been hired to take Fogarty's place and was arriving early next morning.

'And then, maybe I can get some rest,' he grunted, 'unless those police friends of yours start acting up again, Mr Duluth.'

I left the smoking-room with Stroubel. We were strolling down the corridor together when Mrs Fogarty rustled around a corner.

I was surprised to see her. I had supposed that she would have stayed off duty under the circumstances. She looked pale and, if possible, more tight-lipped than usual. But there was a certain indomitable quality about that sallow, angular face. With her, I imagined, personal problems were strictly subordinated to sanatorium routine.

When she saw us, she set her expression to the correct degree of formal greeting and made to pass on. But Stroubel moved to her side and took her bony hand in his. He stared at her with those kindly, sad eyes of his.

'I am sorry,' he said. 'Last night I should not have rung for you. I should have kept my unhappiness to myself just as you kept yours.'

Mrs Fogarty started.

I thought he was being tactless until I remembered that the patients had been told nothing of Fogarty's death. His voice was gentle, rather touchingly apologetic. And yet I could sense once again the subtle, compelling power of personality in the man.

Mrs Fogarty must have felt it, too, for she reacted instinctively. At first her face had darkened, but now she smiled.

'You know you can always ring for me, Mr Stroubel.'

'Even so, you must tell me why you were sad. And I will help you.'

They both seemed unaware of my presence. Stroubel bent forward, his expression suddenly intent, eager.

'You are unhappy now,' he said slowly. 'It isn't – it isn't because of the thing on the slab?'

Mrs Fogarty gave a little gasp. A hand went to her thin throat and then fell limply at her side. Her cheeks had turned a greyish white.

I didn't know what to do. My clumsy experiment seemed to have become a Frankenstein's monster. It had sprung into independent life and was getting out of control.

With a supreme effort the night nurse managed a smile.

'You'd better be getting along to bed, Mr Stroubel,' she said softly. 'Good night.'

The conductor shrugged, turned slowly and wandered away.

Mrs Fogarty and I were left alone.

'I'm terribly sorry . . .' I began.

But I did not finish my sentence. At that moment there were brisk footsteps on the linoleum behind us and Moreno came round the corner. His dark forehead rippled in a frown as he saw the night nurse.

'Mrs Fogarty, I said you need not come on duty tonight.'

He glanced at me swiftly and then back at the night nurse.

'There is no one else to take my place, doctor,' Mrs Fogarty said stiffly. 'Miss Price on the women's wing is sick. The substitute is over there.'

'You needn't worry about staff arrangements. You are in no fit state to be here tonight. You need rest.'

Mrs Fogarty's crisp white shoulders shrugged. 'And the patients?'

'I have arranged for all the room telephones to be connected with your alcove. Warren will have to be on duty, anyway. He can remain in there.'

I could not tell whether the night nurse was grateful, displeased or angry. She stood there a moment staring in front of her with dark, hollow eyes. Then, with a soft: 'Very well, Doctor Moreno,' she hurried away.

I had thought things out and decided that Lenz should be told of what Miss Powell had said in the lounge. It sounded fantastically ludicrous but I had grown to suspect the ludicrous. While Moreno stood there at my side I asked his permission to go to the director.

Instantly he became the model young psychiatrist – the diagnostician of patients and the guardian of superiors. His questioning eyes scrutinized my face.

'Doctor Lenz is very busy at the moment,' he said. 'He is still in conference with the police.'

'But I overheard something which I think Lenz ought to know,' I said determinedly. Then, as he still stared at me in silence, I added, 'I don't think this thing has ended yet.'

'And what do you mean by that?'

'Just that Fogarty's death was a part of something else – something which is still going on.'

'You must be careful not to let your theatrical imagination run away with you, Mr Duluth.' Moreno was regarding his hands fixedly. 'You are in a nervous condition and you still have to be careful.'

'But it's not my nerves!' I exclaimed irritably. 'I know perfectly well that –'

Moreno looked up suddenly. 'If it interests you, Mr Duluth, the police are satisfied that they know the reasons behind Fogarty's death. It had nothing whatsoever to do with the institution or the inmates. Captain Green is ready to believe that the whole affair was a most unfortunate – er – accident.'

His tone was convincing, his gaze was steady.

But I knew he was lying.

13

When Moreno left me, I found that all the others had retired to their rooms. The corridor was deserted as I made my way toward the chain of bedrooms at the far end of the wing.

There is something about an empty passage in a sanatorium – something bleak and forbidding. My irresponsible nerves started to act up and I felt an unreasonable impulse to hurry out of that loneliness, to find human companionship, although if there actually were danger, it was far more likely to lurk in the presence of the other inmates than in the loneliness of the corridors.

I reached the swing door that led to the sleeping quarters and pushed it open. In front I could see the long row of doors that marked the individual bedrooms. To my left was Mrs Fogarty's little alcove – plunged in darkness. I was passing it when I heard my name called. I started, felt a sudden stab of alarm and then cursed myself for a jittery fool.

It was only Mrs Fogarty's voice and it came from the darkened alcove.

'Mr Duluth!'

I moved across the passage and stepped into the small three-walled room. The half light from the corridor crept insidiously in. I could see the night nurse's profile, irregular and shadowy beneath its pale white cap. She sat at a table by the dully gleaming telephone. There was something stiff and sentry-like about her. I could visualize her springing to attention when the telephone rang to summon her to any of the patients.

'What is it, nurse?' I asked. 'I didn't know you were going to be on duty.'

'Doctor Moreno told me not to,' she said quietly. 'But my brother's had so little sleep, I thought I'd give him a few hours' rest before he takes over.' A bony hand moved wearily across her forehead. 'I have quite a headache myself. That's why I'm sitting in the dark.'

It was unlike Mrs Fogarty to entertain a patient in banal conversation at so irregular an hour. But after all she had every reason to be unlike herself that day.

'It's Mr Stroubel,' she said abruptly, almost accusingly. 'You heard what he said – the thing on the slab. Someone must have told him about – about my husband.' Her eyes shone coldly in the semi-darkness. 'You are the only patient who knew.'

If I hadn't felt so guilty, I might have resented her school-teacherish attitude. But under the circumstances I could merely be confused and angry with myself for having caused her unnecessary pain. I blurted out an inarticulate story of my psycho-analytical experiment, doing my best to conceal the fact that it had been inspired by Doctor Stevens. I explained that Stroubel had been referring merely to his grotesque composition on the piano. She listened in silence and was surprisingly nice about it.

'I understand that you meant no harm, Mr Duluth, and I won't report it, but please don't do anything like that again. Jo's death has been a – great shock to me. I could not bear to have the patients worried by it, too.'

'I'll admit I was a darn fool,' I agreed gloomily. 'I only hope I haven't got the whole place upset.'

I had been leaning against the table as I talked, idly fingering the telephone. I jumped when the bell rang with sudden shrillness. Mrs Fogarty started, too. She leaned forward and picked up the receiver. Her face was only a blur but I could tell from her shadowy silhouette that she was holding the instrument a few inches away from her ear in that intense, nervous attitude of a rather deaf person who has difficulty in catching what is said from the other end of the wire.

'Hello, hello, who is it?'

Her voice was brisk and professional, curiously out of place in that vaguely illuminated alcove.

There was no reply.

Once again, she asked:

'Who is it speaking?'

Instinctively I moved closer. My eyes were fixed on the shining receiver. And for months afterwards I was to associate all telephones with that incredible answering voice. It seemed hardly human. Low and distorted, it crackled across to me in a horribly intimate whisper.

And I heard the words as plainly as though they had been breathed in my own ear. They were:

'*I am the thing on the slab.*'

This startling repetition of my phrase might have seemed merely ludicrous; it might have seemed infinitely pathetic as a symbol of all the confused, unbalanced minds in the sanatorium. But it was neither. It was the most unnerving experience in my life. There had been something malignant, evil, about that hoarse voice.

I stood absolutely motionless, hardly conscious of Mrs Fogarty's strangled sob and the dull clatter as she dropped the receiver.

Then, on an impulse, I sprang forward, groped for the swinging telephone, lifted it.

'Who is it?' I shouted. 'What do you want?'

Dead silence, then once more that low, husky whisper. The voice was remotely familiar and yet I could not connect it with any particular individual.

'*There will be another thing on the slab, Duluth,*' it said. '*Take care that it is not you.*'

My lips framed an answer but there was a faint click from the other end of the wire. After a moment I replaced the receiver dazedly and peered through the darkness at Mrs Fogarty. The night nurse was leaning forward, her hands over her face. I had never seen her like that before – without her steel control.

'I'm frightfully sorry,' I said at length. 'All this is my fault. I never thought of you.'

'It's all right, Mr Duluth.' The words came flat, toneless.

'We'd better find out where that call came from.'

Slowly Mrs Fogarty lifted her eyes. I could see them gleaming faintly in their deep sockets. 'We can't, Mr Duluth. All the telephones on the men's wing are connected directly with this alcove – and so is the staff common room. It might have come from anywhere.'

'But didn't – didn't you recognize the voice?'

The night nurse rose. As her fingers gripped my arm I could feel that they were trembling. 'Listen, Mr Duluth,' she said with sudden severity, 'you have done a very foolish, dangerous thing. And this should be a lesson to you. But I do not intend to report it. There has been trouble enough already. And' – her voice sank almost to a whisper – 'I think we had both better forget this, not only for your sake, but for mine.'

I did not understand her, did not understand her words or the strange intensity of her emotion.

'But, Mrs Fogarty, if you recognized the voice . . . !'

'Mr Duluth!' The night nurse cut in impulsively. 'Did *you* have any idea whose voice that was?'

'Why no; I thought it was familiar, but . . .'

'Very well.' Her tone was sharp, defiant. 'Perhaps you would understand more closely if I tell you that I thought I *did* recognize it.'

We were standing very close now and I could make out the lines of her face, gaunt as sculptured granite.

'Well, who was it, Mrs Fogarty?' I asked softly.

She did not answer for a moment.

'I'm rather hard of hearing,' she faltered at length, speaking to herself rather than to me, 'and I have had a very trying time today. That must be why I thought I heard it. And that's why I could never report this to the authorities. You see . . .'

She broke off, and suddenly realization came flooding into my mind. I knew what she was going to tell me, and I could feel the hairs at the back of my neck stirring.

'Yes, Mr Duluth. If I said anything, they would think I was mad. You see, that voice on the telephone – If I hadn't known he was dead, I could have sworn it was my husband speaking.'

14

I left Mrs Fogarty alone and hurried down the deserted corridor to my room. As I undressed and slipped into bed, the sound of her words still echoed in my ears. They had become for me a symbol of the day – a day which had begun with murder and closed with the most commonsensical of the staff believing herself to have heard the voice of a dead man.

As I tossed restlessly, I tried to force my jangled nerves to accept. Reason. I told myself that what both Mrs Fogarty and I thought we had heard was patently impossible. The spirits of the dead might converse with David Fenwick, but they were not likely to speak over the house telephone to so practical and unpsychic a person as the night nurse.

There was only one explanation. For some crazy reason, someone had chosen this particularly beastly way of frightening her – and of frightening me. After all everyone knew I had not gone to my room with the others. Anyone in Wing Two might have heard my footsteps in the corridor and my name called by Mrs Fogarty. It did not require supernatural knowledge to realize that I was in the alcove with the night nurse.

And yet, by removing the menace of the other world, I had only thrown myself more violently back upon the realities of our own private world of the sanatorium. And the realities were none too pleasant. *The thing on the slab!* The phrase had become horrible, sinister now. It repeated itself time and time again in my tired brain. And with it, returning with monotonous regularity, came the image of Jo Fogarty – that gagged, agonized face, that helplessly bound body. Moreno had said that the police thought the death was an accident. I could never believe that. I knew as certainly as my name was Peter Duluth that Fogarty's murder was part of something else – some step in the progress of that unseen force which was jerking all of us like marionettes in a mad puppet show of its own devising.

75

Until that moment I had been able to see no motive for the attendant's death, but now I realized one with sudden clarity. Wasn't it possible that Jo with his love of gossip and personalities had stumbled inadvertently upon some knowledge – some knowledge which made him both dangerous and in danger? And if that were so, wasn't it also possible that I, too, had unconsciously discovered something which put me in the same position? After all, I had been warned by that voice. And something told me its warnings were not to be taken lightly. I felt a growing sense of uneasiness, and my regular night fears started to show up again, too. In my mind that intangible menace had become crystallized now – crystallized into an immediate, personal danger to myself. Danger . . . !

I tried to cut off the train of thought. I sat up in bed, looking at the strip of lighted passage through the open door. Usually I liked the idea of that open door; it was a contact with the outside world; it made me feel safe from the neurotic fears in my own mind.

But that night my fears were external. If there were danger, it would come through that door. On a sudden impulse, I jumped out of bed, hurried to the door and closed it. But when my uncertain fingers felt for the key, I remembered there was no lock. The thought came to me tinged with panic. Slowly I moved back to the bed.

I do not know how long I lay awake in the darkness, listening to my heart beat and cursing myself for an old soak. I almost reached the maudlin state of thinking the prohibitionists were right after all. At any rate I realized I was now paying for my alcoholic excesses with a vengeance that would have satisfied even Carrie Nation herself.

The cure seemed to have become more nerve-racking than the disease. I think that if it hadn't been for Iris, I would have got up then and there, demanded my baggage and turned my back on the Lenz Sanatorium once and for all.

After what seemed like hours I calmed down sufficiently to slip off into a doze. I was half asleep, luxuriating in the new sensation of tranquillity, when I heard footsteps.

Instantly I was horribly awake again. Those footsteps were moving nearer. They were coming to my room. I knew it. I sat up and then froze against the pillows like a dummy.

The door was opening. I saw a crack of light, a fragment of a silhouette. As I flung out a hand for the telephone, I realized that by now Mrs Fogarty would be off duty. If I summoned aid, only Warren would

76

come, and in my jittery state I felt I would rather face this thing alone than with the hostile night attendant.

The door had opened to its full now and was shutting again. I made no sound. The indistinct figure that moved toward me was nothing but a blur in the shadows. I strained my eyes, helplessly unable to identify it with any living person in the sanatorium.

It was so near now that I could feel the cold sweat breaking out on my forehead. Then it spoke:

'Are you awake, Duluth?'

I almost laughed, the relief was so great. It was only old Laribee.

He fumbled for a chair and drew it toward the bed. Ponderously he sat down – a pathetic, ungainly figure in his grey pyjamas.

'I want to talk to you, Duluth,' he whispered eagerly.

My fears had vanished. I only felt curious now.

'But how did you get by Warren?'

'He's out there – asleep in the alcove.'

'Well, what's on your mind?'

He leaned forward. His heavy face was close to mine, and I could see his eyes gleaming.

'I'm not mad,' he said. 'I'm sure of that now. I want you to know, too.'

'Good for you,' I said feebly and without conviction.

But he hardly waited for my reply. He went on hurriedly:

'For several days, I thought I really was going insane. That night I heard the ticker in my room. On the walk I heard my broker's voice speaking in my ear. That's enough to make any man think he's crazy, isn't it? But you found that stopwatch in my pocket. I've been thinking it out and I see it was all a frame-up. They're deliberately frightening me – trying to drive me mad.'

I drew the bedclothes up to my chin and waited for him to go on.

'I know their little game,' he was continuing breathlessly. 'I know why they're trying to frighten me. Shall I tell you?'

'By all means.'

He glanced furtively over his shoulder at the closed door. 'When I came here, I thought I was ruined financially. Everything seemed to be crashing. But I knew there was a little left, and that it would go too if I went on playing the market. And I couldn't stop myself. That's why I made a trust fund and appointed Doctor Lenz as one of the trustees.'

Laribee seemed to consider me only as an audience, so I remained silent.

'The arrangement,' he continued, 'was for him to have control of a quarter of my estate if I were to die or really go mad.' A new crafty note had come into his voice. 'I thought that would make him look after my money better, and take better care of me, too. You see, I didn't think I was rich enough to make it dangerous. That's why I did it.'

He seemed to think this had been a particularly cunning move on his part, but to me it merely sounded crazy.

'Yes,' he went on, 'I thought I was ruined then. But now I'm rich. I've got over two millions. And Lenz knows that, too. If I go mad, he gets half a million for the sanatorium. Half a million!' He lowered his voice again. 'Now you understand, don't you? That's a lot of money, Duluth, and I've found out something else, too. All the staff here have a financial interest in the institution. Now you see why they're trying to drive me insane.' He laughed. 'As if they could succeed! Why, I'm as sane as any man in Wall Street.'

I thought he was probably right on that point. But I could follow his reasoning, too. Lenz himself had told me he would benefit considerably if Laribee were committed to a State institution.

For a moment we sat there together in silence. His burly silhouette was outlined against the white wall. I could even see his sparse hair sticking up like a little boy's.

It was difficult to judge just how crazy he was; difficult, too, to decide whether or not to be sorry for him. I did not like him. In fact, I disliked him intensely when I remembered that tragic expression in Iris's eyes. But, after all, he was old and defenceless. And I myself had seen enough to realize that someone was giving him a pretty raw deal.

'They aren't going to fool me,' he said suddenly. 'I'm still sane, and in my right mind, and I've just made a new will. My daughter was going to get the bulk of my estate. She was co-trustee with Lenz. She'd have come in for over a million if they'd driven me crazy, and she knew it, too. She wouldn't have stopped them putting me away, Duluth – not her.'

He paused, peering at me excitedly as though expecting me to make some comment. I could produce nothing more constructive than a grunt.

'Spent a hundred thousand dollars on that girl's education,' he growled at length. 'And then what does she do? Goes to Hollywood and tries to become a movie star. Calls herself Sylvia Dawn, indeed! The old name was good enough for me. And she never thought of coming East when I was sick, Duluth. Oh, no, it was her career all the time that counted, not her father – no, not me.'

78

But now Laribee was thoroughly absorbed with his domestic grievances. He was talking to himself, rather than to me.

'But she didn't consider her career much when she married that cheap skate last summer. Told me at first he was a medical man. And then it turns out he's just a common vaudeville actor!' His hands were beating an indignant tattoo on my quilt. 'Dan Laribee's daughter marrying a cheap one-night stander, indeed! I guess he was after my money, too. Well, I'll fool them both. They won't get another penny out of me.'

He gave a malevolent little chuckle and then added slyly:

'Now Miss Brush – she's not the type of girl that marries for money, is she, Duluth?'

I said that, having none to speak of myself, I had never given the matter much thought.

'Well, they're all after her – Moreno, Trent, all of them. They're jealous. But it's me she likes. She's really in love with me, Duluth.' He crouched forward, almost speaking in my ear. 'And I'll tell you a secret. We're going to get married. Just as soon as I leave this place, we're going to get married.'

It seemed a curious spot and a curious moment for wedding congratulations, but I did my best.

'I knew you'd sympathize, Duluth. And I know you'll understand when I tell you what I've done.' Once more his head turned furtively toward the closed door. 'I've changed my will. I'm going to leave everything to Isabel. That's why I came here. I've got the will with me. And Isabel lent me her fountain-pen. I want you to be a witness. But we have to be careful.' His laugh was high, excited. 'They'd do anything to stop me if they knew. They'd do anything. They'd even murder me, I think.'

I could not get my own reaction straight in my head. Laribee seemed wilder, crazier than I had ever before seen him, but there was a kind of logic in what he said.

'You might ask why I don't leave this place,' he was whispering. 'Well, I can't leave Isabel here unprotected. There would be danger for her, too, if they knew. You see, they all want her and they all want my money.'

He was fumbling in his pyjama pocket now. His fingers came out, gripping a piece of paper that gleamed in the darkness.

'Here you are. Here's the will. All you have to do is to witness my signature.'

I hesitated a moment. But I did not see that it was my part to object. Although the whole thing seemed completely nutty to me, it obviously meant a great deal to Laribee. And, after all, we were all in the same boat at the Lenz Sanatorium. I felt I ought to stick by my fellow-patients.

My knowledge of legal procedure was hazy in the extreme but it did not seem to matter whether or not the will would be valid.

'I'll sign,' I said. 'But I'd like to be able to see the darn thing.'

'Yes, yes.' Eagerly Laribee's fingers slipped once more into his pyjama pocket and came out clutching a small object. 'I've got matches – a whole box of them.'

I was amazed. All of us were considered potential pyromaniacs. Matches were as difficult to get in the sanatorium as a bottle of absinthe or vodka.

'I got them from Isabel,' Laribee was explaining. 'And the pen, too.'

He struck a match, holding the small flame near the paper. In that flickering light I could see the bluish veins in his red face. I heard his quick, stertorous breathing as I leaned forward to read through the shaky sentences of the will.

The last part alone held my attention.

'My entire estate, both real and personal, to my wife, Isabel Laribee, *née* Brush; or in the event that my decease should prevent our marriage, to Isabel Brush –'

There was something rather pathetic about those stilted, legal phrases. Something slightly ominous, too. The match burned low and another was struck. Laribee handed me Miss Brush's pen, saying almost triumphantly:

'Sign there, Duluth.'

I scribbled my name and the match went out. As the darkness closed in around us again, I remembered an elementary rule of will-making. 'You'll need another witness,' I said. 'All wills have two witnesses, don't they?'

In his excitement, Laribee seemed to have forgotten it, too. He had been folding the paper contentedly, but now it remained poised in mid-air. His voice faltered as he asked:

'But what shall we do, Duluth? What shall we do?'

He sounded so sad – so disappointed – that I felt sorry for him.

'It'll be O.K.,' I said comfortingly. 'I'll get you another witness tomorrow. Geddes is a good sport. He'd do it, I know.'

'Tomorrow? Oh, I can't leave it till tomorrow. We've got to be quick. Don't you see? Quick and secret.'

Laribee fumbled through the darkness for my arm and gripped it pleadingly.

'Get Geddes now, Duluth. Please get him to do it now.'

I did not exactly like the idea of waking up fellow-patients in the middle of the night, but, as I seemed to have become so deeply involved, I thought I might as well see the whole thing through. With Laribee fussing agitatedly around me, I jumped out of bed and moved to the door.

One look down the corridor showed me Warren. The light was on in the alcove and the night attendant was slouched sideways in the stiff chair where his sister had sat. His elbow, propped on the table by the telephone, supported his head.

It was a simple matter to slip next door into Geddes's room unobserved. But it was not so simple to wake him. I had to shake his shoulder violently before I got any response. When I did manage to rouse him, he gave a little alarmed cry and stiffened against the pillow – just as I had done earlier when I heard Laribee's footsteps.

I knew how Geddes' narcolepsy plagued him with nightmares and vague fears of the darkness. I felt rather a brute.

'It's all right,' I whispered. 'It's just Duluth.'

I explained the situation, but he didn't seem to grasp it very well. And I could not blame him. As I outlined it, the whole thing seemed absolutely cock-eyed to me, too.

'But Laribee's all worked up,' I concluded lamely. 'I thought it was the only decent thing to do to help him out.'

There was a moment's pause. Then Geddes murmured with that polite English acceptance of the extraordinary:

'Only too glad, I'm sure.'

He got out of bed, and together we tiptoed to my room. Laribee was waiting eagerly. As soon as we entered, he hurried toward us, waving the paper.

'You just have to sign here, Geddes. Sign my last will and testament.'

With trembling fingers, he lighted a match and handed Geddes the pen. The Englishman yawned: pressed the will against the wall and scrawled his name.

'And now you again, Duluth,' exclaimed the old man urgently. 'I've just remembered – the two witnesses – they must sign in each other's presence.'

Again I went through the formality with Geddes as a very sleepy, confused witness. Laribee snatched the paper and we stood a moment in silence. Then the Englishman muttered:

'If you don't mind, Duluth, I think I'll turn in again. I'm not feeling awfully bright.'

He had moved to the door and was groping for the handle when very slowly it started to open inward. Instinctively he stepped back. We all did. We stared stupidly as the crack of light broadened and a thin, rigid figure stepped across the threshold.

I must have been pretty much on edge for I felt a moment of wild alarm. The man with the bare feet and the blue silk pyjamas seemed somehow uncanny. He drifted rather than walked, as though he were moving in a trance. I did not realize for some seconds that it was David Fenwick.

He closed the door behind him, stood there absolutely still, and said softly:

'I heard voices – voices.'

I was amazed that he had been able to hear us, for his room was some way down the corridor. But I suppose that people whose ears are tuned to the spirits must be unusually sensitive.

There did not seem anything to say, so we all stood there in silence. Slowly Fenwick turned to Laribee, who was still clutching the will in his hand. The young man's large eyes gleamed even in the obscurity. I had the fleeting impression that he could see in the dark.

'What do you have in your hand, Laribee?' he asked suddenly.

The millionaire seemed in a daze. His arm fell to his side and he mumbled mechanically: 'It's . . . it's my will.'

'Your will! So you are preparing for death.'

'Death?' Laribee's voice rose and then faded into the deep silence but I still seemed to hear the word echoing in my ears.

Fenwick had turned stiffly to the door. He walked like an automaton, and his voice, too, had a flat, robot quality.

'You know the warning. I passed it on to you all. There is no need for you to die if you would obey the spirits and beware of Miss Brush.' He slipped into the corridor and his voice trailed back to us. 'Beware of Miss Brush. There will be murder.'

The three of us were still standing there in bewildered immobility when there were swift footsteps outside and an angry voice exclaimed:

'Hey, there, you!'

The door was swung open again and the light switched on. In the blinding illumination I saw Warren standing on the threshold, his steel hand clamped on to Fenwick's delicate arm. The sour, suspicious gaze flashed around the room.

'What's all this about?' he snapped.

We reacted like school kids caught out in a midnight prank. Laribee had stuffed the paper and fountain-pen into his pyjama pocket. I could not tell whether or not the night attendant had noticed them.

'Well, what's all this about?' he was growling again.

Neither Geddes nor Laribee spoke. Someone had to say something, so I shrugged and murmured as casually as I could:

'Just the boys getting together, Warren. Come on and join the fun.'

15

After the departure of my uninvited guests, I had sufficient presence of mind to grope about in the half darkness and retrieve the damning evidence of the match-sticks. Having disposed of them down the wash-basin, I returned to bed and, oddly enough, slept quite soundly.

Next morning I was wakened by the new attendant. In my sleep-bleary state, I thought for a moment that he was Fogarty. It gave me quite a shock. I had another mild shock when I saw the man's face. It was a perfectly ordinary face – youngish and pleasant. But it was exasperatingly familiar.

I tried to place him as we went down to the gymnasium for my pre-breakfast work-out. He said his name was John Clarke, but that did not mean anything. At last I got so mad at myself that I asked:

'Haven't I seen you somewhere before?'

He smiled and said: 'No, Mr Duluth.'

And the conversation ended there.

After breakfast I paid my daily visit to the surgery. Doctor Stevens seemed to have regretted his impulsive frankness of the day before. He was short with me and rather embarrassed. He would have been even more embarrassed if he had learnt the disastrous results of his suggested psycho-analytical experiment.

The sight of the surgical knives glinting in their glass cabinet almost moved me to warn him of Miss Powell's peculiar monologue in the central hall. But in the light of what had followed, that incident seemed almost too trivial to mention. Besides, ever since I had found out his connection with Fenwick, I had lost my whole-hearted confidence in him. I ended up by telling him nothing except that physically I was bearing up remarkably well under the shock of the past twenty-four hours.

Unlike his colleague, Doctor Moreno was as impeccably impersonal as ever when I underwent my official pep-talk in his office. For a while he discussed my condition as though there were no more pressing business in the world than the mental and neural state of an ex-drunk. His masterly self-control intimidated me, and I was taken completely off my guard when suddenly he said:

'With regard to the other matter, Mr Duluth, I have questioned all the patients as carefully as I could. Of course, I made no direct inquiries. But none of them seem to have seen or heard anything to worry them. From what I can gather no one knows anything concerning Fogarty's death.'

'Even if they don't know anything,' I said, 'I only hope someone's doing something about it.'

Moreno looked annoyed. 'If it is any comfort to you, Mr Duluth, all the members of the staff have spent most of their spare time either being questioned by the police or trying to help them. You can rest assured that there has been no negligence.'

I accepted this as a sarcastic dismissal and was about to take my leave when he added curtly:

'What were Laribee, Geddes and Fenwick doing in your room last night?'

It was now my turn to be annoyed. After all, Moreno was probably younger than myself, and I felt he had no right to adopt this dictatorial attitude. Certainly there seemed no reason for me to confide in him.

'I guess they couldn't sleep,' I said, 'and were bored. They came in for a chat.'

I almost reminded him that we paid a hundred a week and ought to be able to do what we liked with our nights. But his studied dignity made such a remark seem merely juvenile. He looked at his antiseptic hands and asked slowly:

'And what was there so fascinating to talk about that you should all have been breaking the regulations, Mr Duluth?'

'There was something that fascinated Laribee,' I said promptly.

'And it was?'

'He was raving about Miss Brush.' I deliberately returned Moreno's stare. 'It's none of my business, of course, but it strikes me she's been leading him pretty far up the garden path, hasn't she?'

His eyes narrowed suddenly and I saw in them that dangerous gleam which I had noticed several times before. Despite his cold suavity, he was pretty bad at concealing his anger. I expected him to snap out at me, but when he spoke, his voice was very quiet.

'You are my personal patient, Mr Duluth. As the authorities have seen fit to give you some of their confidence against my advice, I feel there are several things about this institution which you should know.'

I nodded, admiring the man's control. He obviously thought I was a low-down son of a gun for meddling around in other people's business, but there was no sign of it in his manner.

'One of the things you should realize, Mr Duluth, concerns Miss Brush. She is an extremely efficient young woman and she has by far the most difficult work in the sanatorium. You are an intelligent man, and, as such, you will understand that it is practically impossible for an attractive – er – nurse to look after men who are mentally off balance without certain complications arising.'

'I'm over thirty,' I said, smiling. 'You needn't begin with the birds and the flowers.'

Moreno's tone became a trifle more stiff and pompous. 'For purely psychiatric reasons it may be necessary for Miss Brush to take certain attitudes with certain patients. But whatever attitude she adopts, it is always one which has been suggested and approved by the authorities at our staff's conferences.'

I might have asked him whether the authorities had approved of her lending Laribee a fountain-pen to make a will in her favour. I might also have asked him why, as a doctor, he approved of certain aspects of Isabel Brush's behaviour, when he so obviously disapproved of them as a man. But I did not want to suggest things to him. I wanted him to suggest them to me.

'So Miss Brush is just part of Laribee's treatment?' I inquired naïvely.

Moreno drew in a swift breath. 'I suppose that is one way of putting it, Mr Duluth. But rather a theatrical one. And I must ask you once more to leave the worrying in this matter to those who are directly concerned.'

His lips moved in a brief, professional smile, then he said he would expect me at the same time the next day.

When I was out in the passage, I saw John Clarke again. The new attendant was standing with his back to me, taking towels from a closet. Although he wore the official white coat of the institution, he did not seem to wear it as to the manner born. I noticed, too, that he was dealing very inefficiently with the towels. It was that which gave me the clue. Suddenly everything came flooding back to me.

It had been two years since I had last seen John Clarke. But now that the link had been forged in my mind, I could remember him distinctly.

We had met in those ghastly days after the theatre had burned down during rehearsals for my *Romeo and Juliet* production – those days when my mind was still dazed by the memory of Magdalen in her Juliet robes, trapped and helpless in that sudden, inexplicable blaze.

They had suspected pyromania and the police had been brought in. Clarke had been one of those policemen. And I remembered him because there had been something solid and real about him. At that time he was one of the few human beings I could bear to have around me.

I strolled up to him and said:

'It was pretty dumb of me not to recognize you, wasn't it?'

He glanced at me blankly over the pile of towels and then, seeing who I was, grinned cheerfully.

'I thought you wouldn't forget, Mr Duluth, but I was told not to let on. Incidentally I was talking to Doctor Lenz about you. He said you'd be out in a couple of weeks. That's swell.'

'Meanwhile you've been put in here to keep an eye on us nuts, I suppose.'

He gave me a broad wink. 'I'm just the new attendant.'

'I get you,' I said. 'Who else is in on it?'

'Only Moreno and Doctor Lenz. It was Captain Green's idea.'

'If you felt like talking out of school,' I suggested, 'I'd be very much interested.'

'I'm afraid I'm only a dumb cop,' he replied easily. 'There's not much to tell except that they're working high pressure and we expect something to break soon.'

'You expect something to break?' I echoed.

'That's what we always tell the Press, Mr Duluth.'

He took a firmer grip on the towels and moved away, grinning over his shoulder.

That grin gave me a slight sense of reassurance. Clarke was one of those dependable people who manage to make the ground feel firmer beneath your feet. And it might be useful to have a friend at court. Even so, I thought, it was going to take more than a John Clarke to straighten out this muddle.

And a muddle it undoubtedly was. With every moment I seemed to be becoming more and more involved while I had less and less idea of what it was all about. But, through the most divergent channels, I seemed to have acquired a great amount of information which for the most divergent reasons I was compelled to keep to myself. It seemed only logical that I should try to do something about it. As I have already said, the detective instinct is a very fundamental one – even in ex-drunks. And, after all, I was still in possession of my faculties.

With this resolve fresh in my mind, I seized an opportunity of cross-examining Miss Brush when we were out in the snow for our morning walk.

Although she was not a nut, I felt that she would be the hardest of them to crack. She had completely lost yesterday's pallor and uneasiness. The blond brightness was as polished and hygienic as ever. Nothing, I felt, short of shock tactics could have any chance of success with her.

We were a little behind the others when I began my attack. 'Can I ask you an indelicate question, Miss Brush?' I said.

'Certainly, Mr Duluth.' She tightened the blue scarf around her neck and switched on the famous smile. 'That is, if you don't mind an indelicate answer.'

'There's a rumour floating around that you're engaged to Laribee. Is that true?'

The smile vanished automatically, but I could detect no other change in her expression.

'Because if it is true,' I went on, 'I want to be the first to offer official congratulations.'

Miss Brush paused in the snow. With her white nurse's cap and blond hair she looked the picture of exuberant health. She also looked as if she wanted to slap me.

'Since I've been here, Mr Duluth, I've been engaged to three authors, one bishop, several senators and a couple of charming young alcoholics like you. Unfortunately I'm still – er – Miss Brush.'

'So this is your first experiment with a millionaire,' I said, smiling.

She did not seem to think it funny. For a moment she positively glared at me. Then, with an effort, she became once more the radiant day nurse, the patients' delight. She laid a hand on my arm and said with formidable sprightliness:

'Don't you think you're being rather stupid, Mr Duluth?'

'Frightfully stupid,' I agreed. 'If I hadn't been, I wouldn't be here and I'd never have had the pleasure of making your acquaintance.'

We hurried to catch up with the others.

When we reached them, Laribee joined us. His face was wreathed in smiles and he offered me a mysterious 'you're-in-it-too' look. Feeling in his breast pocket, he produced the fountain-pen with which we had signed the will the night before.

'I had meant to give this back to you earlier, Isabel,' he said. 'Thank you very much. And everything is settled.'

Once again he glanced knowingly at me. But Miss Brush seemed very careful not to catch my eye. With a casualness which seemed a trifle ostentatious, she took the pen and slipped it into the pocket of her coat.

'Thank you, Mr Laribee,' she said coolly. 'I'm sorry the pens in the library didn't suit you. I'm not in the habit of lending mine to everyone who wants to write letters, you know. But, you said you hadn't written to your daughter for several weeks.'

And that was all I got out of Miss Brush.

It was possible, I supposed, that Laribee had faked up some excuse for borrowing that pen, and that Miss Brush was as innocent as she appeared. But one thing was certain. Our extremely efficient young day nurse was very definitely giving me no change.

16

The weather had started to act up. By the time we returned from our walk, there were ugly clouds creeping up from the east and it looked as though we were in for a storm.

The patients always reacted to bad weather. That afternoon we were all jumpy and on edge – even more on edge than we had been the day before. I could have blessed Geddes when he suggested a game of squash.

We obtained permission from Miss Brush, changed, and had John Clarke unlock the court for us. It was a small independent building, standing in a corner of the yard. When we entered a musty smell of disuse invaded our nostrils. Lenz's male patients obviously were not keen on voluntary exercise. In fact, I myself had not been there before, and in my pre-drinking days I had thought I was a pretty good squash player.

As soon as Clarke had left us, we started in. Geddes had said he was very rusty, but I might have known he was just pulling the old British line of modesty. He trimmed me badly and then grudgingly admitted that he had been Fives champion at the Calcutta Rackets Club in '26.

'But this damn' disease of mine mucks up everything, Duluth. Exercise seems to bring it on, too. It's a wonder I didn't drop off after playing just this one set.' He leaned against the wall, wiping invisible perspiration from his forehead. 'It's bally awful, Duluth. Half the time I'm living in a daze. Muzzy, just like a sheep.'

'Or a drunk,' I added consolingly.

Somehow I had a lot of admiration for that man's grit. He was the only one of us never let down in public. I suppose that's what King Edward and the British Empire do for you.

I suggested another set, but he wanted a rest. I had the impression that he was worried somewhere behind that veneer of his. Suddenly he said:

'Did you come into my room last night, Duluth? Or was I just dreaming?'

'I came all right.'

'And was it some business about witnessing that fellow Laribee's will?'

'That's right.'

He started slightly as though he were surprised, as though he had been half hoping I would deny it.

'So it all happened,' he murmured.

His voice echoed around the walls of the squash court, sounding rather eerie as though some of Fenwick's spirits were answering him. I remarked on it and, instantly, he said:

'I've got to get away from this place, Duluth.'

He spoke with curious desperation. When an unemotional man like Geddes talks that way, it worries you.

'You mean they're not curing you?' I asked.

'Oh, it's not that particularly. I didn't really expect them to make me well.' He laid his head with its perfectly combed hair against the wall and stared straight in front of him. 'Of course, it may be my nerves. I thought it was until you told me about that business in your room really happening. You see, it all seemed like a dream. But if that part of it wasn't a dream, the other part can't be a dream either.'

I nodded, feeling a strange, uneasy sensation.

'I remember all that in your room very vaguely,' he went on. 'But I know Warren got me back to bed. For some reason I was frightened. I lay there for a long time in a kind of daze.'

He passed a finger along his moustache. There was something rather pathetic about the way he was keeping his hand from trembling.

'It was some time then that it happened, Duluth. It's so deuced impossible, I know you won't believe it.'

'Go on,' I said.

'I was lying there, half asleep, when I heard that damn' voice – calling my name.'

'Good heavens.'

'But that's not all. At first I thought it was my own voice – just like I did the first time. But then I knew it wasn't because – because I could tell there was someone else in the room.'

I realized that he did not know about all the other people who had heard the voice. He did not even know I had heard it. I could imagine what that visitation must have done to his nerves.

'You'd scared me quite a bit when you came in, Duluth. But this was far worse. I could feel someone there in the darkness but they didn't speak – not after they had called my name.' He shrugged his shoulders slightly. 'I know this sounds like a kid's ghost story, but at last it came right up to my bed – that figure. I could see it quite plainly.'

'A man or a woman?' I cut in sharply.

'I couldn't say. To tell the truth I was trembling all over like an idiot. But I did hear what it said. Very quiet and penetrating: "*There will be another thing on the slab, Martin Geddes. Fogarty was the first. You, Laribee and Duluth will be the next.*"'

The squash court was very quiet when he stopped speaking.

'Of course,' he murmured at length, 'it might just have been Fenwick acting up again, but – well it seemed somehow horrible and – and serious, as though, whatever it was, it meant what it said. I could have called Warren on the house telephone, but ...'

'I know exactly how you felt,' I broke in quickly, feeling a cold tingling up my spine.

'I thought I had to tell you, Duluth,' said the Englishman slowly, 'because it mentioned you and used that queer phrase of yours – the thing on the slab. What's it all mean?'

He gazed at me intently. I could only stare back at him. I was at a loss for words.

'And then there's Fogarty,' he persisted. 'It said Fogarty was the first. He's not here any more. Do you think something happened to him?'

I was glad in a way that Geddes did not know about what I had discovered in the physio-therapy room, glad that I did not have to tell him.

'I expect he's sick,' I said guardedly.

'Sick? Perhaps he is sick.' Geddes twisted the racket fiercely between his hands. 'But it's not good enough, Duluth. Moreno was talking to me yesterday when he took me to the surgery for some of that new drug they're experimenting with. He said something awfully queer about Fogarty. I got the impression he was trying to find out whether any of us had seen him. Perhaps Fogarty was scared like we were and left without warning. From what I know of him, he's not the sort of fellow to think twice about leaving his wife. Anyway, something's going on here and for some reason you and I are mixed up in it. I'm not a coward. I don't mind facing danger when I know what that danger is. But this is so senseless, so intangible. You don't have a chance to fight. That's why I feel I've just got to clear out.'

I could sympathize with him. Having received this second, indirect warning, I almost wanted to leave, too, and go back to the peace and safety of alcoholism. But I had a real reason to stay. I was not going to leave Iris with no one to look after her. I suppose it was conceited of me to think I could do anything to help. But somehow there was no one in that place I could trust. And Iris was hearing the voice, too. She was in danger.

Geddes was speaking again, his tone strangely low. 'There was that crazy spirit warning of Fenwick's. And then the piece of paper in Laribee's book. It's Laribee they're after, I'm sure. But how does that affect us?'

Suddenly a thought struck me, a confused, rather stupid thought. 'Maybe it's got something to do with that will. After all, you and I witnessed it. I'm frightfully sorry if I've been the one to drag you into this.'

Geddes considered a moment. 'It can't be the will. I first heard that voice two days before there was any question of the will. No, there's something else – something they've got against us.'

Neither of us spoke for a moment. You noticed the silence when you stopped talking in that squash court. The vague echoing whispers faded so quickly. I had a crazy feeling that they were real voices, voices that stopped when we stopped – to listen.

'We're both in this,' said Geddes slowly, 'and I think that between us we ought to do our best to find out what's the matter with this place. I'm going to give it two days, and if I don't succeed, I'm leaving.'

He broke off and we looked at each other.

'I said we were two orphans in the storm,' I murmured, smiling. 'It seems as if I was only too right. As for the partnership, it's O.K. by me.'

It was only after I had spoken that I remembered how the powers that be had pledged me to silence on certain aspects of the affair. A moral problem arose which seemed at the moment too complicated to cope with. For the time being, at least, it might be wiser to keep Geddes in the dark as to what I knew rather than to run the risk of displeasing the authorities and having one of the main channels of information dry up. Anyway, after my embarrassing experience in psycho-analysis the day before, I hardly felt myself in a position to take any more unauthorized risks with the mental health of my fellow-patients.

It seemed impossible to start playing squash again. We both appeared to realize it at the same time, for Geddes had moved to the door and was stepping out into the courtyard.

I followed a little behind him. The clouds were banking up overhead, bringing a premature evening.

Geddes had disappeared into the building before the two other figures emerged. I recognized them at once as Daniel Laribee and Clarke. I was surprised to see that Laribee was changed for squash.

Clarke nodded to me pleasantly, murmured something about Miss Brush wanting the financier to take some exercise and went in to clean up the court. Laribee did not follow him. He stood tensely at my side, waiting till the attendant had disappeared.

'There's one thing I forgot to tell you last night,' he whispered. 'You mustn't say anything about those matches. No one knew I took them – not even Isabel. I took them when she was lending me her pen. And she would be angry if ever she knew.'

Rather bewildered, I gave him my promise. His eyes were still on the open door of the squash court some fifteen feet away.

'I don't trust that new attendant,' he said nervously. 'He's always hanging around me. I think he suspects something about the will.'

Before I had time to say anything, he thrust a hand into the pocket of his overcoat and produced a paper.

'I carry it about with me wherever I go,' he muttered. 'But it's too dangerous now. I want you to look after it, Duluth.' He slipped the paper between my fingers. 'They may kill me. They may do anything to get it away from me ...'

'All set, Mr Laribee.' Clarke's voice rang out from the court.

'Keep it safe, Duluth,' breathed the old man pleadingly. 'You've got to keep it. You're the only one I can trust.'

17

On my way back from the squash court, I had to pass near the main entrance of the sanatorium. I was still rather distracted by Laribee's sudden action in giving me his will. More and more I was becoming convinced that this peculiar document had some vital significance in the tangle of mystery and danger which was involving us all.

My conscience told me that it should be shown to Lenz. And my instincts for self-preservation made me more than eager to get the wretched thing out of my own keeping. But, crazy as he was, Laribee seemed to trust me implicitly and he had begged me to be secret. For him, all other men, not excluding Doctor Lenz, were enemies. I did not feel that I could betray him.

The restricted atmosphere of a sanatorium has a remarkable effect upon one's ethical standards. After a few weeks of it, one feels oneself reverting to the ineluctable codes of one's prep-school days. The staff assume in one's mind the impersonal aloofness of martinet school-teachers and the patients become schoolmates and fellow-conspirators. Relationships take on a juvenile intensity and the breaking of a confidence seems as dire and irremediable a sin as does gratuitous tale-bearing to the normal boy.

And so in the case of Laribee's will, there seemed nothing for it but that I should hold the bag, the baby or what have you.

I had just made this Horatio Alger resolution when Lenz himself appeared in the passage-way. He was dressed for going out and carried a black, portentous brief-case under his arm.

Although a great deal of my information had been told me in confidence, there was still a lot more to which no strings were attached. I gladly snatched this opportunity of shouldering them off on to the director.

His large, bearded figure was progressing with processional dignity to the front door. I hurried after him and forced him to notice me.

'Good afternoon, Doctor Lenz,' I said pleasantly.

He paused and smiled indulgently. 'Ah, Mr Duluth, I am glad to see you have been getting some exercise.'

I smiled back. 'I was wondering if you could spare me a few minutes.'

The director shot an almost imperceptible glance at his wrist-watch. 'Certainly, Mr Duluth. But you are overheated. You should not stand in draughts.' A godlike gesture indicated the open door of some nondescript visitors' waiting-room. 'Let us go in here.'

He led me into the room and shut the door carefully behind us. His grey eyes were regarding me with kindly serenity.

'Doctor Lenz,' I said, coming straight to the point, 'the other day you said I might be useful; that you felt there was some subversive influence at work here in the sanatorium.'

His face clouded slightly. 'Ah, yes, Mr Duluth.'

'Well, I've come across a few things that I feel you ought to know.' I did my best to return that level gaze. 'I think Mr Laribee is in danger. I think that somehow all this crazy business – even Fogarty's death – centres around him.'

'But why should you think that, Mr Duluth?' he asked gently.

I told him all the incidents, except that of the will, which directly concerned the financier; the ticking in his room and my finding of the stopwatch in his pocket; the broker's voice on the walk, Fenwick's spirit warning and the piece of paper Geddes and I had found in the old man's book.

As I recounted each detail, Lenz nodded slightly but his eyes never left my face. I had the uncomfortable impression that he was more interested in my personal reactions to the events than in the events themselves.

'That has all been reported to me, Mr Duluth,' he said at length. 'All except the piece of paper which you and Mr Geddes discovered. But I am not surprised at that. Other similar notes have been brought to my attention.'

His very calmness baffled me. 'But how do you account for it?'

'For twenty-five years, Mr Duluth, I have been faced daily – hourly perhaps – with things for which I cannot account. And if you believe these incidents to be directly connected with the distressing death of Fogarty, I feel you should know what I personally think of them. I believe that all the manifestations you mention could have a comparatively simple explanation.'

I was astonished and I must have looked it, for he smiled paternally.

'Since you are in our confidence, Mr Duluth, I will give you an elementary lesson in psychiatry. I do not make a habit of breaking medical ethics by discussing my patients, but the circumstances are most unusual and Doctor Moreno has told me you have been worrying yourself. In your condition I am particularly anxious for you not to worry.'

He made me feel like a small boy who had been interfering impertinently in the affairs of his elders.

'You are right, Mr Duluth, in saying that these warnings seem to be directed toward Laribee, but you forget that there is someone else involved.'

'You mean Miss Brush?' I asked quickly. 'Is there danger for her, too?'

Lenz stroked his beard and I saw in his eyes a faint look of amusement. 'No, Mr Duluth, I do not feel there is danger for anyone in particular. But the mentioning of Miss Brush's name in those messages makes things much more simple for us.' He was very grave again. 'I am afraid that Mr Laribee is beginning to show signs of schizophrenia, which is merely a long word for a split mind – a mind divided between sanity and delusion. His deluded mind tells him he is going to marry Miss Brush. That is harmless enough because it keeps him from worrying about his financial affairs. But his sane mind and his past experience tells him that young women are dangerous, they are after his money. And so, his sane mind warns him against his own delusions. He writes notes to himself, unconsciously acts on the suggestions of the other patients. It is possible that he even talks to himself about it – in such a manner that a man like Mr Fenwick could interpret it as a spirit warning and pass it on again so that the whole thing becomes a vicious circle. You have seen a stone thrown into water, Mr Duluth, seen the ripples spread until the whole pool is agitated. A great many of these trivial incidents might, I think, be explained that way.'

'And the stopwatch?' I asked dubiously.

'That, Mr Duluth, seems to me just another manifestation of the same condition. It is perfectly possible for a patient of Mr Laribee's type to react to his own suggestions as to those of other people. He knows that under his present financial arrangements the sanatorium will come into a certain amount of money should he be certified insane. From that knowledge, he contracts the idea that he is being deliberately driven mad. It is only a short step to the stage where, to justify himself, he creates definite proof of his delusion. He could, for example, take the stopwatch from the surgery, frighten himself with it and in due course forget completely that he was the one responsible for the whole episode.'

As usual the director had succeeded in being interesting, if not completely convincing.

'But there are other things,' I persisted.

I told him about Miss Powell and her soliloquy on knives. Doctor Lenz looked concerned.

'That disturbs me, Mr Duluth, but it disturbs me only as a doctor. You confirm my belief that some of the patients are losing ground. Miss Powell has not talked to herself before, but there is nothing unusual about her stealing.'

'No,' I said. 'I've already seen a demonstration of that.'

'Miss Powell is a kleptomaniac. She is a clever, cultured woman, but she has this strange impulse to steal. There is no desire for gain. She simply steals things and hides them. Of course, she, too, is suggestible. You or I could suggest to her that she take something and she would probably take it. At times her own impulses urge her to theft and then it is possible that she might voice those impulses and speak out loud as you heard her do.'

'So you don't think there's anything behind it all?' I asked. 'You don't think that someone is fooling around with hypnotism or mesmerism – or whatever you call it?'

Doctor Lenz's strangely magnetic eyes met mine. 'Mesmerism, Mr Duluth, is an obsolete quackery which exists only in parlour games and sensational fiction. As for hypnotism – it is only another name for extreme suggestibility. Occasionally it has its therapeutic value as a means of unearthing something which is buried in the patient's subconscious mind. But it is nonsensical to suppose that through hypnotism one could upset another person's ethical standards and persuade him to do anything at all violent – unless, of course, there were a pre-existing tendency toward violence.'

I almost blurted out to him how that voice was trying to work on Iris's suggestibility, trying to capitalize her morbid aversion to Laribee, but I stopped myself in time. The recollection of her pale, sad face had risen in my mind, and the pleading in her eyes when she said: 'Don't tell Doctor Lenz. Whatever you do, don't tell him. He'd keep me locked up in my room. He wouldn't let me work . . .' The memory of her fears of the director made me a little doubtful of him myself. His theories seemed to come a trifle too pat.

'But there's no explanation for that voice,' I said bluntly. 'I heard it and I'm reasonably sane. Laribee heard it as the voice of his broker. Fenwick heard it as the spirits. And now there's Geddes.'

I told him of the two occasions on which the Englishman had been warned. He listened in silence and I had the fleeting impression that his face had turned a shade more solemn.

'I must admit that both in the case of yourself and that of Mr Geddes it is not easy to account for the delusion,' he murmured. 'But I believe there is an explanation even for that. It is difficult – even for a trained physician – to hypnotize another person. But it is easy even for the feeblest minded patient to hypnotize himself. People who are mentally sick are sensitive to atmosphere; what is commonly called psychic. They sense danger or uneasiness around them, especially when they are confined in a sanatorium. They are also very egoistical, and that makes them instinctively centralize that danger in themselves, in their own egos. They imagine things – warning voices, for example – and their suggestibility is greatly increased by their imaginations. It is a sort of self-hypnotism.'

This was a reversal of what the director had told me the other day. He seemed to have an astonishing talent for going to earth in warrens of psychological intricacy.

'Even if that is so,' I said rather accusingly, 'you're not going to make me believe it was self-hypnotism that persuaded a hard-headed man like Fogarty into that strait-jacket.'

'No, indeed.' Doctor Lenz was smiling sadly now – the smile of a man who is constantly faced with things more tragic than death. 'To attempt an explanation of that is not exactly within my sphere as a psychiatrist. I have merely tried to convince you of your mistake in believing that these other, purely psychiatric, phenomena have any connection with the death of Fogarty.'

I stared at him intently, trying to guess what went on behind that bearded, Jovian front.

'But, even so, there must be some explanation for Fogarty's death, Doctor Lenz. The police aren't going to sit around . . .'

'The police,' broke in Lenz rather coldly, 'are already almost satisfied that Fogarty's death was the result of an unfortunate accident.'

'But how on earth . . . ?'

Doctor Lenz glanced once more at his watch. He seemed less interested now that we had abandoned the fertile fields of speculative psychopathology. 'I am telling you this in confidence, Mr Duluth, because I feel it is best for you to know the truth. Mrs Fogarty admits that she and her husband quarrelled on the night that he died. Apparently Fogarty told her he had decided to leave the sanatorium in order to try his luck in your sphere of activity, Mr Duluth – the theatre, or perhaps I should say, the entertainment, world. He wanted her to go with him, but she refused and advised him very strongly against making such a move.'

The director paused. He had, at least, given me an explanation of why Mrs Fogarty had been crying on the night of her husband's death.

'Yes,' he continued, and once more a slight smile moved his mouth, 'in a way, Mr Duluth, I believe that you were responsible for his death. At least, the presence here of a celebrated theatrical man aroused in him those enthusiasms for the stage which are normally associated with younger people. I am reluctant to apply psychological dogmas to the perfectly normal. But we all know that Fogarty was a vain man, intensely proud of his strength. And his wife had just pricked his vanity. It is convincing to suppose that in a moment of pique, he went to the physio-therapy room alone, determined to assure himself of his ability. He tried to perform some trick – possibly a variation of the well-known strait-jacket. And –'

'But the police . . .' I broke in.

'The police, Mr Duluth, have found no evidence to invalidate the theory that Fogarty tied himself up and was unable to free himself. Captain Green has discussed the matter with me exhaustively and, as a psychologist, I can see nothing which may not be interpreted in that manner.'

The director rose with a swift glance at his watch. Obviously this was my dismissal.

As I followed him to the door, I remembered how much the time of such a man is normally worth. He had, I felt, been more than generous. I could only hope that this little lecture would not appear as an item on my next bill.

'Well, Mr Duluth, I am glad to have had this opportunity to talk with you. Come to me at any time, and' – he paused at the door – 'I must congratulate you on your – er – improved appearance. It is gratifying to know that all this mental stimulation has done you no harm.'

A brief, bearded smile. Then he was gone.

As I went upstairs, I tried to figure out whether Lenz really believed what he told me; or whether he had been indulging merely in a little psychiatric tomfoolery to make me feel good. Well, in that at least, he had succeeded. It was impossible to listen to him for long without being more than half-convinced.

And yet my instinct warned me to suspect the disarming logicality of his explanations. I felt that my newly acquired optimistic frame of mind was just what the sanatorium itself was intended to be – a fool's paradise.

18

Once back in my room, I took Laribee's will from my overcoat pocket. The millionaire had begged me to keep it safe, so I looked around for a good spot in which to conceal it. Hiding places were few and far between in those hygienically bare rooms. I ended by slipping the document under the rubber mat which was attached to the floor beneath the wash-basin. I suppose it was rather foolish, but I had reached the stage where nothing seemed particularly foolish any more.

When I strolled down to the smoking-room, everything was surprisingly peaceful. Billy Trent, who had cheered up considerably, offered to shake me a soda after my squash game. Stroubel was sitting at a table, smiling vaguely at his moving hands. Fenwick was playing double dummy with Miss Brush, apparently ignoring the spirits' emphatic warning against her.

For a moment I found myself believing that Lenz had been right – that nothing more sinister had happened in the sanatorium than a tragically unsuccessful strong-man act; and that all the other strange incidents could be explained as the results of normal abnormality.

But the next minute I thought of Iris and the expression on her face when she told me about that voice. It had been twenty-four hours since I had seen her, and in the restricted life of the sanatorium that seemed like several eternities. I was desperately eager for the evening with its accompanying mixed sociabilities. She would have to be in the lounge that night, I reflected. If she wasn't I would raise hell until they convinced me she was all right.

At last dinner was over and tirelessly brisk Miss Brush took us down to the central lounge. I saw Iris as soon as we entered. She was sitting by the piano, away from the other women.

I started excitedly toward her but was blocked by Miss Brush. The day nurse was smiling brightly and asking me to be a fourth at bridge. I said I was sorry; I didn't feel like it. I was almost rude. But still she stood in my way, commanding and statuesque despite her *ingénue* dress of robin's-egg blue.

'Now, Mr Duluth, you mustn't be unsociable. It's going to be very good for you.'

For the first time I regretted that I had reached a stage of convalescence where it was no longer permissible to swear at the staff. She had taken my arm and was leading me toward the bridge table. I had the distinct impression that she was deliberately keeping me from Iris. But short of going berserk and knocking her down, there was nothing I could do about it.

I loathed bridge, anyway, and that game was a nightmare. Miss Brush chatted gaily and played almost as crazily as the two women patients. Most of the time my gaze and my attention were fixed on that corner by the piano.

Iris seemed a bit restless, I thought, but more lovely and mysterious than ever in a dark-green dress with trailing sleeves. Once her eyes met mine and I thought I saw in them a look of pleading. My bidding became even more hysterical. Somehow I had to finish that rubber.

But my partner was a timid little school-teacher – the type that never bids unless she has all the aces and all the kings in her hand. I never even got a break as dummy.

I noticed that Geddes was being more sociable than usual. I wondered whether it was part of his new determination to track down the mystery behind the voice. When I saw him draw Laribee aside, I was sure of it. I was horribly curious to know what they were saying.

'Four spades,' said Miss Brush.

'No spades,' said my partner unconventionally.

'Six spades,' said Miss Brush's partner.

My attention was divided now between Geddes and Iris. As I offered an absent-minded but heroic seven no-trump, I saw Iris rise and move across the room toward Miss Powell. The Bostonian spinster paused in her solitaire to say something. Geddes had left Laribee now and was talking to Stroubel. Nothing is more exasperating than to know things are going on and to have no means of joining in.

I went ten down on my no-trump bid. To my infinite surprise and delight, Miss Brush was annoyed.

'Really, Mr Duluth, I don't think you're concentrating.'

'Very well,' I said quickly. 'Let me get you another partner.'

I rose with alacrity, roped in Billy Trent, who was always delighted for a chance of being with Miss Brush, and hurried over to Iris.

She was back in her chair by the piano now. As I sat down at her side, I could tell at once that something was wrong. Her fingers were playing nervously with the clasp of her hand-bag and there was an expression on her face which gave me a sudden sensation of alarm.

Although we were in the middle of that crowded hall, I gripped her hands and said swiftly:

'What is it, Iris?'

She drew her hands away. I do not think it was because she objected to my holding them. But Moreno had just come in and was hovering near us, looking very waspish and professional.

As she waited for him to move away, her head was bent forward as though she were listening for something which she could not quite hear. Then she whispered:

'It's happened again just now.'

I knew she meant that damn' voice. We were both slightly trembling.

'What did it say?' I asked hoarsely.

'Almost exactly the same thing.'

'About Laribee?'

'Yes. But it said something else, too.'

She turned toward me so swiftly that I could feel her breath warm on my cheek. Her eyes, usually dark and slumbering, were awake with a strange flame.

'If I tell you, you'll only think I'm mad, the way all the others do.'

I took her hands again. For a moment neither of us said anything. It was a comfort to touch her. I think she felt that comfort, too.

When at length she spoke again, her voice was almost calm.

'It said that I must revenge my father's death, that Mr Laribee was responsible and that only by killing him would I ever get well. And then –'

'Yes!'

'It said there was a knife in my hand-bag.'

'A knife?' I repeated dully.

'But I haven't dared to look. I hoped perhaps you would come.'

I suppose it was just my over-wrought imagination. But at that moment everyone else in the room seemed to have stopped talking. I felt they were all listening, watching.

I pulled myself together with an effort. 'Give me the bag,' I said.

She handed it to me without speaking. My fingers were shaking as I fumbled at the catch. At last it sprang open.

Blankly I stared at Iris's tiny handkerchief, her compact – the few little things they had allowed her to keep. There was something pathetic about them. They were so everyday, so normal.

It was the contrast which made the other thing so horrible. Lying among them, strangely out of place in that delicate, silk-lined hand-bag, was a thin surgical knife.

Swiftly I picked it up and slipped it into my pocket. Iris and I looked at each other.

'But it's absolutely impossible,' she whispered.

I knew it was impossible, too. But I was not thinking about that. I was just thinking how someone had done this beastly thing to her.

Then, as we sat there together, I saw that glazed, half-hypnotized expression come back into her eyes.

'They want me to kill Laribee,' she said slowly. 'They're trying to make me do it against my will.'

Her hands dropped to her sides and she added with sudden pleading: 'But you won't let anything happen, will you?'

'Of course I won't. I've got the knife. It's safe. You can trust me.'

Around us in the lounge the sociabilities continued. Vaguely I heard Miss Brush laughing, and then the boom of Laribee's voice. At a table not far off, Miss Powell was shuffling her cards for the solitaire which always came out.

Iris had started trembling again. Regardless of everyone and everything, I put my hand on her shoulder and said quietly:

'You mustn't let them frighten you, Iris. Remember I'm always here.'

'But –'

'There aren't any buts,' I said, and my mouth was very close to her ear. 'I'm going to stand by you whatever happens, because – you see – I love you.'

Her eyes met mine and she smiled. I found myself not giving a damn about the knife, the voice – or anything.

As my lips brushed her hair, I wondered whether this wasn't the craziest of all the crazy things that had happened in Doctor Lenz's sanatorium.

19

Iris smiled again, and that cleared my head, made me suddenly feel very male and purposeful. The knife would completely justify my conviction that something was vitally, dangerously wrong with the sanatorium. I would have to see Lenz again right away.

I told Iris so, and immediately a look of alarm spread across her face.

'No, you mustn't tell him – you mustn't. He'll think I'm worse, keep me shut up in my room. He'll –'

'But he won't think you're worse, Iris. Don't you see? We have the knife. It's a proof.'

She would not be comforted. Her lips were trembling as though she were near to tears. She couldn't stand it, she said, being shut up there in her room.

'He'll have to see the knife, Iris,' I urged. 'But if you like I won't tell him I got it from you.'

That seemed to dispel her fears. She inclined her head slightly and whispered:

'Of course – you must do what you think best. But it's all so dreadful. It makes me feel I shall never get well, never get out of this place.'

I knew exactly how she felt. I was almost that way myself. But I did my best to sound optimistic.

'Nonsense,' I said, 'we'll both be out in a couple of weeks. And what I said yesterday still goes. I'm going to take you with me and put you through the hardest job of training you've ever had in your life. I'm going to make you a big actress – or I bust.'

As I said it, I knew that I meant it. In some crazy way my life was bound up with hers now. Whatever else did or did not happen, I was going to get Iris out of the sanatorium – going to get her well again.

'You stay here and don't be frightened,' I said with an encouraging smile. 'I'm going to see Lenz.'

As I moved away from her, I happened to glance at Miss Powell. Until that moment I had been too confused and angry to be able to think coherently as to how the knife could possibly have been put into Iris's bag. But when I saw the Boston spinster sitting there with a card poised thoughtfully over her solitaire game, those strange words of the night before came back into my mind:

'There are lovely knives in the surgery.'

One thing was patently obvious. Whoever had started this cruel campaign against Iris, was now working either with or through Miss Powell.

I was still musing upon this when the Boston spinster turned to me and nodded an elaborate greeting.

'Good evening, Mr Duluth. Such typically March weather we're having, aren't we? In like a lion, you know!'

She gave a short, nervous laugh and turned back to her card-cheating.

Moreno was the only person who could give us official permission to see the director at unseasonable hours. Neither he nor Stevens was in the lounge, and my first instinct was to hurry out of the room to find them. Then I remembered my promise to Iris to keep her out of it. Everyone had seen me talking to her. If I were to leave at once, I might arouse suspicions which would inevitably involve her.

Curbing my impatience, I spent the remaining minutes of the social hour in being as sociable as it was in me to be, hoping to draw attention from Iris. I took a short but convincing interest in Miss Powell's solitaire and her very positive views on social reform. I looked over Miss Brush's shoulder and confirmed my previous opinion that she was an even worse bridge player than myself. I kidded Billy Trent. And then in turn talked to Laribee, Fenwick, and Stroubel.

I noticed that Miss Brush was observing this sudden accession of brightness on my part. Doubtless she considered it an indication of advancing convalescence.

It was not until we were in the corridor on our way to bed that I had an opportunity for a word alone with Geddes. I was eager to know what, if anything, he had learned from Laribee, but I only had time to whisper: 'I'm going to see Lenz. Something else has happened. Tell you later.'

Then Miss Brush caught up with us.

'Attractive girl – Miss Pattison,' she murmured.

'Yes,' I said guardedly.

'You get on very well with her, don't you, Mr Duluth?'

'Does that have to be recorded on my chart, too?' I asked rather irritably.

She smiled and I thought I could detect a trace of malice in her eyes. 'Oh, come, Mr Duluth, don't take it that way. I was just complimenting you on your taste in brunettes.'

Miss Brush may have been a hard-boiled, efficient nurse, but apparently she was human enough to resent it when one of her little group of worshippers started noticing other women.

Not daring to postpone it any longer, I told her I had to see Lenz. Instantly the smile left her lips and she said rather sulkily that I would have to ask Moreno. Warren appeared at that moment and she told him to take me down to the young psychiatrist's office.

The night attendant looked rested and less gloomy than usual as we went down the corridor together. He was quite friendly, too. I suspected that he had already heard of the police's belief that his brother-in-law's death had been accidental. With the menace of official cross-examination no longer over him, he had apparently decided to forgive me.

Doctor Moreno was closing the door of a small closet when I entered. I had just time to see a familiar bottle and a tumbler, half full. It was Johnnie Walker Black Label, and I envied him. But it was a relief to realize that I did not envy him unduly. A few weeks before I would have jumped on him and wrenched the bottle from him like a hungry mountain lion.

I suppose he saw from my expression that I had caught him out, for he smiled and said almost humanly:

'I wish I could ask you to join me, Mr Duluth.' He indicated a chair near his, but I did not sit down.

'I'd like to, doctor,' I said, 'but I'm afraid I can't stay. I've got to see Doctor Lenz at once.'

Moreno stiffened and the good humour left his face. Like most of us, I suppose, he hated it when people wanted to go over his head to the man higher up.

'Doctor Lenz is speaking at a medical meeting in New York,' he said coldly. 'He will not be back until tomorrow.'

'But I've *got* to see him,' I insisted.

'In Doctor Lenz's absence I am in charge of the sanatorium. If there is anything important, you can take it up with me, Mr Duluth.'

The change of expression on my face must have been unflatteringly obvious, for he continued hotly:

'I think it is time I told you, Mr Duluth, that your attitude toward me and the staff in general has been most uncooperative. I feel you have been holding things back which might have been important. You've been creating a melodrama . . .'

'Melodrama!' I cut in. 'I only wish it was melodrama. But it's all real – horribly real. It's you and this sanatorium that do your best to dehumanize everything. You were on the stage, weren't you? I suppose you played the tight-lipped, science-must-march-on physician. Well, you've been playing it ever since. And you're such a long way away from reality now that you can't understand it when people start behaving like people instead of neurotic puppets whose function in life is to react correctly to treatment and show the correct development on their progress charts.'

Moreno went rather red. 'You are exciting yourself, Mr Duluth,' he said quietly. 'And, from what I can gather, you have been exciting the other patients, too. If you are not careful, you are going to prove more of a hindrance than a help, not only to us, but also to your own recovery.'

As I glared at him, standing there, stiff, almost priggishly neat in his white physician's coat, he seemed to become a symbol of all the red tape, the humouring, and the hypocrisy of that expensive sanatorium. I told him that it was a good job that someone was being a hindrance to the things that were going on. I called him a stuffed shirt and a number of other incoherent but opprobrious names.

He took it very calmly, considering his own annoyance at me. As I raved on I had the uncomfortable feeling that he was going to enter all the epithets on my progress chart as soon as I had left.

His calmness only aggravated me further. I did not care if he thought I was crazy. I did not care if it meant my being shut up for an extra six months. I was getting out of my system all my frustrated loathing of officialdom; it was a very pleasant sensation.

At length I paused for breath and he said quietly:

'If you have finished, Mr Duluth, I suggest we now talk to each other as man to man. I have been considering you as a patient and you, I gather, have been treating me as a doctor. Shall we drop it for an instant?'

'I don't believe Lenz is away,' I said doggedly. 'And I'm not going to talk to anyone but him.'

'You are at liberty to try and find him, but it will only be a waste of time. Look.' He tossed me a medical magazine which announced Lenz as speaker at some meeting that evening.

'Did you have anything *definite* to tell him?' He asked the question with a trace of sarcasm in his tone. 'Or were you just going to talk about a few more mysterious voices which you and the –'

'Definite!' I cut in. 'Would you call it definite if I told you that knives have been stolen from the surgery?'

'I would say it was definitely impossible, Mr Duluth, though I am willing to check up on it.'

'So you don't believe me?'

'I said I thought it quite impossible. Doctor Stevens has charge of the surgery and –'

'All right, perhaps I can convince you.'

I had worked myself to such a pitch that I could hardly control my voice. All my jitteriness had come back. I could only just get my shaking hand into my pocket.

'Look!'

'I am waiting to be convinced, Mr Duluth.'

My hand had come out of my coat pocket and was running through my other pockets – breast, trousers, vest.

'I am still waiting, Mr Duluth.'

His voice was so calm and assured that I was certain he knew what to expect.

I had searched every one of my pockets. There could be no mistake about it now.

The knife was gone!

And then something must have snapped, for the next thing I knew was that I was in bed, and Mrs Fogarty was pouring something sweet and soporific down my throat.

20

Next morning I was kept in bed and coddled. Moreno came to see me early and acted the composed young psychiatrist as though nothing had happened. Miss Brush hurried brightly in and out to make sure I had everything I wanted. I suppose they were trying to soothe my troubled nerves.

But they did not succeed. I tossed and turned, thinking about the knife and what a precious fool I had made of myself. I was still calm enough to be certain that the whole incident in the lounge had not been imaginary. Someone had deliberately stolen that knife from me. There was no doubt of that.

Time and time again I reviewed in my mind my sporadic movements after leaving Iris. There was only one depressing conclusion to draw. In my eagerness not to involve her, I had talked to almost everyone in the sanatorium, giving them all equal opportunity to take the knife from my pocket.

To my surprise, the middle of the morning brought Doctor Stevens. The sight of his plump solemn face led me to suppose that the drama of the night before had brought on some unsuspected physical set-back. But I was soon to realize that his visit was only nominally official. As he poked and prodded, I could see him nerving himself to say something. It came out abruptly.

'I heard from Moreno that David, my – er – half-brother was here in your room the other night,' he said as I rebuttoned my pyjamas. 'You know how anxious I am about him. I thought perhaps you could tell me why . . .'

He broke off and looked rather sheepish. I myself was in too absorbed a mood to feel overmuch sympathy for his family problems.

'Oh, there's nothing to worry about,' I said vaguely. 'A couple of the others were in here and Fenwick heard us. I guess he thought we were spirits or something.'

'I see.' Doctor Stevens drew up a chair and sat down. His fingers found their invariable resting place on his stethoscope. 'As I've started to explain my position to you, Mr Duluth, I feel it's only fair to tell you what I'm going to do. These last few days David has been getting distinctly worse. I've decided that, whatever may be the effect on the other patients, I am going to take him away. He is to leave tomorrow. Of course, it will all be done quietly. There will be no fuss made. I intend to speak to Doctor Lenz about it when he returns from New York.'

'You suppose the police will let anyone go?' I asked casually. 'There's been some pretty funny business around here, you know.'

'I don't understand what you mean.' The cherubic Stevens contrived to look cold and forbidding. 'Surely you are not suggesting . . .'

'I'm not suggesting anything,' I broke in, feeling weary and unable to cope with an argument. 'And I guess you're right, Stevens. This is not exactly the place for anyone who's trying to get well.'

Instead of putting an end to the conversation, I seemed only to have given it fresh life. Stevens started to press me eagerly for an explanation. Had I heard or seen anything that made me believe something was wrong? Had I told Doctor Lenz what I knew? Was it anything about David? I shamelessly denied everything. It seemed the only thing to do.

In his endeavour to force me into an admission, Stevens once more overrode the bounds of professional delicacy. To give me the lead, he remarked:

'You don't think that David is worried because of Miss Brush? I can't imagine why he gave out that warning against her, unless . . .'

'That's because you're not a psychiatrist, Doctor Stevens.'

We both looked guiltily at the door where the day nurse was standing, stern and radiant as the angel with the flaming sword. Her deep blue eyes reflected anger and disapproval. Portentously she moved toward the bed.

'I don't know what started this interesting discussion,' she said, 'but I'm sure Doctor Lenz does not approve of gossip between the staff and patients. You have only been with us a short time, Doctor Stevens, and you will learn eventually that this is a mental sanatorium and that the elementary rules for working here include a certain amount of tact.'

I'd never seen her so alarming before. I could not make out whether her anger was motivated by loyalty to the institution alone or by personal pique at Stevens's unfortunate remark about herself. In any case, the result was an overwhelming victory for the day nurse. Stevens rose, went very red, muttered something inaudible and hurried out of the room.

After he had gone, Miss Brush offered me a dazzling smile of forgiveness, but her eyes were shrewd.

'I'm afraid it was wrong of me to lose my temper in front of a patient, Mr Duluth. But we're all having quite a lot of trouble with Doctor Stevens. He's a bit of an old woman, you know.'

'He was just asking me about his half-brother,' I explained lamely.

'Even so there's no reason for him to discuss anything like that with you.' The day nurse started vigorously to make me comfortable, plumping out the pillows, tugging at the sheets. At length she glanced up and her expression was imposing in its determination. 'You've got to stop worrying, Mr Duluth. If you have a feeling something's not right, you're all wrong. It's just your imagination.'

And that, from Miss Brush, was an order. She pulled down her starched cuffs, rustled her skirts and departed with dignified serenity.

The storm which yesterday was threatening had broken during the night. All the morning, a thick icy sleet poured down outside my window.

After a few hours of solitude, I was granted Miss Brush again. She made her seventh or eighth entrance to announce the fact that there was to be a film showing that afternoon. Movies were a regular part of sanatorium diet and one had been scheduled for that evening. But owing to the storm and the impossibility of giving the patients their outdoor exercise the entertainment had been shifted to immediately after lunch. We inmates were to be given no spare time to mope on our own misfortunes.

'Of course you must come, Mr Duluth,' the day nurse commanded. 'It will do you the world of good.'

'What's the film?' I asked testily.

She smiled. 'Some sort of animal picture. Animals are very soothing, you know.'

'Not to me,' I said glumly. 'I belong to Broadway. I get no kick out of the sex life of the white-tailed baboon.'

'Don't say that until you've seen the white-tailed baboons.'

Miss Brush laughed. I wondered how on earth she managed to keep so depressingly cheerful.

Lunch was brought to me in bed – a wing of fried chicken and some caramel custard. I was only given time to wash the fried chicken from my ears when I was ordered to dress. Hastily I put on my clothes and was hustled into the procession on its way to the cinema.

I spotted Geddes and contrived to loiter at the back with him as the little queue progressed down the corridor. The Englishman's face was drawn and tired.

'Damn' stupid of them to make me see this flicker,' he said morosely. 'If it's dull, I'll go to sleep anyway and if it starts getting exciting, it'll send me off into one of my rigid attacks. Still, I suppose the routine must go on.'

During the idle hours of the morning I had decided that the time had come to let Geddes know all I knew. Lenz's psychiatric quibblings, Moreno's pompousness, Stevens's inquisitiveness and Miss Brush's brisk officiousness, had taught me once and for all to expect neither sympathy nor cooperation from the staff. And I was horribly in need of both. I wanted someone who could talk sense instead of discussing insanity, someone who would believe what I told them instead of bringing my mental condition up as a major problem at board meetings. Geddes was investigating on his own. The two amateurs should go into partnership – and to hell with authoritative red tape.

'Listen,' I began furtively, 'I've got a lot to tell you – things I've known all along but have been too much of an idiot to talk about.'

Geddes paused. Ahead of us the others clattered on their way to the cinema.

'You mean something about that voice?'

'Yes. You know what it said about Fogarty. Well, Fogarty didn't leave the sanatorium. He was murdered.'

'Murdered!' A look of utter astonishment spread over the Englishman's face. 'What on earth do you mean?'

'The police think it was an accident, but I . . .'

'When did it happen?'

'A couple of days ago.'

'Right here in the sanatorium?'

'Yes. In the physio-therapy room some time Saturday night.'

'So that's it.' Geddes's eyes gleamed with an expression of understanding, then they went very grave. 'I see it all now, Duluth, see why they've been trying to drive me away – why they threatened to kill me. God, if only I'd known this before . . . ! Listen, I've got to go to Lenz right away.'

'Don't do that,' I urged. 'Not until you've told me. You mean you saw something or . . . ?'

'Yes, I saw something all right and . . .'

We were both too worked up to have noticed the approach of Miss

Brush. Before we realized it, she was standing about two feet away from us.

'Come on, you two slow-pokes. If you don't hurry, you'll miss the movie.'

She had a talent for appearing at the wrong moment – that woman. I couldn't tell whether or not she had heard anything, but she showed no sign of it. Slipping between us, she took both our arms and led us along like two little rich boys with their expensive nurse-maid.

Of all its modern conveniences, the Lenz Sanatorium was most proud of its cinema. The director himself believed strongly in the tranquillizing effect of certain carefully chosen movies, and in order to extract the maximum benefit from them he had installed a particularly luxurious cinema in a room which had been originally constructed with a theatre in mind.

The greatest difficulty to be overcome in a mental institution is the sense of restriction. Lenz had done his best to re-create the outside world in this theatre so that we could feel we had just dropped over the street to see a show. The place was small, but it seating arrangements were those of the authentic movie houses, with cushioned chairs set in rows. The lighting was controlled from the projection-room and appropriately dimmed and raised from there. And as a final splendid touch, the films were thrown on to the screen from a sound-proof projection-room in the rear so that the whirring of the movie should not disturb the more sensitive patients.

Only one divergence from the normal had been adopted and that, I believe, is a perfectly regular Asiatic custom. The sexes were strictly segregated – women to the left of the aisle, men to the right.

The women were already assembled when we entered. The left of the aisle was alive with femininity, heads bobbing over sanatorium gossip, excited chattering and laughter. I saw Iris immediately. She had an aisle seat next to Miss Powell. Although I did my best to catch her eye, she did not seem to notice me.

The men were milling around, making a fuss about who was to have the best seats. I was eager to get back to Geddes and hear what he had to say, but while I was moving toward him, Miss Brush took me under control again. Before I had time to protest, I was sitting in the last row by Billy Trent.

I was too preoccupied to take much interest in what was going on around me, but gradually everyone became satisfied with their places. The talking subsided into an expectant silence. And from somewhere in the sound-proof projection room, Warren, who acted as projection man, dimmed the lights. I had just caught a glimpse of Laribee's burly figure taking an aisle seat immediately opposite from Iris when the illumination was extinguished altogether.

There was a nervous giggle from one of the female patients, a shuffle of feet, then, in portentous silence, the animal film began.

Wide-eyed gazelles, strangely reminiscent of David Fenwick, were tripping about on the African veldt. A sloth munched a banyan or some such fruit. Baby baboons scratched one another's backs. I found it all rather tame. But the others didn't. Almost immediately the atmosphere was charged with interest. Young Billy Trent in the chair next to me was leaning forward with shining eyes. There was an occasional loud comment of approval from someone on the women's side.

This concentrated, childlike absorption in the excitement of the moment made me realize more than anything else how different were the minds of my fellow inmates from those of the people outside. I realized, too, how easy it must have been for the staff to keep them ignorant of what had been going on around them. They reacted to things violently for a few seconds and then forgot them again immediately.

Billy Trent's face was a symbol of them all. In one minute his expression would change from alarm to joy, from joy to misery, from misery to hilarious amusement. And all this because two blue-faced monkeys were fighting over a bunch of dates.

I remembered what Geddes had said about his reaction to excitement. I had given him enough cause for worry and I was eager to assure myself that my hurried confidence had had no bad effect.

My eyes were fairly used to the semi-darkness now. As I scanned the house, I saw Stroubel rhythmically nodding his finely shaped head. I saw Fenwick staring with luminous eyes. At length I caught a glimpse of the Englishman. He was sitting very straight and rigid like a wax figure. With a slight sinking of the heart, I realized that the prophesied attack had come on.

For a moment I contemplated telling one of the attendants, but I decided that I would only cause an unnecessary disturbance. Geddes would be as comfortable there as anywhere else.

Once more I tried to interest myself in the movie, to forget the complex mysteries of the sanatorium in the light-hearted gambols of the animal kingdom. I would have given anything to see a nice healthy lion devouring a couple of natives. But, apparently, all carnivora had been carefully censored.

Around me, in the darkened room, the excitement was growing more acute. I could almost sense it as an actual, solid presence in the cinema. I seemed to be the only member of the audience to notice that the door behind us was opening.

Swiftly I glanced around to see a large, square-shouldered silhouette on the threshold. He was in half profile, and the straight line of his beard was clearly visible. So Doctor Lenz was back from New York.

Usually there was something reassuring about the sight of that bearded, magnetic man. But I watched him then with a strange alarm. He seemed so real that he intensified the unreality of the animal puppets on the screen and the human puppets around me.

I had an insane impulse to run to him and to tell him everything about Iris and the knife. But at that moment I was distracted by a figure rising in the front row and slipping down the aisle toward me.

As he passed, I recognized Moreno. He hurried to Lenz, and they stood there together by the door, whispering. Somehow, I felt they were worried.

Giraffes were galloping across the screen now – strange, crazy animals – the sort of things you might see in delirium tremens.

I was thinking of delirium tremens, thinking how close I had been to it myself, when an incredible cry split the silence.

It was high, hysterical – like the voice of a terrified woman. And it shrieked the one word:

'Fire!'

For a second I was frozen into my seat. I thought my imagination must have played me some crazy trick, for I was sitting in the back row, and the voice had come from behind me. There was no woman there, I knew.

And then it sounded again – once – twice – three times. It seemed to echo around the room and come from all parts at once.

'Fire! Fire! Fire!'

In the panic that followed I had no time to think, no time to wonder how genuine the alarm had been. Instantly everyone had sprung to their feet. The women were screaming and chairs were clattering backward. Around me the men scrambled for the door. Billy Trent almost barged me over. I caught a glimpse of Miss Brush's uniform gleaming white in that chaotic darkness.

And the movie still went on. The giraffes galloped madly – galloped as though they, too, were trying to escape the menace of fire.

My first instinct had been to get to Iris. As everyone rushed past me,

I began to struggle forward. The giraffes had vanished now and a tapir was blundering blindly across the screen. There was something horrible about the serene progress of the movie in all that crazy confusion.

'Lights!' I yelled, but no one paid any attention. I had forgotten that the only switch was behind the screen and that Warren in the sound-proof projection-room would have no means of telling what had happened.

Lenz's voice was booming resonantly from the door. 'Do not be alarmed. There is no fire. Keep your seats, please.'

That seemed to check the disorder slightly, but the headlong rush to safety continued. Some of the more distracted patients were running pointlessly about as though in the darkness they had lost their sense of direction. Everything was in a hopeless muddle. Screams, gasps, shouted injunctions were raised in a grotesque cacophony.

The film tapir had given way to a flock of flamingos. They were flapping toward the front of the screen – growing larger and larger until at any second I expected to feel gigantic feathery wings enveloping me.

As I pushed forward, I heard Warren's voice from somewhere, crying agitatedly:

'What's the matter? What's going on here?'

'Get back and switch on the lights, you fool.' I recognized Moreno's answering voice, sharp and angry. 'And stop that damn' film.'

Somehow I had managed to stumble through two or three rows now. I was peering around anxiously for Iris when I tripped over something lying on the floor. I bent down and was just able to make out the figure of Geddes, sprawled there among the overturned chairs. I touched him. His arm was as rigid as steel.

I had to stand over him to keep the stragglers from trampling on him in their blind dash for the door. I thought I recognized Miss Powell, fluttering by me like an agitated moth. And then I felt a hand on my shoulder, and Clarke's voice spoke in my ear.

'Is that you, Mr Duluth? You'd better help me get him out.'

'But who shouted fire?' I asked breathlessly.

'No one knows. Can't think why Warren doesn't switch on those darn lights. And be careful with Mr Geddes. If we jerk the muscles it may bring on a spasm.'

Together we lifted Geddes and carried him through the jumble of overturned furniture to the door. Instantly another attendant came up and the two of them took Geddes away. I was left there in the passage, blinking at the dishevelled array of my fellow patients, whom Lenz, Miss Brush, and a few other officials were doing their best to reassure.

Immediately I scanned the crowd for Iris. She was not there. Feeling an unaccountable apprehension, I hurried back to the door of the cinema and swung it open.

Warren had switched on the lights now. Bright illumination poured down from a chandelier in the ceiling, paling the suspended screen images of the stationary movie. I could see only too clearly what the darkness had concealed.

The room was empty except for two figures. They sat close together in aisle seats, strangely isolated in that confusion of overturned chairs. One of them was Iris, and she was perfectly still as though carved out of stone. Her eyes were lowered, fixed intently upon something which lay in her lap.

In uncontrollable fascination, my gaze turned to the second figure, sitting so near to her across the narrow aisle. I say sitting. Actually, he was crouched in an awkward, unnatural position, half supported by the back of the chair in front of him.

It was Daniel Laribee.

As I stared, his body slipped jerkily forward – moving slowly, woodenly until it collapsed to the floor.

I felt that Iris had not even been aware of him until that moment. But at the sound of that heavy falling body, she started. Then, with a little scream, she picked up the thing which had been in her lap and threw it blindly from her across the room.

I am vague about what happened next. I know I rushed forward to try and do something for her; to hide, if necessary, the thing she had thrown away. But Miss Brush was too quick for me. While I was still stumbling through the chairs, she had run from the door and was picking it up.

Her eyes flashed to Laribee and then back to the thing in her hand with an expression of growing horror. Very slowly she moved to Iris.

I shall never forget that picture; Isabel Brush leaning tensely forward, her blond hair ruffled around her face; and Iris, sitting there perfectly still, stretching her hands in front of her in a gesture of extreme disgust.

I could not tear my gaze from those hands – so fragile and white beneath the scarlet stains of blood. I could see the blood on her dress, too, soaking into the grey material.

Footsteps sounded behind us now and the rest of the staff came trooping in. Most of them hurried toward Laribee, but Moreno moved to our side and the three of us stood there in silence. Suddenly Iris seemed to become conscious of our presence. She glanced up wildly and screamed.

'Look, doctor.' Miss Brush was holding out the thing which she had picked up from the floor. 'I saw her throw this away.'

Moreno stared blankly. I felt the blood pulsing in my temples. In her hand, the day nurse was gripping a thin surgical knife. Its blade was crimson with blood.

'Miss Pattison,' said Moreno quietly, 'what does this mean?'

Iris turned her face away. 'I – don't – know – what – happened,' she said very deliberately and softly.

'But you had that knife and Mr Laribee –'

'Laribee!' Iris swung around, her eyes suddenly desperate and alight with fear. 'So it did happen? He is dead! And – I suppose you think I did it.'

I wanted to push forward, to comfort her and tell her not to be frightened, but somehow I could not move. It was as though we were all caught up in some spell.

Slowly Iris lifted a hand to her face. Her shoulders quivered and I could hear her sobbing quietly, hopelessly.

'I don't know what happened,' she faltered. 'I can't remember. I didn't want to kill him. I've been trying not to do what they said. It's . . . it's all so terrible . . .'

At that moment the motherly figure of Mrs Dell hurried over. She brushed us aside and before any of us spoke again, she had slipped an arm around Iris's waist and was leading her out of the room.

Someone closed the door behind them.

I turned to the little group that was bent absorbedly over the prostrate figure of Daniel Laribee. I saw Doctor Lenz's bearded face pressed close to the millionaire's vest. I saw a little pool of blood darkening the floor in the aisle.

'Stabbed in the back!' The exclamation came from Doctor Stevens, who crouched at Lenz's side.

I caught Moreno's expression as he crossed to join them and I knew at once that Laribee was either dying or dead.

So it had come at last – this major tragedy to which all the minor incidents of the past few days had seemed inevitably to be leading. Laribee had been killed – stabbed to death during an innocent animal movie.

There had been that cry of fire, Warren's failure to switch on the lights, the resulting chaos. Were those things merely accidents? Or were they all part of that deliberate plan – that plan which had so brutally and relentlessly involved Iris and now, it seemed, had actually planted the knife on her.

'Who was it called fire?' Lenz's voice cut angrily into my thoughts.

No one answered for a moment. Then Moreno said quietly: 'I thought it came from somewhere at the back of the hall not far from where we were standing.'

Lenz bent over the body again. Swift comments rippled among the others. Had it been a man or a woman who had cried out? There seemed no agreement.

I stood on the fringe of the group, apparently forgotten in the confusion. At length Miss Brush glanced up and saw me. She still held the knife in her hand, and, as she moved toward me, she looked like an imperious Lady Macbeth after the murder of Duncan.

Her deep blue eyes stared penetratingly into mine.

'There is no need for you to be here, Mr Duluth,' she said. 'You'd better go back to your room.'

21

So it had come at last! Despite the horrible thing that had happened to Iris, Laribee's death brought with it a strange feeling of relief. It was like the hysterical ending to an over-acted, over-sensational play.

Now that he was dead, the financier seemed somehow small and pitiful. I thought of his delusions of poverty; his strange relationship with Miss Brush; that pathetic midnight will.

And the will, I reflected suddenly, was still lying under the rubber mat in my room. It might prove important; it might help to convince the police that Iris had no part in the affair. I decided to go and get it immediately.

As confused and anxious I passed through the building on the way to Wing Two, everything was in a state of bedlam. Patients were roaming around haphazard and talking excitedly together about the alleged fire. Like a lot of children they all seemed to have found exactly the places where they had no right to be, and the sexes were inextricably mixed. Attempts at supervision were merely nominal, and the fleeting glimpses I caught now and then of the staff showed them to be as disorganized as the patients.

There was no one on duty in Wing Two. But that did not surprise me. I was surprised, however, when I found Laribee's will lying under the mat, exactly where I had left it. By now the normal and expected seemed more startling than the unexpected and abnormal.

As I slipped the paper into my pocket, I remembered my interrupted conversation with Geddes just before the movies. He had wanted to tell me something about Fogarty's death – something that explained why he had received those strange warnings.

I hurried to his room to find him stretched out on his bed, where the attendants must have left him. He was still asleep, and, despite my eagerness, I did not like to wake him. It would probably have been impossible anyway, for his face muscles were still stiff, even though the rigidity had loosened slightly in his body.

Leaving him, I wandered down to the smoking-room. Some of the others were there, and Billy Trent was very excited at the discovery of a box of matches. He was striking one after another and proudly offering to light cigarettes for all comers. The scene was almost ludicrously reminiscent of an illicit schoolboy smoking-party.

I found a fairly remote corner and sat down, tormenting myself about Iris. The police could not consider her as a serious suspect, I told myself. They might learn of her feelings about Laribee and the part he played in causing her father's suicide. But no one could be stupid enough not to connect this recent death with that of Fogarty. And surely she would not be suspected of trussing up and murdering the day-attendant.

But whatever happened, there would be questions, probings. It was for her sanity as much as for her safety that I was worried. I knew how she would dread the inevitable police grilling, and she would be so helpless to defend herself. I thought of that sad, delicate face – like the petals of a flower crushed beneath the heavy boots of policemen.

I was racking my brains for some course of action, when David Fenwick glided toward me. His dark, ethereal face was alight with some hidden excitement.

'You heard that voice calling fire, Duluth?'

I nodded impatiently, but he drew up a chair and sat down, carefully arranging the meticulous creases of his trousers.

'That's bad,' he whispered, shaking his head. 'When a manifestation of that type occurs, things are in a very difficult condition.'

I did not feel up to arguing with him. If he thought some malicious phantom had given a fire-alarm, I wasn't going to bother to contradict him. In my anxiety, it was an effort even to have to speak.

'I'm going to tell you something,' he was murmuring. 'This sana-torium has a very unfavourable atmosphere. Between you and me, I'm leaving tomorrow. My bro – I mean, Doctor Stevens is going to arrange it for me.' A sensitive hand fingered his pastel tie. 'I suggest you leave, too, Duluth. I don't think it's safe here – not safe at all.'

I looked into his large, shining eyes, trying to read what, if anything, lay behind this unexpected admonition.

'I'm O.K. here,' I said shortly.

'You are?' Fenwick smiled mechanically. 'Well, I have warned you. And if you have any particular friends here, I think you should pass the warning on.'

At that moment there was a confused, scuffling sound. I looked up to see Billy Trent stuffing the matches into his pocket and the others hastily stubbing their cigarettes. The door had opened and Warren was stepping into the room.

He glanced darkly around him and moved to my side.

'They want you, Mr Duluth,' he muttered. 'Right away in Doctor Lenz's office.'

As I hurried out into the corridor, I heard his voice exclaiming sharply:

'Which of you took those matches?'

Except for the addition of Clarke and the absence of Stevens, the group in the director's office was the same as it had been after Fogarty's death. But that time I had been invited more or less as an honoured aide. Now, from the cold, official glances of the police, I gathered that Captain Green regarded me as a potential accessory before – if not after – the fact.

It seemed that Lenz had just been telling the captain of my visit to Moreno the previous evening.

'And after Mr Duluth left, doctor,' snapped Green, 'did you make a check-up in the surgery?'

'Yes, captain.' Moreno's handsome Latin face was masklike. 'I did not altogether believe Mr Duluth's story. But I got in touch with Doctor Stevens immediately and we went to the surgery together.'

'And a knife was missing?'

'Yes.'

'Did you do anything about it?'

'Naturally. We realized the potential danger and spent half the night hunting for it. Stevens told me that Miss Powell had complained of sinus trouble in the morning and had gone to the surgery. I thought that she must have taken it.'

'You seem pretty careless about your knives around here,' grunted the captain.

'On the contrary. But Miss Powell is a kleptomaniac and they are unbelievably cunning. She hides things under cushions as a rule. We looked in her usual places, on the divan in the lounge and the large armchair in the women's library. Miss Brush and Mrs Dell even searched the patients' clothes this morning while they were still asleep in bed. But we found nothing.'

Green turned sharply to me. 'Well, Doctor Moreno says you had that knife in your pocket at one stage, Mr Duluth. Who took it from you?'

'I haven't the slightest idea,' I said lamely. 'Practically everyone had a chance.'

'Could Miss Pattison have taken it, for example?'

'It's hardly likely, seeing she gave it to me in the first place.'

After I had spoken, I cursed myself for a fool. Obviously, Green had set a trap for me and I had walked into it, both feet at once.

'So you got it from Miss Pattison!' The captain's voice was almost too gentle and considerate. 'And then Miss Brush saw the same girl throw it away after the lights went up at the movies.'

There was a smugness in his tone as though the case were already solved and forgotten. As usual, I lost my temper.

'Don't you see it's just a frame-up?' I cried. 'Anyone with an atom of sense would realize that Iris Pattison's as innocent as – as Doctor Lenz here. Someone's been working on her – using her as a cat's-paw.'

Rather incoherently I went on to tell them how Iris had heard voices urging her to kill Laribee. I got dramatic, semi-hysterical, and the more ardently I championed Iris, the more damning a case I was making against her. If Green had doubted it before, he must have been certain now that she was dangerously insane.

To my relief it was Lenz who finally came to my rescue. His voice sounded tired and rather dejected. 'I agree with Mr Duluth,' he said quietly. 'I cannot believe that Miss Pattison is responsible for this second tragedy. Of course, I find Mr Duluth's theory of deliberate persecution rather hard to credit, but Miss Pattison *is* suffering from a mild form of persecution complex and it was unquestionably aggravated by the presence of Mr Laribee here in this institution. As I see it, Miss Powell must have stolen the knife and secreted it in Miss Pattison's bag, either accidentally or deliberately. Miss Pattison saw it. She is very suggestible and she imagined the rest – the compelling voices and the external force willing her to murder.'

'But that doesn't explain how she got the knife back,' persisted Green, 'or why she had it in her hand after the lights went up. And I understand that she more or less confessed to Doctor Moreno.'

'That is only natural, too,' broke in Lenz again. 'Miss Pattison had thought and worried so much about Laribee that when the tragedy actually occurred she would have had a moment of believing that perhaps she herself had been willed in some way into performing it.'

'Strikes me there's going to be a lot of psychological bunkum in this case,' growled the captain. 'Of course, it may all be a plant, but I've got to see that girl, Doctor Lenz. I've got to find out what she was doing the night Fogarty was killed. It's obvious now that we were all wrong about that first business. Fogarty was murdered just as sure as Laribee.'

'I agree with you,' said Lenz slowly. 'And I admit that I myself was completely mistaken when I supposed him to have died by accident.'

'Then let's have that girl in here.'

'Don't let him see her, Doctor Lenz,' I exclaimed imploringly. 'She's only a kid and she's scared to death. They'll drive her mad if –'

I broke off as I saw the stern expression on the director's face. 'You can rely on me, Mr Duluth, to protect the patients under my care.' He turned to the police officer. 'I cannot allow anyone but an alienist to see Miss Pattison at the present time.'

'Very well,' snapped Green. 'I'll get Doctor Eismann here. He's working on a case at the moment, but I can have him here by ten o'clock tonight. He's the State alienist, and if he finds anything –'

'If he finds anything unexpected in her condition,' put in Lenz quietly, 'or if he finds that I have misrepresented the true facts, I am willing to close my sanatorium.'

I could not bear it when they talked about Iris that way – when they referred to her as just another mental case. I loathed the thought of a State alienist prying into her mind. Somehow, I told myself, somehow I would have to do something – think out some way of bringing the real solution to light before that alienist arrived.

I was shaken out of my thoughts by Clarke's voice.

'Doctor Lenz,' he was asking deferentially, 'would it be possible for someone who wasn't really – er – mad to get into a place like this? I mean, sort of fake it up without you knowing?'

'It would be possible.' Doctor Lenz passed a hand over his beard, and his eyes were kindly. 'Just as you policemen can never tell how criminal a man is, so we doctors cannot tell exactly how mentally sick a person may be. Sanity is a relative term. One cannot put the living brain under a microscope. Our first rule is to believe everything the patient says. Then we observe his actions carefully. With time and experience one reaches a true diagnosis.'

'To put it in plain English,' said Green, taking up the point, 'if Miss Pattison had wanted to kill Laribee and not get blamed for it, she could have come here and strung that line about someone trying to drive her crazy. Even if she was as sane as a sentry, she could have put on an act which would have fooled you doctors. She –'

'She'd have to be a very clever actress,' cut in Moreno, surprisingly. 'She's been here six months.'

It was the word 'actress' which gave me my first constructive theory. I had been racking my brains to find something, however tenuous, to work on. And here was a perfectly good idea absolutely thrown at my head.

'Talking of actresses,' I broke in excitedly, 'Mr Laribee had a daughter who was an actress in Hollywood. Has anyone got in touch with her?'

'My office has phoned the Los Angeles police,' replied Green shortly. 'I've no doubt she'll come east for the funeral.'

'She'll come east for over a million dollars,' I said with growing enthusiasm. Then a second idea came tumbling on the heels of the first. I turned to the director. 'Would you let me use your phone, Doctor Lenz?'

He shot a questioning glance at Green.

'We can't have anything said about this on the outside,' said the captain. 'I promised Doctor Lenz, and I don't want it to get into the papers until we've got something definite.'

'But,' I urged, 'I swear I won't mention the case. You can listen to every word I say.'

'Who do you want to talk to?'

'Prince Warberg, the producer. I want to find out more about that daughter of Laribee's. Warberg can give you the dope on anyone who's stood five minutes behind the footlights.'

'Why waste time?' asked Moreno with a shrug. 'After all, presumably she is in California, and the murder was committed here.'

'And the motive is here,' I persisted. 'I can imagine there are quite a few people who'd consider murdering their father for a million dollars – or their father-in-law for that matter. The daughter's husband was an actor, too; and no one's seen him, not even Laribee. And he either is, or has been, a doctor. That makes him a very logical person to be in a sanatorium.'

I must have been a most insufferable nuisance, and my suggestion was the merest shot in the dark, but for some reason of his own Green capitulated. Perhaps it was the hope of saving himself some work; perhaps it was the name of Prince Warberg, the best-known producer in New York; or perhaps he was just humouring a nut's hunch.

'O.K.,' he said, 'call this Warberg fellow, but don't mention anything about the case, see?'

I sprang avidly to the telephone.

'Listen, operator. This is a personal call to New York . . . I want Prince Warberg . . . yes, *the* Prince Warberg . . . I haven't the slightest idea where he is. Try his apartment: the Actors' Club; and then start working through the theatres and bars . . . yes, you know what bars . . . What? . . . no, I'm not trying to be funny. Only find him for God's sake.'

Knowing Warberg's elusiveness, I did not envy the operator at her task, but I consoled myself by marshalling supreme faith in the telephone company.

The others had listened intently while I called, but as soon as the receiver was back on its hook, they started to talk again. Green announced glumly that Miss Brush would have erased all other finger-prints from the knife. He went on to argue about the seating arrangements in the cinema and, from Moreno's account, sketched a plan of Laribee's chair and those of the patients and staff who had been nearest to him. It seemed that Stroubel had been sitting in the seat directly behind the financier, but Lenz pointed out rather coldly that deduction along these lines would be more than useless. In the confusion, anyone could easily have left their seat and stabbed Laribee without being observed.

'But that fire-alarm?' said Green. 'Surely one of you must have noticed where it came from?'

Lenz shook his head. 'Opinions seem to differ. I think several people must have taken up the cry.'

'And the lights weren't put on for quite a few minutes,' continued Green. 'I don't understand that, either.'

Moreno explained the nature of the sound-proof projection-room, and, when Green plied him for further details, sent John Clarke to find Warren.

The night attendant looked particularly grim when he entered. His dark, deep-set eyes flicked to the captain's and then settled their gaze on the floor.

'I'm told that all the lights in the cinema are controlled from the projection-room,' said Green.

'Yes, sir.'

'Why didn't you turn them on as soon as you heard the fire-alarm?'

'I didn't hear the alarm,' muttered Warren. 'That room's sound-proof.'

'Well, what did you do?'

'There's a small window, sir, looking into the cinema. I happened to glance through and saw people milling around. The film runs with-out being watched. I went down to the theatre to see if anything was wrong.'

'Without switching on the lights?'

Warren shrugged. 'Of course. How was I to know what had happened?'

'And did you actually go into the cinema?'

'A few steps. Then Doctor Moreno told me to go back to the projection-room and turn on the lights.'

'So that's all there is about it?'

'That's all.' Warren turned his sour gaze on Doctor Lenz. 'If you're through, sir, I'd better be getting back to the patients. They're being rather difficult.'

'O.K.' Green nodded curtly to the door.

The night attendant had only just left when the telephone rang. I thanked heaven when I heard Prince Warberg's voice from the other end of the wire.

'For God's sake what do you want?' he asked pleasantly. 'I thought you had been painlessly put away.'

I couldn't stop him kidding me for a while. He said I would break jail that instant if I could smell his breath over the wire. He said that since my official demise he had had Broadway sewed up – him and a few other fellows. At last I managed to cut him short.

'Know a movie actress called Sylvia Dawn?' I asked hurriedly.

'Vaguely.'

'Well, find out everything about her. What parts she's had, how good she is, what she looks like – everything. And you're so damn' prosperous, you can call Hollywood long distance. If she's actually there, I don't want to know anything about her. She's got a husband. Some sort of a hoofer. Find out all the dope on him, too. And when I say find out, I mean find out.'

'My poor dear Pete,' muttered Warberg calmly, 'are you as bad as all that?'

'And while you're about it, check up on whether the husband's a doctor and, if so, where he graduated and where he is now.'

'Listen, I'm a hard-working man.'

'Do it,' I threatened, 'or I'll die and haunt you.'

'For the love of Pete . . . !'

'Well, do it for the love of Pete. And for mercy's sake, wire me the whole set-up before nine-thirty tonight.'

He started to swear, which was an infallible sign that he had capitulated. Then he started in about a new play, and I hung up.

This short talk with Warberg had stirred in me again the old longing for the theatre – for Broadway, greasepaint and the fuss of first nights.

With sudden satisfaction I realized that this day with all its incredible and horrible incidents had done something to me. I no longer felt weak and flabby. It was as though the vital necessity for action had restored to me the ability to act.

Doctor Lenz's office seemed gloomy in the darkening March afternoon. The director's face was gloomy, too, and pale as he rose to his feet. The others had risen, also, and we all stood there a minute, motionless, like actors holding a pose just before the curtain drops.

At length Lenz spoke solemnly, magisterially. 'One thing I must insist on. And this applies to you all. As far as possible, things must go on as usual for the patients. There will be the same routine this evening, the customary social gathering. In spite of the extreme seriousness of the situation, I will not have the inmates disturbed any more than they have been already. Moreno, will you ask the staff to see that everything is carried on just as though nothing had happened?'

Jupiter had spoken. There was nothing more for mortals to say.

On my way back to the men's ward, I felt an overwhelming urge for a cigarette. As my hand went into my pocket, it touched a piece of paper and brought out Laribee's midnight will. I had forgotten all about it!

I was just going to hurry back to Green when I felt stealing over me that sensation of delight which we all feel when we are consciously defying the forces of law and order. I was keeping material evidence from the police, but I did not care. At least, I possessed one thing which I could use in my effort to save Iris from the probings of that grim-sounding State alienist.

But how I could use it, or what I could do with it, I had not the remotest idea.

22

When I reached Wing Two, I started searching for Geddes. I was horribly eager to find him. Now that I had determined, in movie parlance, to sweep into action, he was my only possible confederate. He had knowledge, possibly valuable knowledge. If I could get it before Lenz and the police, there was just a chance . . .

But in the common rooms where the others were still roaming more or less at random, the Englishman was nowhere to be seen. I decided to try his room, though his attack should have been over by now and I knew that he hated staying in bed longer than was necessary.

I hurried through the still deserted corridors. The evening had closed in on us and no one had thought to turn on the passage lights. As I moved through the wan half-darkness, I felt a strange sensation of alarm – an alarm which grew steadily as I left the others farther and farther behind. One day, I told myself, I would write a horror play about a man alone in an empty sanatorium, looking for something or someone that he could not find. Alone, with no companion but a Voice.

Which reminded me suddenly that our own particular Voice had never lied. It had warned Geddes. It had coupled his name with those of Laribee and Fogarty. And if anyone had wanted to harm him, what a perfect opportunity he would have now, when the sanatorium was in chaos, when everyone could get everywhere and the staff was occupied, when Geddes was alone there, sleeping in his room.

I ran down the last few yards of the corridor, threw open the Englishman's door, and switched on the lights. I was dazzled, but only for a second. Soon I could see all too clearly.

Geddes was still lying on the bed, but not in sleep as I had seen him before. While I paused motionless on the threshold, I heard once again those ominous words he had repeated to me in the squash-court.

' "Fogarty was the first. You, Laribee and Duluth will be the next." '

Even in my dazed state, I could tell that Geddes was bound almost exactly as Fogarty had been. There was no strait-jacket, but he lay on his stomach, his hands crushed somehow beneath him. And around his neck, tied viciously tight, was a twisted surgical bandage, a bandage which was also attached to his legs. He was pinioned in that same brutal, ghastly way. His mouth, like Fogarty's, had been gagged with a handkerchief.

For the fraction of a second I stood there, feeling that all power of motion had permanently left me. Then, I thought, I caught a slight movement, a twitching in the muscles of the neck which was being drawn gradually backward by the feet, just as Fogarty's had been. His eyes were staring, desperate. But, thank God, they were not the eyes of a dead man.

That brought me back to my senses. Springing forward, I fumbled like a fool with the bandages. Their toughness was amazing. My agitated attempts to untie them must have almost choked Geddes, but at last I got him free.

He was in a complete daze, unable to speak, scarcely able to move. I stretched him, somehow, on his back and started to chafe the ugly red marks around his throat and wrists. For a long time I sat there, moving my hands over his body. I do not know if I did any good, but I was too bewildered myself to think of trying to find someone else to help me. It was very quiet – quiet with that deep, preternatural silence of a place deserted by all animated life.

Gradually, I could feel him relaxing beneath my fingers. At last, he drew himself painfully into a sitting position and flexed the muscles of his shoulders. Life had come back into his eyes, and his gaze moved slowly to the pile of bandages on the floor.

But when he tried to speak, the words did not come. I brought him a glass of water, and that seemed to help. He drank it eagerly and croaked with a wry smile:

'I thought bandages were supposed to be instruments of mercy. They seem to make pretty effective instruments of torture, too.'

I was thinking the same thing myself. I had always supposed bandages to be fragile, ladylike things, but, twisted in that way, they had the strength of steel cable.

As I stared at them, coiled there on the floor, I remembered Mrs Fogarty's words on the night of the dance. I could see her handing Miss Powell's treasure-trove to Doctor Stevens. 'This accounts for everything but a stopwatch and two bandages.'

Well, we could account for the bandages now. Vaguely I wondered whether they had been destined for this sinister purpose from the beginning, just as the stopwatch and the knife had been for theirs. The criminal at large in the sanatorium seemed certainly to have extracted the uttermost out of Miss Powell.

With an effort, Geddes had risen to his feet and was staggering to the mirror. With one hand he started to pass a brush across his hair; with the other he tried to shake some of the creases from his suit. I questioned him eagerly.

Of course, he could remember nothing. The last thing of which he had been conscious was the film. Baboons or something, he said. After that, everything was blank except for an unpleasant nightmare about a python strangling him to death. He had wakened up from it to find himself bound and helpless – as helpless as he had been in the grip of that dream python.

'I must have come to just a few minutes before you arrived, Duluth,' he said shakily. 'You saved my life.'

We grinned at each other and looked a bit embarrassed. But I realized that he was only too right. I found myself marvelling at the ruthless efficiency of that amazing personality in our midst. It had been only by the purest luck that I had discovered Geddes when I did. If the session in Lenz's office had kept me a few minutes longer, that slow, agonizing torture might have been successful for a second time. And once again the murderer might have established for himself a watertight alibi, right here under the very nose of the police. In fact, I reflected with sudden disgust, had it not been for the Englishman's cataplexy, which kept his muscles unusually rigid, he might easily have been already dead when I came to him.

'I'd better get Miss Brush or someone to doctor those bruises,' I said.

'No. I'm all right.' Geddes sat down on the bed and glanced at the weals on his wrists. 'I want to get things a bit straight in my mind first. I can see now why that damn' voice warned me, why they were so anxious to do me in, but why on earth didn't they strangle me outright instead of playing that crazy antic?'

'Fogarty was killed that way,' I said bluntly.

'He was!' The Englishman stared at me in horrified astonishment.

'Yes. And for God's sake tell me if you know anything that would help to explain.'

Geddes's eyes had taken on a steely hardness. 'They must have tried to murder me,' he said slowly, 'because they thought I knew who killed Fogarty.'

I felt a moment of wild hope. 'But do you?'

'No. That's the damnable part of it.' He smiled slightly. 'I've gone through all this for nothing. On Saturday night, just after the dance, I happened to want Fogarty – wanted to ask him if he could switch my hour with young Trent's. I went down to the physio-therapy room on the off-chance he'd be there.'

I nodded.

'When I reached it, I heard voices. One of them was Fogarty's so I pushed the door open and glanced in. I couldn't see anyone. They must have been in an alcove. But I called Fogarty's name and the talking stopped right away.' He shrugged. 'Then I noticed some clothes lying on the floor. We all knew Fogarty's reputation with the ladies. I thought something like that must be going on and tactfully withdrew. Didn't give the matter another thought, although I see now why Moreno tried to question me about it.'

'But didn't you recognize the other voice?'

'Afraid not. One doesn't think about things like that at the time. I have the vaguest notion it was a woman's voice, but perhaps that's just because I associate the whole business in my mind with a woman.'

'You must have got there just before the murder,' I said. 'It's easy enough to see what they had against you. They knew your voice and thought you'd seen or heard something.'

The Englishman grunted. 'I can understand that, all right, but I can't imagine why they were satisfied with warning me at first. I'd have thought that once they'd made up their mind to it, they'd have disposed of me right away.'

'Not necessarily. You weren't much of a danger to them so long as you were just a coddled patient who hadn't been told of Fogarty's death. As you admit yourself you'd forgotten the incident completely. It was only after I spilt the beans that you started being a real menace. I'm afraid that, as usual, I was more or less responsible for this. Someone must have overheard us outside the movie.'

For a moment neither of us spoke. Then Geddes remarked slowly: 'There's another thing that puzzles me. How on earth was it possible for me to be trussed up here all that time without one of the staff finding me?'

It was only then that I remembered how his attack had come on a short while after the movie began. He still knew nothing about the fire-alarm, Laribee's murder and the consequent crazy confusion. Swiftly I started in and told him from the beginning all I knew of what had been happening in the sanatorium. It was astonishingly comforting to be able to shoot my mouth off. I even told him about Iris and my own rash determination to do something for her before that alienist came at ten o'clock.

At first he seemed a bit dazed, but gradually he managed to piece things together.

'So they murdered Laribee and then hurried up here to do me in,' he exclaimed grimly. 'Double murder in an afternoon's pretty ambitious. You were threatened too, Duluth. You've had a bit of luck.'

'Don't congratulate me yet,' I said, grinning. 'I may not last out the night. But listen. I've made up my mind to raise hell until I've found out who's back of this. I was hoping you might do a bit of helping.'

Geddes sat very still a moment. Then a hand moved to the red bruises on his throat.

'I'd decided to leave,' he said slowly. 'I'd had just about enough of this sanatorium. But if there's anything I can do, why –'

'That's decent of you.'

'Decent!' he echoed. 'Don't you suppose I'm as eager as you to get my hands on that swine? Apart from anything else, he tied me up when I was unconscious. That's one little trick I don't feel any too good-tempered about.'

He was as visibly indignant as I had ever seen him. Something about the set of his jaw comforted me.

'Two against the world,' I remarked. 'It's very touching but what are we going to do?'

'Well, what have we got to work on?'

'Precious little. There's that hunch of mine about the son-in-law. Maybe he's masquerading here somehow.'

'Perhaps he is. And the daughter, too. It's a damn-fool notion. But she's an actress, you say, and Laribee was pretty mad. She might have done something to herself so that he wouldn't recognize her.'

'Sounds fairly far-fetched,' I said. 'But I guess we're out after something pretty crazy, anyway.'

'Of course, there's the staff,' said Geddes musingly. 'In a way, that's a more hopeful field. You say they all have a financial interest in the sanatorium, and old Laribee's death brings in a half million. It's absurd to suspect Lenz himself, but some of the others –'

'Yes,' I broke in eagerly. 'And as we're being disrespectful, how about Miss Brush? If that will were valid –'

'I'd forgotten the will. You say you've still got it and no one knows you have. Surely, we can do something with that.'

I felt we were getting somewhere, teetering on the brink of a workable idea. It was Geddes who straightened it out first.

'Listen,' he said, 'we can assume fairly certainly that the whole business originally centred around Laribee. Whoever killed him must have been after his money. Well, they'll be wanting that will, won't they?'

'What do you mean?'

'Listen, practically everyone on the staff of this place benefited by Laribee's former will. If one of them murdered Laribee, he'd be desperately eager to find the new will and destroy it, just in case it could be proved valid. If, on the other hand, we're looking for someone who benefited by the new will, they'd be just as anxious to get hold of it and use it to claim the money. That's pretty straight reasoning, isn't it?'

'Gosh, yes,' I said enthusiastically. 'So we do have a trump card, after all. But how on earth can we play it?'

Geddes passed a reflective finger across his moustache. 'If only we could plant it somewhere – plant it in some place that only the murderer would know. It's rather like Daring Dick, the Ace Detective, but –'

'Got it in one!' I cut in. 'We know that somehow or other our criminal at large must have worked on Miss Powell to steal things for him from the surgery. When I heard her talking about her projected attack on the knives, she said, "I can hide them in the musical place." Obviously that's the spot where he gets her to conceal her stolen goods.'

'Yes. And he'd take damn' good care that no one else knew where it was. But what next?'

'This thing's going to be as simple as breathing,' I exclaimed. 'We plant the will in the musical place, let the murderer know it's there – and just wait for him to take it.'

'Unfortunately,' said Geddes with a smile, 'as we don't know who the murderer is, we can hardly let him know what we've done.'

'Then we'll have to tell everybody,' I persisted. And tell them in such a way that it'll be so much nonsense to everyone but the person we want – a sort of adaptation of my celebrated psycho-analytical experiment.'

'And how do we do that?'

For a moment my fountain of inspiration seemed to become clogged, but soon it spouted up once more.

'Got it again,' I said excitedly. 'We can take another cue from our versatile adversary. I'm certain he worked through Fenwick, faked up that phony spirit message to suit his own purposes. Why shouldn't we invent a spirit message, too? With any luck we could persuade Fenwick into believing we'd received an official announcement from the astral plane, that Laribee has made a new will and put it in the musical place. We could easily convince him it was his particular duty to impart the news to everyone individually. The guilty person's bound to go to the musical place on the off-chance. The others'll just accept it as Fenwick's usual hooey.'

'That's pretty ingenious,' remarked Geddes after a pause, 'but it'd only work with the patients. If the man we're after's on the staff, he'd smell a rat right away. We'll have to think out something less fishy for them. Listen, you're more or less in their confidence, aren't you? Why don't you tell them some story? You could make out you saw Miss Powell pinching something from Laribee's pocket just before the movies and heard her whisper something about the musical place. It's rather thin, but they're used to swallowing anything in this institution.'

'Positively brilliant!' I rose and started to pace up and down that small, silent room. 'If ever a cock-eyed scheme deserved to work, this does! I'll hide the will in the musical place. Fenwick and I can circulate the messages and then' – I glanced at him eagerly – 'can you imitate one of your attacks?'

'I could hardly make a poker of myself, but I could pretend to go to sleep.'

'Swell. Everyone's used to your going asleep at odd moments. We can plant you right there by the musical place and then you drop off into a doze. Why, they'd take that will from under your nose and not give you a second thought.'

'The perfect plan,' murmured Geddes wryly, 'to catch the almost perfect murderer. But ...' he broke off and I saw a smile move across his lips. 'Damn us for idiots, Duluth! We've forgotten the only important thing. We haven't the slightest idea where this absurd musical place is.'

I felt like a pricked balloon. 'Probably near the radio,' I said weakly.

'Or the piano – or the gramophone at the far end of the room,' muttered Geddes. 'I'm afraid this is where we start all over again – unless we could shanghai Miss Powell. She'd be able to tell us.'

'I doubt it,' I said dejectedly. 'I don't know much about psychology, but I'm pretty certain that she has no more idea where the musical place is than we have. All that side of her nature's subconscious or something. When she's normal, she instinctively drives it out of her mind.'

Geddes jumped up from the bed. 'Why not crib another of our friend's tricks and work on Miss Powell's subconscious mind, Duluth? Have you got any jewellery?'

I indicated a ring on my finger.

'You say she steals things while she talks to people,' continued the Englishman quietly. 'And she hides them in definite places. With any luck –'

'– we could get her to take the ring and put it in the musical place,' I broke in quickly. 'Fine and dandy!'

I think that if I alone had figured out that scheme, built up as it was on an elaborate groundwork of conjecture and other people's psychoses, it would have seemed incredibly, hopelessly fantastic. But I had lived so long among crazy people that nothing seemed particularly crazy any more. Besides, there was a matter-of-factness about Geddes. Any plan with his O.K. must have a certain amount of logic.

'I think we'd better perform our miracle tonight, Duluth,' he was saying calmly. 'We'll get to the central lounge about eight o'clock, that gives us two hours before the alienist comes. You can start work right away on Miss Powell, and I'll get Fenwick to circulate the spirit message. Then we plant the will and I go to sleep. You'll just have to give your story to the staff and we'll be ready.'

'But even if someone does take the will,' I said with sudden doubt, 'do you suppose that's enough to convince the police?'

'It's enough to get them thinking,' muttered Geddes. 'And that's all we can hope for at the moment.'

He stared once more at his bruised wrists and fingered them gently.

'Think I ought to report this, by the way?'

Finally we agreed to say nothing about the attack on Geddes for the time being. It would probably result in his being questioned by the police just when our plan was to go into action.

As we gathered up the bandages and hid them temporarily under his mattress, I noticed the handkerchief which had been used to gag him. It was lying on the floor by the bed. I picked it up, and then gave a little grunt of surprise. The white cotton was stained with blood.

'You've been bleeding,' I said.

Geddes moved forward and took the handkerchief from me swiftly. There was a puzzled frown on his forehead.

'That's not my handkerchief,' he said slowly. 'I always use brown silk ones. Bought them in India for about ten cents each.'

'But there's blood on it, anyway.'

'I wonder –' Geddes turned to face me. 'Take a look at me, Duluth. See if I've been bleeding anywhere.'

I examined him carefully. His throat was still red, but there was no sign of any cut or abrasion inside or outside his mouth. We stared at each other blankly.

'He couldn't have been such a fool!' exclaimed Geddes at length. 'He'd never have used his own handkerchief to gag me.'

'It's just possible,' I said excitedly. 'He'd have been in a hurry and –'

'But the blood!'

'Exactly,' I exclaimed. 'It looks as though we've been given a break. Don't you see? That's most likely Laribee's blood. That handkerchief must have been used to wipe the fingerprints off the knife.'

We were still staring at each other like a couple of kids who have discovered buried treasure.

'We'll have to tell the police,' said Geddes at last. 'This is too important to hold back.'

'O.K. We'll tell Clarke. He's a good fellow and an old pal of mine. We'll need his help tonight if anything comes of our little act. I'll give him the handkerchief and ask him to find out who it belongs to.'

'Fine.' Geddes had turned to the mirror and was surveying his crumpled appearance despondently. 'That settles everything except my trousers. I suppose you couldn't get your friend Clarke to press them, too!'

23

It was almost time for dinner when we broke up our conspiratorial conclave and I returned to my own room. Discipline seemed to have returned almost to normal. Both Miss Brush and Mrs Fogarty were bustling around as though day and night had joined forces to dispel the clouds of unrest. The patients were still speculating excitedly about the supposed fire, some of them declaring that by now the cinema must be a charred ruin, but their healthy appetites prompted them to appear punctually for the evening meal.

Clarke was standing outside the dining-room in his attendant's white coat. When he saw me, he grinned confidentially and whispered:

'Boss says business as usual tonight.'

'Anything new?'

'Nope. They're combing the theatre and they've examined the knife. Green was right. There's no prints there except the Brush woman's and a few of Miss Pattison's.'

'How is Miss Pattison?' I asked anxiously.

'All right.' His face was sympathetic. 'She's in her room and Lenz won't let the chief see her – not yet.'

I felt in my pocket and produced the bloodstained handkerchief. 'I've found something,' I said quietly.

He took it and examined it.

'There are three full cases of Johnnie Walker in my apartment,' I went on. 'I won't be needing them when I get out. They're yours if you'll find out who that handkerchief belongs to.'

He looked at me doubtfully.

'You don't have to keep anything from Green,' I urged. 'Only just hold it until I give the word.'

Clarke nodded and put the handkerchief in his pocket. 'O.K. I'll do it this evening. Anything else?'

'Yes. I'm hoping for a show-down later on. If I ask you to watch a certain person, will you stick on to him like a leech while I go to Green?'

'For three cases of Scotch,' said Clarke cheerfully, 'I'd spend the evening watching old man Lenz himself.'

He was moving away when a sudden thought seemed to strike him. 'Listen, Mr Duluth,' he said hesitantly. 'That show-down of yours – you'd better make it snappy. Doctor Eismann's coming at ten o'clock, and they're going to take Miss Pattison away.'

'You mean take her away from the sanatorium?'

'That's what Green's planning to do right now.'

He must have guessed my feelings from the expression on my face, for he added with some embarrassment: 'Maybe I could fix it so's you could see her for a minute or two.'

Clarke was one of those men you meet so seldom that you almost forget they exist. They restore your belief in the essential decency of people in general, and the police force in particular.

'It's pretty much against orders, of course,' he was muttering. 'But Mrs Dell's a good sport.'

'Listen,' I said brokenly, 'someone ought to give you a golden halo.'

He grinned. 'Three cases of Scotch will do for the time being,' he said.

He told me to follow him at a discreet distance and led me along back passages whose existence I had never before so much as suspected.

The women were all at dinner, so their wing was more or less deserted. But my sense of guilt peopled the corridors with terrifying female monsters who, at any moment, might spring out on me and apprehend me for this most cardinal of sanatorium sins. Once there was an actual rustle in the passage ahead. Instantly Clarke signalled me into a lavatory, and I stood there, holding my breath, as official heels clattered past the closed door. Those were some of the most harrowing moments in my life.

But at last we reached our destination. With mock caution, Clarke stationed me in a small alcove while he went to dicker with Mrs Dell. They had, of course, locked Iris up. He had to get the key.

Waiting seemed depressingly like eternity, but at last he reappeared.

'Three minutes exactly,' he whispered. 'And if Moreno comes, hide under the bed, or Mrs Dell says there'll be a couple more murders.'

He unlocked the door and with a grin closed it behind me.

Iris was sitting by the window, gazing across the sombre evening parkland outside. When she saw me, she rose, moved impulsively toward me, and then paused.

'You . . . !' she whispered.

My heart was beating so loud that I felt everyone in the building must be hearing it. I tried to say something, but I couldn't think out the words. I only knew that I loved her and that she was there.

Then she moved again and somehow she was in my arms. Neither of us spoke. We just clung together like a couple of mutes.

And so passed the first of my precious three minutes.

At length Iris drew away and I could see her face. I was amazed and delighted that the tormenting sadness had left her eyes. They were shining now with a bright, healthy indignation.

'Do you know what the police are going to do about me?' she asked bluntly.

I hesitated, and her fingers tightened on my arm.

'You've got to tell me. None of the others will. Mrs Dell treats me like a baby – keeps stalling me off. Don't you see? I've got to know the truth.'

There was a new determination in her voice – a determination which elated me beyond words.

'They're sending for someone to talk to you,' I said guardedly. 'He's coming about ten o'clock tonight.'

'You mean a police doctor?'

'Why – er . . .'

'So they do suspect me!' Iris tossed her head indignantly, and once more the anger blazed in her eyes. Then her shoulders moved in a slight shrug. 'But I don't really blame them. There was that knife – and I acted so foolishly. But it all seemed like some horrible nightmare. I didn't know what I was doing – or what I had done.'

'Of course, darling.'

'But I know now,' she said suddenly. 'I can see it was all a frame-up. That's why they scared me with those voices. They tried to make me so confused and miserable that – that when it all actually happened, I'd be crazy enough to take the blame. It almost worked – but not quite.'

She turned her head away and when she spoke next her voice was perfectly calm. 'You'll think this is the maddest thing of all, but somehow I can see everything straight now; see how dumb I've been, worrying over things that really were so unimportant. Something happened to me today. I know there's danger. Maybe the police will take me away – even arrest me, and . . .'

'They're not going to,' I cut in, feeling absurdly light-headed. 'I'm hardly athletic enough to escape with you down the drain-pipe, but I'm going to move heaven, earth and the sanatorium to see that man doesn't get you tonight.'

'Let him come,' said Iris with a slow smile. 'Let them all come. I'm ready to fight back now. I don't know whether Lenz would call it good psychiatry, but what I needed to snap me out of it was a pretty violent shock. Well, I've had the shock – and I'm grateful, whatever the consequences.'

We stood there, smiling at each other. I never thought things were going to break that way. It seemed too good to be true.

'Good girl!' I whispered. 'Give 'em all you've got. And I'm launching a little attack of my own tonight. Between us, we'll lick them all.'

'You and I,' said Iris softly. 'What could be crazier?'

She was very near. Her lips were warm when they touched mine. That was the first time I had ever really kissed her.

When she drew away, her eyes were still smiling.

'By the way,' she said, 'I don't think I ever caught your name.'

'Peter,' I said. 'Peter Duluth.'

'Peter Duluth!' She looked blank for a moment. 'So you really are Peter Duluth, and all that you said about the theatre –'

'– was on the level,' I cut in. 'I told you from the start I wasn't screwy. At least, not that screwy.'

She stood there, looking at me. Gradually the smile faded from her lips; and a faint expression of fear crept into her eyes.

'You'll do what you can, won't you, Peter?' she said pleadingly. 'I'm trying to be the *ingénue* with a stiff upper lip, but it's not going to be any too pleasant if – if they take me away.'

That brought me violently back to earth, reminded me that, in spite of the seeming miracle of Iris's recovery, the situation was as serious as it had ever been. I was going to reassure her, tell her that everything would be all right, when the door burst open and Mrs Dell appeared with a tray of supper.

She scolded me roundly, and she scolded the absent Clarke. She scolded herself, Moreno, and everyone else in the institution. But she didn't scold Iris. In fact, she treated her as kindly as if she had been her own daughter.

I could have kissed her.

I was shockingly late for dinner, but I did manage to whisper my thanks to Clarke when I got back to the dining-room.

'Forget it, Mr Duluth,' he muttered, smiling. 'I saw you get one tough break two years back. I don't want to see you get another. I thought you'd like to have a minute or two with her before they take her away.'

Take her away! Now that I was back in the world of cold facts, eating my rapidly cooling liver and bacon, I realized how horribly near to the climax we were. Once the police had Iris to concentrate on, they would slacken their activities and, unless I over-estimated our adversary, he would be covering his tracks pretty quickly. It seemed as though the situation would take a distinct turn for the worse unless the lunatic plan conceived by Geddes and myself bore fruit.

As the liver was removed to give way to some artistic contraption of ice-cream, I discovered a fundamental fact about myself. If anything happened to Iris now, it would mean the end of me. Clarke would never get those three cases of Scotch. My expensive cure would be utterly wasted. The last stage of Peter Duluth would be infinitely worse than the first.

24

One has heard so often of the bright smile that masks the aching heart – the dainty shoes that hide pinched feet. But these well-worn clichés seemed to have been freshly invented to describe the members of Doctor Lenz's staff when we all assembled in the main lounge that evening. Jove had nodded, and there was to be business as usual. The patients' routine must go on.

It was not one of the formal evenings, but Miss Brush's dress was almost indecently gorgeous. It was a sort of tiger colour. At least, it made her look like a magnificent, if somewhat tired, tigress. Her smile was as bright and professional as ever, but I noticed that it went on and off at regular intervals, revolving like a lighthouse beacon. Once or twice I saw her smiling at no one at all.

Moreno was very smartly dressed, and he had obviously determined to be affable if it killed him. The women patients seemed thrilled by his unusual attentions, and I heard my little schoolmistress say he looked exactly like George Raft. He smelled like an excellent brand of Scotch when he came near me. Apparently he had been working on the interesting bottle I had seen the night before in his office.

Warren had put on a clean white coat and pomaded his hair down to a festive flatness. His smile seemed a little more genuine than the facial contortions of the others. Perhaps he felt that Laribee's death freed him once and for all from any suspicions with regard to Fogarty's 'accident'.

Even poor Mrs Fogarty had turned up trumps. And, like Queen Elizabeth, she had donned her best in the hour of deepest need. Her best was a rather faded mauve, which suited neither her face nor figure; and the blobs of rouge on her high cheek-bones only threw into relief the dark lines beneath her eyes. Though so recently a widow, she knew her duty. The patients' routine must go on.

And for the patients, things were going on very happily. They seemed surprisingly cheerful and normal. The fire-alarm had given them something to talk about, had been an exciting incident in their uneventful lives. None of them, I felt sure, knew that Laribee's dead body was lying somewhere not fifty yards away, and that the place was still full of policemen. And none of them seemed to care that Iris was up there alone in her room. None of them except myself.

The thought of Iris brought me back to the business in hand. And my business was with Miss Powell. She was the first link in the chain, and without her nothing could be accomplished. Our plan could not even begin until I found out the whereabouts of the musical place.

The Boston spinster was dressed rather daringly in red and yellow. A tribute perhaps, to the flames which had almost destroyed us all. She was easy enough to see, but hard to get alone, for she flitted from group to group, discussing fire insurance and the enormous premiums one had to pay on the houses in Commonwealth Avenue. She was as fickle and frivolous as her costume. I was beginning to be seriously alarmed lest the shock of the afternoon had cured her kleptomania and made her as normal as the others seemed.

'The danger of fire in Boston slums –' I began enticingly when finally I had her cornered between the victrola and a radiator.

That got her. There was no more difficulty now in luring her away to the couch where we had first sat together. She came like a lamb and treated me to a brilliant discourse on slum clearance, housing problems and social reform in general.

I had one bad moment when I heard Miss Brush suggesting a bridge game and saw her looking expectantly in our direction. No one showed any interest, luckily, and I was able to concentrate on Miss Powell.

Not once did she appear to look at the ring on my finger, although I twiddled it invitingly, and even pulled it over the knuckle so as to make her work more simple. At last I became so carried away by the torrents of her garrulity that I found myself staring at her in a kind of horrified fascination. I had tried to hypnotize her, but she had succeeded in hypnotizing me. The well-bred voice flowed smoothly on. Her eyes, I swear, never left my face.

'So you see, Mr Duluth, the overwhelming problems which the new administration will have to face.'

I saw them only too well. I saw also to my astonished relief that at last my ring was gone. Her gaze had not faltered. I had not felt so much as the touch of a butterfly wing on my finger. But the ring was gone. I swore that if ever I got back to a world of sanity, I would promote this woman – make her a limited company, and her fortune and mine would be assured. She was a genius.

'. . . Bostonians jib at their obligations to society.'

And I was jibbing at mine. She had the ring. Now I would have to make her hide it in the musical place. I knew her predilection for cushions as a means of concealment. I am afraid I was ungentlemanly enough to put my feet up on the couch so that it would be impossible for her to slip the ring underneath. She was far too much of a lady to comment upon my rudeness.

And then I started to work on her, trying somehow to throw a message from my mind to hers.

'The musical place,' urged my brain. 'Put it in the musical place.'

Apparently I was neither psychic nor hypnotic. Her loquacity went on unabated. It was something about teachers' salaries being disproportionate to their responsibilities.

At length I realized that I would have to resort to something more crude. I turned my head away from her.

'The musical place,' I mumbled.

Then deliberately I looked down at my denuded finger.

At last! An expression of alarm had crept into her eyes. She did not stop talking, but her hands shifted uneasily toward the cushions. I pressed my foot more firmly against them.

As the look of alarm in her eyes grew more intense, I felt thoroughly ashamed of myself. It was a vile thing to exploit the frailties of this poor bewildered creature, to capitalize the weakness of my fellow patients. But the murderer had done so, and had forced me to imitate him. That was another score I had against him.

I glanced anxiously at the clock. It was eight. We had only two hours before that State alienist arrived.

'The musical place,' I muttered again desperately.

Miss Powell had risen to her feet, and, though her voice went mechanically on, the sentences were halting, jumpy.

'Our – only – Republican – hope – is –'

She had turned and was almost running across the room. Once again I noticed that hunted look in her eyes as she saw me following.

She made straight for the piano. I could not catch the movement of her hands, but I knew instinctively when she had disposed of the ring. Her face brightened and she even continued her sentence where it had broken off. I was afraid I was in for another discourse, but luckily she decided upon solitaire and left me.

The identity of the musical place, this mysterious cache where Miss Powell must have concealed, first the knife, and now my ring, was absurdly simple. And yet it was exactly the kind of place where no one would think of looking, underneath the ornamental cloth which covered the back part of the piano. It could have been used only for thin objects. Even my ring betrayed its presence by a slight bulge. There was another bulge, too, and I thought for a moment that I might be on the brink of an important discovery.

I looked cautiously around the room, but no one was watching me. Then I slipped my hand under the piano cloth and brought out both objects. My ring was one of them, all right. The other thing was a silver pencil – my own pencil. She had got that too, though how she managed to snitch it from my breast pocket will always be a mystery. But I said that woman was a genius!

I turned my back on the piano, and, with a stealth and cunning that even Miss Powell might have envied, I took Laribee's will from my pocket and slid it under the cover. The first part of our scheme had been accomplished now. The will was in the musical place and no one, I was sure, had seen me put it there.

Geddes was alone when I sauntered over and whispered the news.

'Good,' he said. 'Now, I'll work on Fenwick while you take the staff. Nod to me when it's O.K., and I'll go to sleep by the piano. If anyone takes that will, I'll nod three times, and then the fourth nod will be in the direction of the person who took it.'

Despite the desperate issues at stake, there was something childishly exhilarating about this little plot. In fact, its very importance made it that much more exciting. It seemed like a parlour game, yet it was being played with a real murderer, and the forfeit might be the electric chair.

I was rather apprehensive about my job of tackling the staff. But Miss Brush and Moreno were talking together, so I had a chance of killing off my first two birds with one stone.

Miss Brush forgot to smile when I approached. I had the distinct impression that she, as well as Moreno, had fortified herself alcoholically for a difficult evening.

'I've just remembered something,' I said jauntily. 'Something about Laribee.'

'S-sh!' Doctor Moreno looked quickly around to see if any of the patients were within hearing.

'It's probably not important,' I continued, 'but, when we went into the movies this afternoon, I thought I saw Miss Powell take a paper out of Laribee's pocket.' I gave a gulp at my own mendacity. It all sounded so very thin. 'And I believe I heard her murmuring something about a – a musical place.'

Moreno's face was impassive.

'I thought it might mean something to a psychiatrist,' I continued. 'I don't profess to understand it myself.'

'You said it was a piece of paper?' Miss Brush's voice was tense and jerky.

'Yes.' I stared boldly into her dark blue eyes. 'Perhaps it was the paper Laribee wrote when you lent him your fountain-pen.'

'That was a letter to his daughter.'

Miss Brush turned her head away and I could not see her expression.

Moreno made some pompous remark about informing the authorities and gave me an icy dismissal.

My next attack was upon Stevens. He was standing by himself in a corner watching his half-brother with anxious eyes. I asked casually whether he had arranged Fenwick's departure, and he went very red.

'Owing – er – to what has just happened, Duluth, the – er – authorities seem to feel that no one –'

'By the way,' I broke in, 'just before the movies Miss Powell . . .'

Doctor Stevens did not seem to pay a great deal of attention to my implausible history of the spinster and the will. He shook his head vaguely and was muttering something inaudible when Geddes came up. The Englishman said he felt a bit drowsy. He did not think it would be a bad attack and he asked Stevens's permission to stay in the lounge even if he should go to sleep.

'Very well, Mr Geddes. Ask Doctor Moreno to take you to the surgery. He will give you some of those tablets.'

I knew that Stevens and Moreno were treating Geddes with some new kind of stimulating drug and I knew it did not help much. I only hoped that if the Englishman's attack were genuine and not part of our scheme, it would keep him awake long enough for him to perform his duties as watchman.

Meanwhile I had to continue my own duties by telling my unlikely story to the other members of the staff. From Mrs Fogarty I got a sad shake of the head and:

'Miss Powell, poor thing! And she has such a good mind.'

I moved to Warren and had just finished my little sentence when I noticed Clarke slip unobtrusively out of the room. I wondered if he would be successful in tracing the owner of that bloodstained handkerchief. I

149

wondered if it would mean anything if he did. Then I saw that Geddes had returned and was looking at me hopefully from the other end of the room. I nodded to show him that I had done my part. He strolled with admirable nonchalance toward the piano, and, setting a chair in a strategic position, sat down and started to look sleepy.

The trap was set now and the stage cleared for action. It remained only for our unknown star to play his part. I felt the double thrill of a producer and a member of the audience as I stood there, leaning against the wall, waiting, watching.

And as I watched, I noticed a curious phenomenon. Earlier in the evening the patients had all seemed so normal and cheerful that a casual observer entering the room would certainly have given them higher mental rating than the harassed staff. But gradually the atmosphere seemed to change. Eyes that had been bright began to lack lustre; conversations were less brisk. It puzzled me at first, and then I realized that Fenwick was the cause. Geddes must have done his work well, for the spiritualist was moving from group to group, beckoning people aside – whispering. And, wherever he went, he seemed to leave a trail behind him of uneasiness and heightened nervous tension. Several times I heard the name of Laribee. The patients were, for the first time, asking about the absent member – wondering why he was not there.

Seeing the effect of our crazy spirit warning, I realized once more what a cruel, unfeeling thing it was to work on the susceptibilities of the mentally sick. But I thought of Iris again and glanced anxiously at the clock. Twenty-five minutes to nine.

'Where's Laribee, Pete?'

Billy Trent was standing at my side and his youthful eyes were clouded. 'At lunch today he promised to explain how to sell short on the market. And now Fenwick says that . . .'

'You'd better stick to the soda fountain, Billy,' I broke in. 'I'll take a banana split.'

Young Trent did not answer for a moment. He was looking down at his shoes.

'You know, Pete,' he said at length, 'that's all bunk about me working in a drug store. I've realized the last few days that –'

Then he went on to talk about how he hoped to get back to college in the fall – about football. It was sane, sensible stuff, and just what you would expect from a nice kid of twenty-something. I was glad to think he was getting better, that his mind had been too healthy to be affected by all the beastly things which had been happening in the sanatorium.

Fenwick glided toward us now, and his voice was as hollow as one of his own spirits. As he spoke, I realized suddenly what a good actor he would have made, with his startling face and his vivid gestures. I could not tell how sincerely he had accepted Geddes's announcement, but he sounded just as genuine as he had done the night when he announced what to him had been a first-hand spirit message.

'They have spoken again,' he began, and his delicate hand played with his tie. 'Laribee has made a new will and . . .'

'I heard all about it,' I cut in quickly.

Fenwick started slightly, lowered his luminous eyes and moved toward Stroubel. Faintly I could catch his words as he whispered in the conductor's ear.

I could see that the staff were worried by this subtle change in the patients. Stevens hurried toward his half-brother and started to talk earnestly with him. Miss Brush redoubled her efforts to get up a bridge game, but met with no success. Mrs Fogarty circulated her mauve cheerlessness, and Moreno grew so jovial that it must have hurt.

But their combined efforts could not undo Fenwick's work. The spirit message and the fact that there was no explanation for Laribee's absence had disturbed the patients almost to a pitch of hysteria.

I think we should all have been sent prematurely to bed, and our plan would have been wrecked, if Lenz had not come in at that moment. The very sight of his beard seemed to produce a sedative effect. Perhaps it was because he was wise enough not to try to look falsely cheerful or fatuously optimistic. The expression on his godlike face was such as we might all hope to see on the final day of reckoning, an expression which said:

'Things have gone a bit wrong, my children. But there's nothing *really* serious to worry about.'

And he knew another psychiatrist ruse to calm jangled nerves. Music! I saw him approach Stroubel, and then the two of them moved over to the piano. Lenz held up his hand and smiled around the room with magic benevolence.

'Mr Stroubel has kindly consented to play for us.'

He made a sign to Warren, who fetched a stool and opened the piano. For one dreadful moment I thought he was going to remove the cloth. I saw his fingers close around it. Then Stroubel distracted him by fussily handing him a vase of flowers to take away.

Geddes was in place, feigning a most realistic doze. I could detect no movement from him as the great musician drew up the stool and sat down.

He played the *Moonlight Sonata*, and, although I have never liked Beethoven in sentimental mood, I must admit that the music got me. It got the others, too. Anxious creases smoothed out on their faces, and eyes shone as though reflecting the soft moonlight of the music. Laribee, the sanatorium, their worries, real or imaginary – all were forgotten.

After Stroubel had finished, Lenz slipped out of the room. But the others crowded around the piano. Even Fenwick, who thought Beethoven dreadfully unaesthetic, hovered close. Stroubel seemed unwilling to give an encore, though both Miss Brush and Moreno went over and urged him.

But Mrs Fogarty was a favourite of his, and her plea was more successful. At her request, the old man sat meekly down and gave us a Brahms rhapsody which was breathtaking in its speed and brilliance.

When it was over, the piano became the pivotal point of the whole room. Geddes must be having a tough job, I thought, keeping an eye on that mob. Finally I went over myself, and, pushing my way through the others, took up my position near the end of the piano, close to the musical place.

My fingers went sneaking under that ornamental cloth. They fumbled a moment and found – nothing.

The will was gone! Someone had taken it. Someone who must be within a few feet of me – one of those men and women crowding around Stroubel. The plan had worked.

Geddes was still in his chair, apparently asleep. I felt almost sick with the fear that perhaps he really had gone off into one of his trances or that the confusion had been too much for him. I stared at him eagerly, hardly daring to approach him.

Suddenly, his dark eyes opened. They found mine and his head nodded three times. Then he shifted his position slightly, turned and nodded in the direction of a man who was moving away from the piano.

There was no doubt as to whom he meant. But now that I knew at last, I could hardly believe the truth.

As unobtrusively as possible, I moved towards Geddes and breathed the name of the person toward whom he had nodded.

'Yes,' came the whispered reply. 'He took it all right, and it's in his breast pocket. Watch him.'

Feverishly I looked around for Clarke. He had come back into the room and was standing alone by the door. His face lit up as I told him who it was that I wanted him to watch.

'I've got to go to Lenz right away,' I said hurriedly. 'Don't lose sight of him for an instant. I believe he's our man.'

'Shouldn't be surprised,' said Clarke. 'You see, I've been making a search and I found this.'

He took from his pocket a clean, folded handkerchief. I saw at once it was the same general size and texture as the one which had been used to gag Geddes – the one which was stained with Laribee's blood.

'It was in *his* room,' Clarke whispered.

We smiled with grim satisfaction.

'Well, that just about clinches it,' I said.

25

Leaving Clarke on the job, I strolled back to Geddes, who had left the group around the piano now and was waiting expectantly for me in a corner. I told him how Clarke had discovered the owner of the handkerchief and he gave a low whistle.

'So our balmy plan did work!' he murmured.

As we stared at each other, I had a moment of acute nervousness. I felt like a schoolboy who had looked up in the answer-book the solution to an algebra problem but still had no idea of the reasoning which alone could establish that solution. As a case for the police, ours seemed pitifully slim. But a glance at the clock showed me ten minutes past nine. There was nothing for it but to go to the director and try to brazen it out.

'Come on,' I said. 'At the risk of having our necks officially wrung, we've got to take this to Lenz right away.'

Geddes fingered his own neck where the red bruises still showed above his collar. 'I'm game for anything,' he said grimly. 'And if there's any neck-wringing, I hope I get a ring-side seat.'

Avoiding the eye of the tiger-coloured Miss Brush, we slipped to the door of the lounge and started along the passages toward the director's office. My nervousness had vanished now. I felt excited and unreasonably sure of myself.

Doctor Lenz was alone when rather precipitously we burst into his office. He sat behind his desk, his bearded face bent absorbedly over a book. Our entrance must have made as much noise as a miniature hurricane, but he paid us no attention until his paragraph was finished. Then, very solemnly, he closed the book, laid it on the desk in front of him and said:

'Well, gentlemen?'

Geddes and I glanced at each other and, at a slight nod from the Englishman, I took the plunge.

'Listen, Doctor Lenz,' I began, 'we've got an idea about these crimes. In fact, we're pretty sure who committed them. You've got to give us a hearing right away. You see –'

'One moment, please, Mr Duluth.' The director raised a large hand and gave me a pontifical stare over his reading spectacles. 'Am I to understand that this theory of yours implies an accusation against one particular individual?'

'It certainly does,' exclaimed Geddes and I in unison.

'Very well.' Portentous fingers removed the spectacles and slipped them into a leather case. The director's eyes fixed us both with the utmost intensity as though, without having heard it, he could gauge to perfection the significance of our information. 'I am prepared to have confidence in you,' he said at length, 'but I would not consider taking the responsibility of hearing what you have to say before the police have been notified. If you have sufficient faith in yourselves, I feel that Captain Green should be informed immediately.'

'We're perfectly ready,' said Geddes.

'Sure we are,' I agreed.

The director's mouth moved in a faint, indulgent smile – the smile of a deity observing the intellectual struggles of the terrestrial.

'I do not know what discoveries you have made,' he said slowly, 'but before we have the captain come here, there is one thing I would like to ask you. It is more than possible that you can account for the circumstances of Mr Laribee's death. But does your theory explain the motive for killing Fogarty and also the means by which he was tied in that strait-jacket?'

'We can make a pretty shrewd guess at the motive,' I said swiftly. 'Fogarty must have found out something that made him dangerous.'

'I agree with you, Mr Duluth. But, this man you are about to accuse – how did he get Fogarty into the strait-jacket?' The director's paternal smile returned. 'That is the type of evidence which, more than anything less tangible, is apt to convince the police.'

I felt a little dashed. 'We haven't had much time to think this out,' I faltered. 'As for that angle of it, I'm afraid I haven't the slightest idea.'

'You haven't?' Lenz fingered his beard and then added abruptly, 'But do not let that concern you. It so happens that I also have been giving the matter some thought. And, thanks to this admirable book, I have come upon what I believe to be a satisfactory explanation of that point.'

He picked the book from the desk and held it out for our inspection. It was written by some German-sounding professor and the title was *Witchcraft and Medicine*.

'A scientific treatise upon hocus-pocus,' he murmured. 'A very healthy diet for the too ambitious psychiatrist.' He opened the book with loving fingers and laid it down again on the desk. 'There is a chapter here upon the magic of the theatre, Mr Duluth. You might be interested in my application of its content to the death of Fogarty. I feel it would strengthen whatever case you have to give to the police.'

As usual, the director's personality had had a markedly subduing effect upon myself and Geddes. We had come to talk, we remained to listen. We stood there in silence while Lenz's eyes scintillated at us, half serious, half amused.

'Our major problem,' he began serenely, 'is to divine how any man without superhuman strength could manage to truss up a person of Fogarty's powerful physique. To me, the solution is simple now that I have read that book.' His tone lowered in mock solemnity. 'It is merely a question of magic.'

I nodded weakly. Geddes bent forward and started to skim through the pages of the book.

'Let us review the case,' continued the director. 'We may presume that the murderer, for reasons best known to himself, realized that Fogarty had become a menace to his schemes. He decided to kill him, and he knew enough psychology to realize that we all have our heel of Achilles. He planned to attack Fogarty in his own individual weak spot, his enthusiasm for the theatrical.'

I glanced quickly at the clock, but the director seemed to feel no sense of time or emergency.

'Mrs Fogarty told us,' he went on, 'that on the night of his death, her husband announced his intention of leaving the sanatorium for the entertainment world. At first I thought that his rather foolish ambitions had been aggravated by your presence here, Mr Duluth. I now feel that there was another subversive influence which made him choose that particular evening. I believe that on that Saturday the murderer had given his first prick to the heel of Achilles.'

The director turned to me. 'Now, you, Mr Duluth. You are a man of the theatre. How would you set about planning to kill a person of Fogarty's type? You would play on his vanity. You might, for example, offer to teach him a trick which would be profitable for his projected career as a stunt-artist. That book, *Witchcraft and Medicine*, describes a certain well-known trick called the strait-jacket trick in which the artist trusses himself up in a strait-jacket and then, as if by magic, extricates himself.'

'You mean,' broke in Geddes excitedly, 'the murderer promised to show Fogarty that trick, got him there helpless, and then tied that cord around his neck?'

'Exactly.' Lenz nodded gravely. 'But the procedure would not have been quite as simple as that. Fogarty was, in his way, a shrewd man. I cannot believe that he would have let himself be tied up by anyone unless the person who was teaching him had first demonstrated the trick himself. And that is what I believe happened. I think that this man and Fogarty went together to the physio-therapy room and that the – er – murderer performed the strait-jacket trick in front of Fogarty. And . . .'

'But he'd have to be a regular Houdini to do that!' I exclaimed.

'On the contrary,' said the director almost apologetically. 'That book shows how elementary the trick is. Anyone, knowing the secret, could perform it.' He picked up a pencil and tapped on the desk. 'In fact, I myself should be able to make a very creditable attempt. Perhaps you would like me to demonstrate.'

He looked up with an almost impish smile. Both Geddes and I agreed rather dazedly that we would be delighted to witness a demonstration.

'Very well,' he murmured. 'I will play magician for you.'

He pressed a button and, when Warren appeared, he sent the attendant for the institution's only remaining strait-jacket. Within a few minutes, Warren returned and with rather surly bewilderment handed the jacket to Lenz.

'Thank you, Warren.' The director nodded his head benevolently. 'And by the way, Mr Duluth and Mr Geddes have something which they are eager to talk over with the police. You might ask Captain Green if he could spare a few moments from his work in the laboratory.' He turned to me. 'I feel that those members of the staff who can leave their duties should also be here in case there are any little matters that need corroboration.'

'Let them all come,' I exclaimed. 'We'd willingly talk before a whole medical convention.'

'Very well, Warren. Would you please ask Miss Brush, Mrs Fogarty, Doctor Moreno and Clarke to come here, too? And ask Doctor Stevens to take charge of the male patients.'

After the attendant had gone, Lenz held up the wicked-looking canvas jacket.

'You must imagine, please, that I am a magician,' he began impressively. 'I hope to show you that it is possible for anyone to have himself bound into this jacket and then make his escape.'

As he spoke, he did look remarkably like a wizard with his important beard and his thick, bushy eyebrows.

'I'm afraid,' he went on, 'that I am a trifle too elderly to care to try this experiment on myself. But you, Mr Duluth, perhaps you would be kind enough to act as what we might call the prestidigitator's guinea-pig.'

I stepped forward and, with a great show of mystery, Doctor Lenz started to bind my shoulders into the jacket. He had succeeded in rendering me completely ineffectual when he paused.

'On second thoughts,' he said, 'I am particularly anxious for you to witness the experiment, Mr Duluth. Another guinea-pig would be preferable. I will ring for Warren.'

Geddes, who had been watching absorbedly, now rose from his chair. 'There's no need for that,' he said with an amused smile. 'Why not try on me?'

'I was going to ask you, Mr Geddes.' The director's face clouded. 'But I think that for a narcoleptic it would be taking an unwarranted risk.'

'Oh, that's all right,' persisted the Englishman. 'Moreno gave me some of that new drug, benzedrine sulphate, about half an hour ago. I'm not likely to go off in an attack or anything.'

Lenz reflected for a moment, and then his satisfaction at mystifying us both seemed to override his sense of sanatorium discipline.

'Very well, Mr Geddes. Let us try.'

While Geddes moved to the desk, the director handed me the jacket.

'Mr Duluth, I want you to strap this on to Mr Geddes as firmly as you are able.'

Obediently I slipped the straps tight. It was rather complicated, but at length I managed. Geddes looked as helpless as a trussed turkey. He grinned.

'You're going to be a genius, doctor,' he murmured, 'if you can tell me how to get out of this.'

Lenz seemed almost boyishly pleased. 'Oh, I assure you it's simple. It's merely ...'

He broke off as the door was pushed open and Captain Green entered with two of his officers. Behind them, came the staff, Mrs Fogarty, Miss Brush, Moreno, Warren and John Clarke.

The captain was staring at us as though we offered him a final proof of the world's insanity.

'What on earth are you doing with that strait-jacket?' he asked.

Lenz patted Geddes's shoulder. 'Mr Geddes and Mr Duluth believe they have solved your mystery for you, captain. I was adding my penn'orth of knowledge to theirs in a little demonstration.'

While the director was speaking, my attention had been distracted to the Englishman. I noticed that he had gone white, and I saw that familiar, glazed expression slip in his eyes.

'Look out . . . !' I exclaimed, but my voice trailed off.

The muscles of Geddes's face had contracted and, beneath the binding strait-jacket, his body stiffened visibly. I was just in time to spring forward and break his fall as he lurched to the floor in one of his seizures.

Instantly the staff was galvanized into efficiency. While Green shouted astonished questions, Warren and Moreno picked up the unconscious Englishman and carried him into a small examining-room which opened out from Lenz's office. We all hurried after them as very carefully they laid him down on a couch.

I had never seen Lenz so concerned. He bent over Geddes, shaking his head and murmuring that this was the first time in his professional career that he had wantonly jeopardized the health of a patient.

'Keep back, all of you,' he commanded. 'You, Warren, open the window. He needs plenty of fresh air, and he should come round shortly. Just fresh air and quiet.'

As the attendant hurried to the window, I moved to the Englishman's side. It was always rather beastly to see him in that condition, but now I felt a genuine alarm. Not only was Geddes my friend, he was also my chief witness and my partner. I would now have to face the police single-handed.

'Aren't you going to take him out of the jacket, Doctor Lenz?' I asked sharply.

'No, no.' Lenz was taking the Englishman's pulse. 'In a case like this, it would be most dangerous. The muscles are unnaturally constricted by the strait-jacket. If we were to take it off, the gradual passing of the seizure might bring on a serious muscle spasm. Please, all of you, get back into the office.'

As a body, we returned to the director's room, and with a parting glance at the patient, Lenz followed.

Green had been watching the proceedings with the avid interest of a layman confronted with a rare medical phenomenon. He now started to ask questions, and Lenz briefly explained the nature of narcolepsy and cataplexy, adding a word of regret on his rashness in using Geddes as the subject of his experiment.

'My only excuse,' he concluded, 'is that I felt a demonstration was really important for the solution of the case. I had not considered how the surprise of your sudden entrance might easily bring on a narcoleptic seizure. I am afraid that now we shall have to postpone my demonstration until Mr Geddes comes round.'

He crossed back to his desk and sat down. Somehow this familiar movement seemed to restore his composure. Within a few moments he was once more very much the serene and omnipotent god. He smiled a trifle sadly at the little group of staff and police who were still gathered questioningly around his desk.

'As I already told you,' he said, 'Mr Duluth and Mr Geddes have worked out a theory which they want you to hear. Unfortunately, Mr Duluth will have to expound it alone now. But before he begins, I want you to know that I personally have no more idea than you what course he intends to adopt or whom he is going to accuse. Needless to say, I feel sure that he will succeed in interesting us.'

The director produced his spectacles and very deliberately perched them on his nose.

'There is one more point. I myself have a little theory which I think is going more or less to agree with that of Mr Duluth. It involves a certain inmate of this institution. I am going to ask Warren to go downstairs and keep him under rather close observation.'

This remark was received with the silent uneasiness which the director seemed to expect. He took a piece of paper from a drawer and scribbling a few lines on it, handed it to the night attendant.

'I want you to watch this person, Warren,' he said calmly. 'If Doctor Stevens should question you, please show him that note. And when I ring the bell, I would like you to bring that particular person to us here.'

The night attendant read through the note and gave a spontaneous grunt of surprise. Lenz smiled, and as Warren hurried out of the room, he turned politely to me.

'Now, Mr Duluth, if you are ready . . . !'

26

The temporary loss of my ally had somewhat unnerved me. But the last few minutes had brought with them certain compensations. While the director was performing his demonstration, my eyes had fallen once more upon that ponderous book which lay on his desk. *Witchcraft and Medicine* – the title had given me an idea, an idea which, like the key-piece to a jig-saw puzzle, suddenly made clear in my mind the pattern behind the whole bewildering series of events.

It had been a puzzle for fools, and I saw now that it was its very foolishness which had saved it from being absurdly obvious. I felt indecently self-confident. I could even return the captain's implacably official stare without the trace of a jitter.

I glanced from him to John Clarke. His reassuring nod told me that he had performed his part of the job to his own satisfaction. The stage was set – and promisingly so.

My prospective audience had settled down in various parts of the room now. Miss Brush had taken herself and her tiger-coloured ensemble to a chair by the window. Moreno, very spruce in his undress uniform of blue serge, leaned against the wall; while Mrs Fogarty, like a mauve, mournful ghost, had progressed to a leather settee. Clarke and Green sat together with the two officers beside them.

The captain started the ball rolling by glancing swiftly at his watch and muttering: 'I don't know what all this is about, but so far as I'm concerned the case won't get any further until Miss Pattison's been interviewed. Doctor Eismann will be here soon, and the girl's going back with him to police headquarters' – he smiled grimly – 'unless, of course, Mr Duluth has it all figured out.'

'No,' I said, 'I haven't got it all figured out.' I was standing by the desk within the sphere of Doctor Lenz's benign presence, and felt as secure there as though I were a repentant sinner shrouded in celestial wings. 'There are a lot of technical details which I don't pretend to have fitted in. But you're a policeman, and that's your job, just as psychiatry is the province of Doctor Lenz here. I believe in every man sticking to his last. I'm a theatrical producer by trade and it's as a theatrical producer of sorts that I want to attack this thing. You see, an idea's just come to me and it's right up my own alley.'

'Shoot,' said the unimpressed Green.

'We all have to take things the way they hit us,' I said. 'And the thing that hit me in the beginning was that Voice. When I first heard it, I was in a pretty jittery state and naturally I thought it was all part of my own craziness. And then, later, when I found out that Geddes, Fenwick and Laribee had all heard it, too, I switched opinions and started thinking there must be some funny sort of hypnotism floating around. But you can't hypnotize people into hearing imaginary voices, can you, Doctor Lenz?'

'I hardly think so.' The director looked up with a faint trace of amusement in his eyes. 'At one time, as you know, I felt there might be a purely psychopathological explanation for practically all the disturbances. But I myself have been forced to change my opinion. The manifestations were a little too wholesale for any kind of hypnotism.'

'Exactly.' I turned what I intended to be a successful self-confident gaze upon the captain. 'You may think we're all just a bunch of nuts and that it makes no difference what we did or didn't hear. But that Voice was real all right. Even Doctor Lenz heard it this afternoon when it entertained us to a fire-alarm in the cinema. I should have guessed what was back of it then if I hadn't been a supreme dumb-bell.'

Except for Clarke and Lenz, no one seemed to be showing much sympathy. The staff regarded me with that alert, strained expression which they adopted when watching for symptoms. Green and his men looked frankly impatient.

'Maybe there is something to be said for the show business, after all,' I went on. 'It seems to have given me a slant which you non-Thespian people missed. You see, I've knocked around burlesque shows. I've been in half the dime music-halls in the country. I've spent days at the big fairs, looking for that elusive thing called talent. And in all those places I've come across a particular kind of artist. He wasn't the type that interested me. He's not well paid. In fact, he's rather out of date. But he'd be a riot in a mental hospital.'

A stiff rustle from Mrs Fogarty made me pause. The night nurse was leaning forward, her gloomy face suddenly creased with interest. 'I see what you mean, Mr Duluth. And that would explain the telephone call when I thought that Jo . . .'

'Precisely,' I broke in. 'Mrs Fogarty has the idea. I refer, of course, to that delight of our less sophisticated forebears – the ventriloquist.'

'Ventriloquist!' echoed Green.

'Yes. The man who can throw his voice. I've seen dozens of them, and they have a lot of cute tricks. They're not only able to make their own voice appear to come from any place they want. They can imitate other people's voices, too – men, women, babies, farmyard animals, anything you like.' I turned to Lenz. 'It was the title of that book about witchcraft which gave me the idea. I know it sounds pretty cock-eyed, but I think that the murderer who's been playing havoc with all your patients, myself included, is nothing but a dime magician.'

The expressions of the staff were showing increasing alarm for my sanity. Everyone stared at Lenz as though waiting to see whether or not he would give me the official stamp of his approval.

The director leaned over the desk and nodded encouragingly. 'I am in complete agreement with you, Mr Duluth. That was my idea, and I think it very intelligent of you to arrive at the same conclusion without having read Professor Traumwitz's learned thesis.'

Green seemed to be qualifying his contempt for me. I could almost see his brain according a modest raise to my mental rating.

'Don't you see how it all fits in?' I asked enthusiastically. 'A ventriloquist could make infinite whoopee in a place like this. He could be Miss Powell's inner self urging her audibly to steal that knife. He could become a disembodied Voice, issuing panic warnings to Geddes and myself. He could be Laribee's broker, whispering stock-market crises in his ear. He could be the spirits themselves, prompting Fenwick to broadcast messages from the astral plane. And when he needed confusion in the cinema he could switch on full power and shout 'Fire' with the tongues of men and of angels.'

'Can you pin all this on any one person?' cut in Green sharply.

'I think so. But humour my theatrical instincts for a while, captain, and maybe I can build up a character you will recognize for yourself. Let's assume to start off with that our bogey-man is a ventriloquist. Does he have any other attributes? I think he does. There's been a lot of hocus-pocus going on, hasn't there? A stopwatch was hidden in Laribee's room and later slipped into his pocket at the dance. A knife was planted in Miss Pattison's bag and then lifted again from right under my nose. All that requires a certain amount of sleight-of-hand. Well, ventriloquists have to earn their bread and butter in their unbuttered times, and they usually do so by giving a double bill. Most of them take up conjuring as a side line.'

'Aren't you making this mythical individual a little too versatile?' broke in Moreno coldly.

'No. This all may sound miraculous to the uninitiate, but nothing's been done around here that the humblest of pickpockets or parlour magicians couldn't have carried off with one hand tied behind his back. The only half-way smart thing he did was the strait-jacket trick, and Doctor Lenz has promised to explain later on that that wasn't particularly smart, either.'

'Yes,' remarked the director solemnly, 'I go along with you entirely, Mr Duluth. But he has a third conspicuous talent, hasn't he?'

'I was coming to that, sir,' I replied. 'It's obvious that he made the most professional use of us patients and our individual neuroses. He was able to work on Miss Powell's kleptomania. He knew enough about Geddes and myself to realize we were scared of the dark. He even exploited Miss Pattison's neurotic feelings about Laribee. I think it's reasonable to suppose that he had a certain knowledge of medicine and psychiatry.'

Lenz inclined his head. 'Once again, Mr Duluth, I agree. In fact, I believe I have an even higher opinion of his abilities than you.'

'Good.' Lenz's approval had given me a surprising elation. I felt carried away like a successful after-dinner speaker. 'We're getting places now, aren't we? We are dealing with someone who was a vaudeville artist and also some kind of medical man. Now there's only one person in the case who happens to have just those two attributes.'

'So you're back on your son-in-law theory!' commented Green guardedly.

'Yes,' I replied. 'And why not? It seems a pretty logical one.'

'Very logical,' broke in the director once again with a smile. 'It appears that we have remarkably similar minds, Mr Duluth.'

'Of course,' I continued, a trifle smug in the security of official approval, 'any youngish man here in the sanatorium could potentially be Laribee's son-in-law. Laribee himself told me he'd never seen the guy, and, although he was both an actor and a student of medicine, he doesn't seem to have been particularly well known in either capacity. No one was likely to recognize him. It was the perfect set-up.'

'So you think he came here from California to kill the old man for his money?' snapped Green.

'More or less. Laribee told me his will left most of his millions to his daughter. He also told me that, by the financial arrangements he made before he came here, Sylvia Dawn and Doctor Lenz would have complete control of the money if he was ever certified permanently insane. The son-in-law had as dandy a motive as you policemen could ever hope to find. There's all the difference in the world between being married to an obscure movie actress and having a millionairess for a wife.'

'But, Mr Duluth' – once more the director's voice rose in serene comment – 'you don't think the son-in-law originally planned to kill Mr Laribee, do you?'

'No,' I said emphatically, although the idea had only that moment come to me. 'I don't think he was that ambitious at first. I think his initial idea was to drive the old man bughouse. It was less dangerous and almost as profitable. Besides, his chief asset was his ubiquitous voice. Ventriloquism's a cinch for sending your father-in-law off his nut, but it's not so hot as a lethal weapon.'

I was still a little surprised at the fluency of my own thoughts. It was almost as though Lenz by his pointed interruptions were performing a Svengali act on me. Anyhow, just as Svengali controlled the audience for Trilby, the director's surprising patronage had assured me the attention of the police now.

'He started off,' I went on, 'by getting poor bewildered Miss Powell to steal that stopwatch from the surgery. Then he scared Geddes and me with a Voice prophesying murder, and, as he expected, one of us, myself as it happened, started to act up, distracted the staff and gave him the opportunity to sneak the stopwatch into Laribee's room. Laribee, of course, thought it was the tape-ticker and had a distinct set-back.'

'And then, Mr Duluth?'

'The next little performance was the broker's voice whispering news of a stock-market crash. It was cruelly, horribly clever. As the director would put it, the son-in-law was working on Laribee's heel of Achilles. And it looked as though things were going to pan out. Then, I think, he went a little too far. He planted the stopwatch on Laribee for a second time and the old man found it, started realizing it was all a put-up job.'

'Exactly,' remarked the director, his faintly amused gaze settling on my face. 'I think that was a false move, Mr Duluth. But, even so, you must remember that the prognosis for Mr Laribee's permanent recovery was always very grave. Why did not the son-in-law have patience and wait instead of altering his plans to murder?'

'Because something else came up,' I said. As before, the words slipped out pat, but I had the feeling that it was Doctor Lenz who had supplied the inspiration. I turned to the day nurse, who was leaning forward, her arms folded across her tiger-coloured breast.

'This is where Miss Brush steps on to the scene. The son-in-law must have found out that Laribee was very fond of her. In fact, he had asked her several times to marry him. Now a second marriage would have meant the collapse of everything. A new wife and stepmother would almost certainly have entailed a new financial arrangement – particularly as relations were rather strained between Laribee and his daughter. There was only one thing to do and that was to remove the menace of Miss Brush. Consequently, our versatile friend worked on Fenwick to deliver that spiritualistic warning against her, and he himself slipped poison-pen notes into Laribee's books. He was hoping either to turn the old man against her or to have her transferred to the women's wing where she would be safely out of the way.'

'And he almost succeeded,' exclaimed Miss Brush with impulsive indignation. 'Why, of all the absurd . . . !'

'Laribee's proposals may have seemed absurd to you,' I broke in. 'But the son-in-law would have had to take them darn seriously. Anyway, I think it was his failure to remove you that made him switch his plans to murder.'

Captain Green glanced at the clock. So did I. The hands pointed to a quarter to ten.

'Don't worry, captain,' I went on hurriedly. 'God knows I'm as eager as you to get this over before ten and I'm coming to Miss Pattison right now. Once the son-in-law decided on murder he must have put in a lot of heavy thinking. And he figured out the most ingenious plan. He'd learned about Miss Pattison's fixation against Laribee. Therefore, he started a ventriloquist campaign, urging her to kill him and finally put the knife in her bag. His idea was to get her so bewildered and confused, poor kid, that when he did the actual killing, and planted the knife on her, she might easily think she had committed the crime in some forgotten moment of madness. The whole business made her a hell of a good suspect whatever happened, and, with any luck, he could slip away from the sanatorium in all the fuss without starting any questions.'

'That's pretty logical,' grunted Green. 'But where does Fogarty fit in?'

'Right here. You see, the son-in-law, in spite of his smartness, didn't get much of a break. Fogarty must have found out something. I don't know what – but it's quite possible that with his passion for vaudeville he'd seen the son-in-law somewhere in his professional capacity and later recognized him here in the sanatorium. Obviously he had to be disposed of.'

For a moment I caught the expression on Mrs Fogarty's face and I continued quickly.

'Well, he got rid of Fogarty all right, but we all know what happens to the best laid schemes of mice and men. Having removed one danger, the son-in-law found he'd only contracted two more – myself and Geddes. Out of sheer muddle-headed, post-alcoholic curiosity, I blundered on to the scene. I began to be interested in Miss Pattison and looked like spoiling his scheme for making her the chief suspect. I had to be coped with but, luckily for me, I wasn't important enough to rate murder.' I glanced once more at the gaunt, intent figure of Mrs Fogarty. 'I was merely warned over the telephone in a particularly unpleasant way. I suppose he hoped that both Geddes and I would clear out of the sanatorium and stop being damn' nuisances.'

'What's this about Geddes?' queried Green tersely.

I felt a little guilty. 'I'm afraid Geddes and I have been holding something back. I guess that's obstructing justice or something, but we thought it the only thing to do. You see, Geddes was far more of a menace than I.'

Quickly I related the facts of the Englishman's unconscious embroilment in the plot and the incidents which had led finally to the brutal attack on him that afternoon and our discovery of the bloodstained handkerchief.

For the first time my audience showed their surprise audibly. A ripple of startled comment ran across the room. I could see the cold, official stare coming back into Green's eyes.

'So you thought it was best to hold back attempted murder from us, did you?' he said when I had finished. 'Strikes me all of you've been holding back a darn sight too much. Those voices, warnings and all the other crazy things – I heard nothing about them.'

'I think you have given yourself your own answer,' said Lenz calmly. 'You called all those things crazy and that is precisely why you were not told about them. You must remember that this is a mental hospital and daily we are faced with things which seem just as bizarre as the incidents to which Mr Duluth has given such an excellent pattern. We on the staff are professional psychiatrists. Mr Duluth, on the other hand, is an amateur. When these events occurred, he was naturally suspicious, whereas we, who have been trained to accept the abnormal as the normal,

167

merely explained them away as the symptomatic behaviourisms of individual patients.'

Captain Green seemed to capitulate before this imposing array of polysyllabics.

'All right,' he said grudgingly. 'But who the hell is this son-in-law? And has Mr Duluth any real evidence?'

'I think I know who the son-in-law is,' I said softly. 'And I've got evidence all right.'

It was rather embarrassing to have to disclose another obstruction of justice, but rather lamely I ran through the pathetic incidents of Laribee's midnight will and our intricate plan which had culminated in the document's removal from the musical place.

'I can see now,' I concluded, 'how anxious the son-in-law would have been to get hold of that will. Of course, it was only a scrap of paper, signed and witnessed by a bunch of nuts. But there was just the chance it might be proved valid. And if it was, Miss Brush would have come in for all the money. The whole elaborate song and dance would have gone for nothing.'

'And you know who took the will?' asked the captain briskly.

'Yes. And Clarke's been watching him. He hasn't had a chance to get rid of it.'

The captain's gaze moved to the young detective and then switched back to me. 'And what's the other evidence?'

Clarke rose. 'I traced that handkerchief to the man who took the will, sir,' he said quietly.

'You did?' bellowed the captain. 'Well, who is he?'

'Just a moment,' I put in. 'Let's run through what we know about him once again. Apart from being a vaudeville actor and a man of some medical knowledge, he must obviously have come from California, where he met and married Sylvia Dawn, neé Laribee. He's presumably quite young and he can't have been here at the sanatorium very long. All those qualifications fit the man who took the will from the musical place. I'm expecting that telegram from Prince Warberg soon. It ought to give some physical details to clinch the matter of identity.'

The following silence was taut and expectant. Everyone shifted in their chairs; glances met glances and flicked uneasily apart. It had been a long, winding trail, but I could see the goal very close now.

John Clarke had moved across the room and was pausing by Doctor

Lenz's assistant psychiatrist. He held out his hand, and when he spoke his tone was incisive:

'You'd better give me that paper, Doctor Moreno.'

27

Moreno did not move. His dark face remained studiedly impassive. There was nothing to betray his feelings except the faintest gleam in his eyes.

Everyone else in the room was staring at him now – staring either in astonishment or apprehension. I myself felt slightly nervous. However strong one's convictions, it is not pleasant to accuse a man of murder.

Only Doctor Lenz seemed completely composed. His bearded face was alert as he watched Clarke move a little nearer the young psychiatrist.

'I said you might as well hand it over, Doctor Moreno.'

Moreno lifted an eyebrow. 'Am I supposed to understand what you mean?'

'I think you will find it in your breast pocket,' said Clarke softly. 'Of course, if you want help, I can . . .'

With an elaborate shrug, Moreno felt in his pocket and brought out a sheaf of papers. He glanced through them and finally selected one.

'This does not belong to me,' he said, handing it casually to Clarke. 'Perhaps it is what you are looking for.'

The detective read through the paper and carried it in silence over to Green. Then he produced a large envelope from which he took two handkerchiefs.

'This is the handkerchief used to gag Mr Geddes,' he said quietly. 'The other I found among Doctor Moreno's personal belongings. They're obviously the same make.'

The captain examined the handkerchiefs carefully and then read the document. 'So all the money was to go to Miss Brush,' he grunted. 'I guess this will's not worth much, but I can see why Laribee's son-in-law'd want to get hold of it.' His gaze settled on Moreno. 'Have you anything to say?'

The young psychiatrist shook his head. 'Nothing that isn't so child-ishly obvious that it's scarcely worth mentioning.'

'Even so,' said Green grimly, 'I should mention it.'

'Very well.' Moreno shot me a cold, indifferent look. 'Mr Duluth is my patient and the regulations of this institution state that the patient must always be right. But as Mr Duluth by his histrionic ability seems to have put himself outside the category of patients, I presume I can tell him frankly what I think of his accusation.'

'I'd be delighted,' I said.

'In the first place, Mr Duluth, your evidence seems rather trivial. You yourself have invested this sanatorium with a murderer who can practise everything from voice-throwing to the most dexterous sleight-of-hand. Surely it would be simple for so talented an individual to plant the will in my pocket and also to borrow one of my handkerchiefs for his own purposes.' He smiled a trifle maliciously. 'The very fact that I still have the will in my possession should prove that I am not this versatile conjuror. If I had been, I should doubtless have secreted the document in Doctor Lenz's beard or Captain Green's pocket by this time.'

I felt slightly nonplussed.

'And as for the will itself,' continued Moreno, 'Captain Green admits that it is almost certainly invalid. I cannot believe that your intelligent murderer would have risked so much to retrieve so worthless a document from your quaintly termed musical place. Personally I would never have dreamed of doing such a thing – particularly after you had told me that implausible story about Miss Powell and the will. In fact, if I may criticize your whole scheme, I would call it so much theatrical poppycock.'

'It's easy to deny you took the will,' I said rather angrily. 'But the fact remains that you haven't been here long. You did come from California. You are a medical man, and at one time you were an actor. That seems like quite a lot of coincidences, doesn't it?'

'Quite a lot, Mr Duluth.' To my surprise, Miss Brush had turned towards me with the brightest of her bright smiles. Her voice was soft and sweet. 'I think you have worked out a splendid theory. I also admit that Doctor Moreno fills the bill very nicely. As you say, he comes from California, he is young, he is an excellent psychiatrist and at one time he was a very promising actor. But – unfortunately – he fails in the final test, Mr Duluth. He is not Mr Laribee's son-in-law.'

I gazed at her stupidly. Green barked:

'How d'you know that?'

'I'm afraid I have indulged in no brilliant deductions,' replied Miss

Brush lightly. 'I can't even lay any particular claims to feminine intuition. But I do know Doctor Moreno isn't Mr Laribee's son-in-law for one very adequate reason. You see, he happens to be – my husband.'

My self-assurance which, during the past few minutes, had been slipping fast, now collapsed completely. I went very red and felt as conspicuous a fool as I had ever felt in my life.

'Of course,' continued the day nurse, switching on once again her disarming smile, 'we have only been married two months. I should hate to suspect Doctor Moreno of bigamy, but you never can tell with these Latin races, can you?'

The awkward silence which followed this remark was mercifully short-lived. It was broken by a stifled male laugh. I looked up to see John Clarke blowing his nose with that intensity which is always adopted to cover inappropriate amusement. Once more his laugh broke out – clear, unmistakable. With an apologetic glance at Captain Green, he rose and hurried out of the room.

My embarrassment turned to a sensation of complete desertion. My one remaining ally had now abandoned me.

'I seem to have amused him,' said Miss Brush mildly.

There was another brief pause in which Green turned sharply to Doctor Lenz.

'Is what she says true?' he asked.

The director's eyes were twinkling. 'To the best of my knowledge. I myself attended the wedding and had the great honour of giving the bride away.'

'But why – why does she call herself Miss Brush?'

'She does so at my suggestion. It is a purely psychological move. Miss Brush's personality has an excellent therapeutic effect upon the patients. We all feel she would have less curative value if she were known to be a married woman.' The director smiled benignly upon the day nurse. 'Any man might be forgiven for considering bigamy after knowing Miss Brush. But I do not think that happened in the case of Doctor Moreno. Not only did he graduate with the highest distinction, he also has an excellent record from every other point of view.'

By now I realized I had met my Waterloo. But once a suspicion had arisen in the captain's mind, he could not dismiss it lightly. He had turned back to the will and was reading it through again.

'I guess we may have to count Doctor Moreno out as Laribee's son-in-law,' he said suddenly. 'But this will leaves over a million to Miss

Brush. Strikes me that if he's her husband, he has a pretty darn good motive for killing Laribee, anyway.'

'As you seem to be anxious for suspects and motives,' broke in Miss Brush with alarming sweetness, 'why not consider me, captain? After all, I should have an even stronger motive than my husband.'

'This is no time to be funny,' snapped Green.

'That's what I should have thought,' continued the day nurse imperturbably. 'But really, it was you who started it. You must admit that it's ridiculous to take that crazy will seriously. Why, if I murdered every patient who left me money, I'd have a dozen deaths to my credit already. Only last month a distinguished banker bequeathed me the Empire State Building. And some time in December I was offered a cheque that would have balanced our national budget.' Her voice grew stern, official. 'Don't you see you're wasting your time with that foolish will?'

She rose like a good-humoured but very gorgeous tigress and strolled across the room. Before Green had time to do anything, she had plucked the document from his hand and was tearing it into tiny pieces. She tossed them like artificial snow to the carpet.

'That's what I think of the will,' she remarked cheerfully. 'Material evidence – or no material evidence.'

For a moment Green stared at her dumbfounded. Then his neck went very red.

'I've had about enough of this monkeying around,' he exclaimed truculently. 'This isn't a circus, and if anyone else starts acting up, I'll have them arrested right away.' He swung round on the director. 'What I want is some straight evidence, Lenz. Do you or do you not think Doctor Moreno's the guilty party?'

'Frankly, I do not.' The director shot me an indulgent glance. 'I think Mr Duluth has given us a brilliant précis of the motives behind these crimes. I also believe he is right on practically every point. His only mistake, as I see it, was to suspect Doctor Moreno.'

This was the first sympathy I had received since my collapse. I felt grateful, though still very crestfallen.

'No,' Lenz was continuing, 'I cannot think Doctor Moreno guilty. Mr Duluth, very naturally, stressed the theatrical side of this affair. And I am inclined to stress the medical. It is clear to me that the man we are looking for is not a very sound psychiatrist, and Doctor Moreno is an extremely accomplished one. No expert would have been as ambitious as Mr Duluth's exposition has shown the murderer to have been. Doctor

Moreno knows far too much, for example, ever to have attempted to influence Miss Pattison in that particular manner.'

'I am grateful for the appreciation,' remarked Moreno, whose facial rigidity had relaxed slightly now. 'It is a relief to have this business discussed intelligently.'

The director did not move his gaze from me. His expression was rather apologetic now. 'There is also one other rather conclusive fact which Mr Duluth overlooked. Mr Laribee was on the walk when he heard his broker's voice. In our daily routine none of the psychiatrists ever accompany the patients when they take their exercise. In that particular instance Doctor Moreno could not possibly have been present.'

Lenz had found the worst flaw in my argument against Moreno, and I saw that once and for all he had blown it higher than a kite.

His voice was running on placidly. 'You have yet to witness my strait-jacket demonstration, captain. I think that should make things a little clearer.'

He rose and moved into the adjoining examination-room. Soon he returned.

'In all this excitement, we have forgotten our patient,' he said. 'Mr Geddes has recovered from his attack. He should soon be with us, and then I shall be free to use the strait-jacket to explain my point.'

'To hell with the strait-jacket and your demonstration!' cried Green, whose patience was rapidly slipping from its monument. 'I don't give a damn about who got who into a strait-jacket. All I want to know is – if you don't suspect Moreno, who do you suspect?'

'You will remember,' replied the director mildly, 'that before Mr Duluth began his exegesis, I sent Warren downstairs to keep an eye on a particular inmate of this sanatorium. My own deductions had led me up a very similar path to that of Mr Duluth. I, too, felt that the murderer must be Mr Laribee's son-in-law, but instead of suspecting Doctor Moreno, I suspected this other individual. Perhaps if Mr Duluth had had more time to think, he might have come to the same conclusion. Like Doctor Moreno, this other man is young. He comes from California. And I surmise he must have some knowledge of medicine. You will see for yourself that he is a most accomplished – er – actor.'

Amid suitably impressed silence, Doctor Lenz leaned over the desk and put his finger on the bell.

'I told Warren to bring this man here when I rang,' he explained pleasantly.

The director had built up to a far more sensational climax than mine. His sonorous voice had instilled into his audience a dramatic intensity. We all started when, almost immediately after his ringing of the bell, the door opened to reveal Clarke and Geddes.

'Ah, Mr Geddes, I do hope you feel better now,' exclaimed Lenz. 'You and Mr Clarke are in time to witness the demonstration, after all. I was just telling these people what an admirable plan you and Mr Duluth worked out. My only criticism is that I believe you had the wrong son-in-law.'

'It's quite possible,' said the Englishman with a sleepy smile. 'We were both pretty mixed up, anyway.'

As the two newcomers crossed to the wall and stood there together, the director turned back to Captain Green. 'You have an extremely intelligent young man on your staff,' he said with seeming irrelevance. 'Personally I should strongly recommend Mr Clarke for promotion, for it was he who really gave me the clue to this mystery.'

'What d'you mean?' asked the captain.

'This afternoon when we had our session here,' continued Lenz, 'he asked me if one could pretend insanity convincingly enough to delude the authorities. I told him one could but, on thinking the matter over, I realized that there was one particular thing which no one could do. It is easy enough to simulate symptoms, but, however skilled in medicine one may be, it is practically impossible to fake a convincing reaction to treatment – especially when one does not know what treatment one is getting. My own candidate for son-in-law has been doing just that. Ever since he came here, his response to treatment has been puzzling all of us on the staff.'

While half-audible queries from his audience sputtered like damp fireworks, the director rose pontifically to his feet.

'We are ready now for the demonstration,' he announced. 'As you recall, it was my contention that a person could get out of a strait-jacket unaided. Well, look.'

He crossed to the door of the little examining-room and threw it open. His gesture was so dramatic that I completely forgot how Geddes's reappearance in the director's office had already proved his point.

The others seemed to have been affected in the same way. We all crowded around Lenz and followed eagerly the direction of his pointing finger.

The examination-room was, of course, empty. On the settee, grey and limp, lay the strait-jacket.

'As you see' – Lenz was tapping the walls, a solemn, satisfied wizard – 'there is no second door to this room, no secret panel. Of course, the window was open and someone might conceivably have come through it to assist Mr Geddes's escape. But that drain-pipe is very difficult to climb up.'

'And very difficult to climb down,' murmured Geddes with a smile. 'It almost ruined my suit.'

Green spun round on him. 'You mean you really got out of that thing?'

The Englishman nodded. 'Yes. Thanks to Doctor Lenz.'

We were all moving rather dazedly back to our seats when the door from the corridor opened for a second time and Warren marched in accompanied by Doctor Stevens.

The night attendant was almost unrecognizable. A long cut above his lip had been lavishly painted with iodine. One cheek was so swollen that the eye was practically invisible. His lank hair hung rakishly over his forehead.

While we stared at him in blank stupidity, he fumbled in his pocket and produced a telegram.

'For Mr Duluth,' he muttered.

Eagerly I tore open the envelope and saw Prince Warberg's name at the foot of the paper. As I read through my fellow producer's message, I blushed once more to the roots of my hair. Now and now alone had the full extent of my folly dawned upon me. And yet there were crumbs of comfort. My reasoning had been dead right. I had merely applied it to the wrong man.

'He fought like a wild cat,' Warren was saying indignantly to the director. 'I had a pretty tough time holding him, and he didn't play square or I wouldn't be messed up like this.' His gaze switched to Clarke in reluctant admiration. 'If it hadn't been for Clarke coming and helping, I guess he'd have got away.'

The young detective looked rather sheepish. The rest of us stared from him to Warren to the plump figure of Doctor Stevens. Captain Green was completely at sea by now and very annoyed about it.

'Can't someone around here talk straight?' he complained.

Lenz turned to him gravely. 'I said that you had an excellent man on your staff, captain. I think Mr Clarke deserves public congratulation. At the time I could not understand his unexpected explosion of mirth, but I see now that he had to provide himself with some reason for leaving the room. I gather that he guessed my particular explanation of the crime and was intelligent enough to go out and help Warren. That was one of the quickest bits of thinking I have ever encountered.'

His bearded face positively beamed as he bowed with ceremonious dignity to Clarke.

'I suppose that the bulge in your pocket is a revolver?' he asked calmly. 'I trust it is fully loaded and that you have Mr Geddes well covered.'

'Yes, sir, ever since we came in.'

Doctor Lenz could not have hoped for a more successful audience reaction. Everyone in the room focused astonished attention upon that little tableau by the wall – the flushed young detective with his hand thrust in his coat pocket, the calm, lounging figure of the Englishman.

'Excellent, Clarke.' The director's tone was affectionate. 'But I think it might be a good move to handcuff him also.'

He turned to Green, throwing out his hand in a rueful gesture.

'You see, captain, this is where Mr Duluth and I differ. Mr Geddes is the man whom I believe to be Mr Laribee's son-in-law.'

28

The Captain seemed to find words too much for him, but at a nod from Clarke, one of the officers managed to control his confusion sufficiently to step forward and slip a pair of handcuffs on to the Englishman's wrists.

Geddes himself made no move. His face was as expressionless as Moreno's had been when he had been the centre of accusation.

'Melodrama in one act by a successful charlatan,' he murmured.

Doctor Lenz looked at him and then at his manacled wrists. He gave a little sigh.

'Mr Geddes is right. I'm afraid I have been something of a charlatan with my demonstration, but I – er – saw no other final curtain for the melodrama. You see, I deliberately led you all astray. That learned thesis, *Witchcraft and Medicine*, does not give one a magic formula for the strait-jacket trick. In fact' – he looked mildly apologetic – 'it states emphatically that no one but a natural contortionist such as Mr Geddes could succeed in performing it.'

'But how . . . ?' broke in Green.

'I see that I have been guilty of confusing you all,' continued the director. 'I merely hoped to persuade Mr Geddes, the natural contortionist, into giving us a *demonstratio ad oculos*. He was kind enough to oblige me. I already had my suspicions when he and Mr Duluth came to me this evening. And it dawned on me that he would be exceptionally eager for an opportunity to – er – escape. I suggested the little strait-jacket episode, hoping he would volunteer as a subject and make an exit through the examining-room window. He was kind enough to satisfy me on that head, too. He proved his guilt not only by wanting to escape, but also by being able to escape. I had already written instructions to Warren to keep a close eye on him and to wait on guard beneath the window.'

'And was he hard to handle when he came down that drain-pipe!' remarked the night attendant grimly. 'Contortionist, indeed! I'd call him an eel.'

'But I still don't know what made you suspect Geddes in the first place, Doctor Lenz,' put in John Clarke.

'Simply because he did not react correctly to the drugs we have been giving him. Doctor Stevens and Doctor Moreno have been writing a paper on narcolepsy and they have been worried that Mr Geddes was the only unsuccessful case in their series treated with benzedrine sulphate. I see now that he was obliged to simulate his attacks whenever it suited his purposes.'

'But that fit he threw . . . !' exclaimed Green incredulously.

'A most convincing fake, captain – and learned from the fakirs.' Lenz picked up *Witchcraft and Medicine*. 'The most valuable thing I gleaned from this excellent volume was that the Indian fakirs can induce a state of rigidity in their muscles which makes them look like corpses. They can go at will into what appears to be a profound slumber. In fact, they could act very satisfactorily all the symptoms of narcolepsy and cataplexy. And, as we all know, the fakirs are the most – er – accomplished conjurors and illusionists in the world. Mr Geddes comes from India. Obviously, with his potentially profitable gifts of ventriloquism and contortion, he was a very diligent pupil.'

For the first time since the director had started to speak, Geddes showed some signs of interest. He smiled contemptuously and turned his suave gaze upon me.

'Of course I come from India, Duluth,' he said, 'but the rest is all so bloody silly. Can't you explain to them what a farce it is?'

I was still holding Prince Warberg's telegram in my hand. I felt anger rising up in me as I looked into the Englishman's eyes.

'Yes,' I said slowly, 'I can explain the farce all right but it's rather embarrassing to have to let the world know just how much the joke was on me. I might have guessed from the beginning that, since your room was next to mine, you were the only person who could have scared me with that voice the first night. I might have guessed that all the warnings you pretended to get were just a fake build-up to give you an excuse for getting away when the getting was good. I certainly should have guessed the truth from that psycho-analytical experiment of mine. You were the only person who showed a murderer's reaction to the thing on the slab.'

Green started to say something, but I went on, ignoring him.

'Incidentally, I've just figured out what it was that Fogarty found out about you. He'd been to England and he told me once your face was familiar. He must suddenly have remembered how he'd seen you on the boards in London as Mahatma, the Oriental Wonder or whatever you called yourself. I guess he was very thrilled when the great maestro himself offered to teach him the strait-jacket trick.'

Geddes glanced indifferently at his manacled hands. 'It might be a good idea, Duluth, if you told the police how I myself was attacked this afternoon.'

'I've already told them,' I said grimly. 'But I didn't realize then just how simple it must have been for an expert contortionist to tie himself up in a few bandages. Of course, it was generous of you to help me out with that musical place business, but I see now what a break it was for you. Just as soon as you knew we were getting on to the trail of the son-in-law, you realized you'd have to leave in a hurry. That phony scheme gave you a chance to plant the will on Moreno when he took you to the surgery for your medicine. With any luck you'd have made your get-away after all. Too bad Doctor Lenz wasn't as dumb as I was.'

The Englishman shrugged. Even then he showed no sign of being disconcerted. The British control which I had found so praiseworthy in the past still seemed unshakable, in spite of the handcuffs and the surrounding group of policemen. My anger had reached a pitch beyond my own control now.

'So we were just buddies!' I exclaimed. 'And it was all too, too sweet. But I happen to be sentimental enough to feel rather nasty when a pal goes back on me. You may have been a whiz as Mahatma, the Oriental Wonder, but to me you're just a new low in scum. What you tried to do to Miss Pattison was one of the filthiest, cruellest tricks I'm ever likely to come up against in a long, long time.'

I was all set to get really opprobrious when the captain interrupted me.

'What's in that telegram you've got?' he exclaimed materialistically. 'That's what I want to know.'

'Oh, yes, the telegram,' I said ironically. 'I'd momentarily overlooked that clinching piece of evidence. Listen to this.'

I smoothed out the crinkly paper and read:

JUST GOT SYLVIA DAWN IN HOLLYWOOD LONG DISTANCE DARN
YOU STOP SEEMS HARMLESS AND SHOULD SAY PUNK ACTRESS
STOP VERY CONCERNED ABOUT HUSBAND WHOM SHE THINKS

HAS DESERTED BECAUSE WENT EAST SOME MONTHS AGO AND
LEFT NO FORWARDING ADDRESS STOP HUSBAND ENGLISH BORN
INDIA THIRTY-FOUR HANDSOME SMALL MOUSTACHE WHEN
FEELS LIKE IT STOP NO ENGAGEMENTS THIS COUNTRY BUT
SOME SUCCESS IN ENGLAND IN TWENTY-NINE AS MAHATMA
ORIENTAL MAGICIAN OR WONDER STOP CONJUROR CONTOR-
TIONIST AND ALL THAT STUFF NO GOOD THESE DAYS NOT EVEN
TO YOU STOP SYLVIA SAYS ONE YEAR CALCUTTA MEDICAL
SCHOOL STOP PHOTOGRAPH COMING AIR MAIL STOP SYLVIA
ALSO SAYS IF YOU KNOW WHEREABOUTS PLEASE TELL BECAUSE
PULLING OUT HAIR BY ROOTS STOP DON'T SAY I'M NOT GOOD
FRIEND STOP ARE YOU REALLY THAT CRAZY STOP

SIGNED PRINCE . . .

I broke off suddenly. All the others were staring in fascination
at Geddes. Mrs Fogarty gave a slight cry of alarm as suddenly the
Englishman stiffened and lurched forward on to the floor. It was typical
of those narcoleptic cum cataplectic seizures which I had witnessed so
often before and which had so often aroused my sympathy.

'How unfortunate!' I exclaimed. 'The telegram has brought on another attack.'

It must have been the essential doctor in Stevens that made him bend
anxiously over the Englishman as the others dashed forward. There was
a general confusion of arms and legs.

I shall never know exactly what happened next. It was impossible to
tell whether or not Geddes had slipped out of the handcuffs. But one
hand, at least, seemed to be free. With incredible speed, he struck
upward at Doctor Stevens with the manacles and sent him spinning
across the room. Then, in a flash, he was on his feet.

'Stop him!'

The captain's voice rang out rather fatuously, but the rest of us
were still too dazed for any instantaneous response. Dodging in and out
with amazing agility, Geddes passed Green, Mrs Fogarty, Miss Brush
and Moreno. While we were still milling pointlessly around, he had
reached the examining-room and was making a dash for the open
window.

'Stop him!' shouted the captain again.

This time we were galvanized into action. I was caught in the general
rush as everyone started in pursuit.

'Well, even if you don't fight fair . . . !'

181

I heard Warren's exultant voice as we all crowded into the small examining-room. By the window two figures were battling frenziedly.

'Don't shoot!' yelled Green to no one in particular.

For an instant I caught a glimpse of Warren's bloody face as his arms clamped like a strait-jacket around Geddes's shoulders. His expression was one of triumphant ecstasy.

'Got him this time!' he panted.

Swiftly Clarke and the two officers sprang forward, and at length the three of them managed to pinion the wildly struggling body of the Englishman.

We all stood around, gazing rather stupidly. There was a lot of pointless exclamations and gasps. Then, cool and clarion, Doctor Lenz's voice rose above the cacophony.

'This should be a lesson to us all,' he said. 'Never trust to handcuffs when you're arresting a magician.'

The State alienist had come and gone. Green and his men had gone, too, taking Geddes with them. The director's office seemed strangely quiet as, one by one, the staff began to disperse to their various duties. Doctor Moreno and his ex-Miss Brush were the last to leave. I stopped them at the door.

'My apologies are as heartfelt as my congratulations,' I began. 'I only hope that your being married –'

'S'hush, please!' Miss Brush smiled at me with warning sweetness. 'You'll get me fired, Mr Duluth, if you ever so much as mention marriage. In the interests of psychiatry I have to go on being the professional wicked woman. But not quite as wicked as you probably thought that night when you saw Doctor Moreno in my room and I lent you his bedroom slippers.'

'I'm afraid I'm a bum detective,' I said, smiling back at her. 'The clue of the missing slippers went clean over my head, even though they were right there under my feet.'

In perfect unison the Morenos displayed their perfect, hygienic teeth.

'And after having insulted your wife by failing to see the obvious, Moreno,' I went on, apologetically, 'I blithely accused her husband of murder.'

'Psychiatrists are often called worse things than that,' he replied equably. 'And really I'm not surprised at you thinking me a man of violence, Duluth. You were, I believe, a witness to several violent exhibitions of domestic discord between my wife and myself. I am unreasonable, I suppose, but at times I feel she takes her – er – professional duties a little too seriously. Even a psychiatrist is not immune to personal jealousy, especially' – his dark eyes caressed his wife's face – 'when he is still practically a bridegroom.'

Miss Brush took his arm and led him affectionately forth.

Of course, she couldn't resist one dazzling glance at me over her shoulder. Married or single, Miss Brush would always be – er – Miss Brush, the patients' delight. And probably she would always take her professional duties just a shade too seriously.

I was about to follow them when Lenz called me back. His benignly bearded face was smiling. With a slightly foreign gesture he indicated a chair.

'Well, Mr Duluth,' he said quietly, 'I am very happy that some good has come out of these two tragedies. Your own recovery is one of the things that makes me happiest. By your brilliant logic tonight you showed that your mental processes have emerged unscathed from their temporary cloud. And – if you will forgive me – you showed me that you have a splendid mind, the kind of intelligence that the world needs.'

'The kind of intelligence which goes just so far,' I said despondently, 'and then draws the wrong conclusion. Exactly what you'd expect from a drunk.'

'Not at all, Mr Duluth. It was worthy of the most – er – teetotal of persons.' He emitted the nearest approach to a chuckle which his Jovian dignity would permit. 'You must not underestimate your deductions since they were the same as my own.'

'But you got the right man,' I said.

'Ye-es.' The director's voice was rather hesitant. 'I came upon the correct solution eventually. But, to tell you the truth, until this evening I was suspecting someone quite different.'

'You were?' I asked suddenly alert.

'I knew from the start that we were dealing with a very sane, very talented and very intelligent person. I'm afraid I underestimated the mental and physical acrobatics of Mr Geddes.' He leant forward as if to whisper an Olympian secret. 'I feel you should know that I do not make a practice of taking patients into my confidence on sanatorium matters. I only did so in your case through a scientific miscalculation far more unpardonable than your own.'

'But who did you think . . . ?'

'I did not see how it could be anyone but yourself, Mr Duluth.'

I sat there staring into those twinkling grey eyes as dazedly as on that first night when I had been sitting in the same chair, wrapped in Miss Brush's blanket.

Then the humour of it all struck me flat between the eyes and I started to laugh like a fool.

'So you set a subversive influence to catch itself!' I exclaimed weakly.

'I apologize for my mistake, Mr Duluth, but at least, it proved to be good therapy. I think the activity helped you.' The director passed a hand reflectively across his beard. 'Strangely enough, I believe all these disturbances have helped the other patients, too. They seem more alert, more interested. That is something new in my experience as a psychiatrist.'

'The Murder Cure,' I said, smiling. 'That's a swell new appeal for the sanatorium prospectus.'

Lenz did not speak for a moment. He was tapping his silver pencil on the desk. 'My only regret, Mr Duluth,' he said at length, 'is that you will be leaving us so soon. The regret is personal, of course. Professionally, I am bound to be delighted.'

A week or two ago I'd have given anything to hear him say that. But now his words depressed me.

'Yes,' he was murmuring, 'you could of course leave us tomorrow. But I am going to ask you to stay on for a while as my guest. You were kind enough to help me in the past, now there is another little matter . . .'

'Another subversive influence?'

'No. This problem is a patient. A patient who needs only an interest in life to ensure complete recovery. I was hoping that perhaps you could supply that interest.'

Slowly, serenely, he rose to his feet and moved toward the door. As he paused a moment on the threshold, he looked once again like the very Adam of conjurors about to produce from nowhere the primeval white rabbit.

'I would like you to talk to the patient in question.'

With a slight, valedictory nod, he was gone.

I knew, of course, what he had meant. And somehow the knowledge brought back to me the tingling nervousness of a Broadway first night. I was all keyed up and excited, but I wasn't jittery any more. At last the door opened and I sprang to my feet.

'Iris . . . !'

'Peter . . . !'

She didn't move. Neither did I. We just stood there, looking at each other. I don't know why or how, but I guess it was the same way people in love have looked at each other ever since the world started spinning on its cock-eyed axis.

Or – in our particular case – like a couple of nuts.

For a complete list of books available from Penguin in the United States, write to Dept. DG, Penguin Books, 299 Murray Hill Parkway, East Rutherford, New Jersey 07073.

For a complete list of books available from Penguin in Canada, write to Penguin Books Canada Limited, 2801 John Street, Markham, Ontario L3R 1B4.